HER◉ES

REBORN

EVENT SERIES

COLLECTION TWO

HER●ES

REBORN

EVENT SERIES

COLLECTION TWO

DUANE SWIERCZYNSKI
KEITH R. A. DECANDIDO
KEVIN J. ANDERSON
AND PETER J. WACKS

TITAN BOOKS

Heroes Reborn: Event Series Collection Two
ISBN: 9781785652714

Published by Titan Books
A division of Titan Publishing Group Ltd
144 Southwark St, London SE1 0UP

First edition: April 2016
10 9 8 7 6 5 4 3 2 1

This edition published by arrangement with Bastei LLC,
Santa Monica, USA

A CIP catalogue record for this title is available
from the British Library.

Printed and bound in the USA.

TITANBOOKS.COM

HER⬤ES

REBORN

EVENT SERIES

BOOK ONE

CATCH AND KILL

DUANE SWIERCZYNSKI

The family that slays together stays together
—Popular saying

LUKE is pissed because, weirdly, the traffic is bumper to bumper. A shimmering sea of cars stretching all the way up I-75 to the horizon, as if everyone were driving straight into the sun.

It isn't supposed to be this way. Not in this direction at this time of day. Luke squints, trying to make out the problem ahead. An accident? Lane closed due to construction? Or something worse? The only reason he's driving is because Joanne's jaw hurts. Usually she prefers to be the one behind the wheel. But Luke questioned the wisdom of driving one-handed while holding an ice pack to her face.

"You okay?" he asks.

"Can't you find a way around this mess?" she asks. "We shouldn't be stuck here like this."

"There's nowhere to go."

Luke wishes traffic were moving for a number of reasons. For one, they really need to get out of Atlanta as quickly as possible. But it would also give him something to do other than replay the last hour in his mind over and over again, wondering if they missed something.

Memory's a tricky thing. After a while, you can't

be sure if you're inventing certain details, maybe subtracting others. Even now, his memories of that frenzied, 10-minute span inside the Shelby house seem to contradict one another.

And that uncertainty triggers his obsession with all the tiny forensic details. Luke can't help it; he's a detail man. Always has been. Seeing the little things everyone else misses has always been the key to his success. Some of his patients, he knows, come to see him instead of an M.D. If something's going wrong in the rest of the body, Luke is almost always able to see the earliest indications somewhere in the mouth. He's sort of a modern-day soothsayer with a D.D.S. A *toothsayer*.

So where's that keen eye for detail now? Come on, think, buddy. You've got nothing better to do. You're stuck in traffic.

The wife—did she bite one of them? Scratch her nails across his arm?

Did Luke step through the remnants of dinner and leave a boot print?

Sure, they set everything on fire. But would fire be enough to erase all the traces of those they left behind?

The car ahead of them lunges forward a few feet, then stops dead. Then it begins to roll forward a few more feet, and a few more. Luke grows hopeful. Here we go. Finally. But then, without warning, the taillights flash deep red and Luke stomps on the brake a little too hard. Joanne bucks in her seat. Almost immediately her hand goes to her mouth.

"Ow!"

"Sorry."

They crawl forward another few feet, then slam to another halt. This is insane. This is purgatory on asphalt. This, Luke thinks, will never, *ever* end.

"I was wondering," Luke finally says.

"Wondering what?"

"If we forgot something. You know, back at the Shelby house."

"What do you mean, *forgot something*?"

Luke can hear the annoyance build in her voice. She hates it when he dances around the point. So he comes out and says it.

"I mean something forensic. Like a hair, or skin under fingernails."

"The bitch didn't claw at me. She got in a lucky punch."

It was a frenzied couple of minutes, that's for sure. The idea was to catch the Shelbys right before they sat down to dinner. *If somebody was going to kill us, when would they do it?* Joanne had asked. Luke had understood what she was getting at right away. The best time to kill a distracted, childless couple is in the hurried time between arriving home from work and preparing dinner.

So the two of them watched the Shelbys long enough to establish their pattern. They both arrived home between 5:45 and 6 p.m. The wife would open a bottle of wine or mix a pitcher of martinis while the husband took care of dinner—which either meant pulling something from the freezer and microwaving it or ordering something online. This meant that dinner a.) would be ready within ten minutes or b.) would not arrive before 6:30 at the earliest. Which was a generous window of time, considering most murders barely stretch beyond the 10-second mark.

Tonight had been a wine-and-microwaved meal kind of

night. Joanne knocked on the front door, doing her best to look like a concerned neighbor, while Luke went around back to the deck that led up from the pool area right to the kitchen. The distraction, and then the kill.

The husband was the Evo. The rumor was that he could manipulate microwave and cell-phone radiation and wireless signals. He liked to impress people with his tricks at cocktail parties and barbecues, which is how Luke and Joanne first heard about him.

(Pro-tip: if you're an Evo, don't show off to friends with Facebook accounts. No matter how cool you think you are.)

And sure enough, there he was, standing in his fancy kitchen, his hands stretched out palms down over a frozen dinner resting on the counter. He looked like a faith healer trying to exorcise demons from his supper—eyes closed, hands trembling a little. The creepy thing was, the dinner was cooking under his hands. Plastic cover trembling, sauce bubbling. Luke could smell the heavy aroma of cheese, even through the glass.

Luke saw the box on the counter and noticed that the couple was eating vegetarian tonight. Pasta, brie, and asparagus. Trying to keep the middle-aged flab off, he supposed. Well, consider the battle won. You two won't gain another pound.

Especially after you're brain-dead.

The hit went off just as planned—at first. Joanne knocked, distracting the wife, sending her to the front door. The moment she walked away, Luke slid open the deck door, startling Mr. Microwave. His hands shifted away from the frozen dinner, and the surface of the counter beneath them began to ripple.

Luke lifted his gun and fired twice—two chest shots—before the guy could even think about raising his mitts and sending some of that heat Luke's way.

The double impact of the bullets sent the husband flying backwards. He reached out towards his half-cooked supper as though it might save him. His fingers caught the edge of the plastic tray and pulled it off the counter, sending cold pasta and congealed brie flying. Meanwhile, he smacked the back of his head on the edge of the Formica countertop on his way down. His body landed among the remains of his intended meal.

Dinner's ready, honey.

Mrs. Shelby, however, was much more quick-witted than her husband. She'd just opened the front door when the shots rang out. The plan was for Joanne to do the same to the wife—take her out with two torso shots. But before Joanne could lift her gun, the wife slammed the door shut in her face. Joanne pulled the trigger anyway, firing *through* the door, with no way of knowing whether the bullets had found their target.

She lowered her gun and blasted apart the doorknob, then kicked the door in.

The wife was waiting for her.

Knocked the gun out of her grip with one hand, then landed a lucky punch on the left side of Joanne's jaw. Which just pissed her off. This Evo-harboring bitch was going *down*.

But Luke had already cleared the distance between the kitchen and the living room. He took out Mrs. Shelby with a shot to the chest, and one more to the head just to be sure. As far as they knew, Mrs. Shelby didn't have any powers. But that might just mean she was better at hiding them.

Five minutes later the house was on fire and Luke and Joanne were peeling away from the scene of the crime... right into hideous traffic on I-75.

So the double murder is fresh in his mind as they inch along the highway. Luke feels no remorse about the Shelbys. Maybe they were perfectly nice people, but that doesn't change the fact that they were too dangerous to be allowed to live.

But because the hit went a little sideways, he finds himself endlessly picking over each moment. In his haste to reach the wife, did he step through some of that brie and pasta crap on the linoleum floor? Perhaps even leave a useable shoe print that the police could trace back to him?

(No, the fire would take care of that… right?)

Round and round he goes until the sound of panic in Joanne's voice snaps him out of it.

"Oh, bloody hell," she says.

"What?"

She's craning her neck out the window to see down the road, but Luke's view is obstructed by a delivery van.

"What is it? I can't see…"

"A police checkpoint."

"Oh shit. Already? How is that even possible?"

"Calm down," she says. "We don't know it's for us."

"Should I try to find an exit?"

Joanne looks. "There are no exits. Besides, that would look more than a little suspicious, don't you think? Careening through traffic in a desperate bolt for a ramp?"

"Maybe one of us really has to use the bathroom… Aw, shit! This is not good. Not good at all."

"Will you calm down?"

As they edge towards the checkpoint—Luke can see it now—it's impossible for him to remain calm. On the plus side, he's no longer obsessing over the crime scene. Instead, he finds himself imagining ways they might escape a police checkpoint. There was the *ram-our-way-through* method, in the hope that the cops haven't set up strips of spikes on the asphalt. There was also the *shoot-our-way-out* method, though they'd almost certainly be outmanned and outgunned.

Or there was simply surrender and arrest. But that wasn't a real option, because that would be admitting that everything—including his marriage—was over. This road trip is the only thing keeping it together.

"We've got to do something," Luke says.

"Just wait until we're closer," Joanne says. "See what we're up against."

"We're up against the police, that's what we're up against!"

But as they inch closer, they see that isn't quite the case. Sure, it's technically the Atlanta PD bringing traffic to a crawl. And they're stopping every third car—or fourth. The selection seems random.

Each cop, however, is accompanied by a worker in a lab coat holding a pouch of sterile swabs. A window goes down, and the lab rat hands the cotton swab to the driver—and the passengers, if any are present. Then the swab is handed back to check the result. The test seems to work fast.

The test to see if anyone traveling along this highway happens to be an Evo.

"What are they doing?" Joanne asks.

"I've read about this," Luke says. "They've just started doing it in major cities. Random searches for Evos."

"They can tell that with a swab of your cheek now, huh?"

"Yeah. I wish we could get a hold of some of those testing kits. It would make our job a lot easier."

Job. As if this is what they do for a living.

In a sense, though, it is.

They lurch forward, three car lengths at a time, then one, then three again, since the cops only seem to be stopping every third or fourth car. They were probably told to make it random, but Luke can already tell that they've fallen into a predictable pattern. And with some quick counting, he realizes they'll probably be fine.

And they are. They pass through the checkpoint without a swab or even a lingering stare. No one suspects a thing. A cop waves them on. Luke stares at the boxes of Evo tests piled up on the side of the road, wishing he could grab one or two.

They continue up the highway. All of Luke's fretting about being arrested was for nothing.

Of course, the point isn't merely to stay free.

The point is to stay free so they can find their next target.

THE TARGET is late for work.

Again.

She doesn't know she's the Target. To her, she's just another 16-year-old high school junior who—unless she pulls off a miracle in the next few minutes—is going to be looking for another after-school job in the near future.

Mr. Baraniuk made that much clear during her last "employee evaluation." If she's late one more time, even by a single minute, she's *gone*. And she can pretty much forget about a recommendation.

Right now it's 60 seconds until Mr. Baraniuk will be expecting her to appear in front of him, ready to don her apron and dish out candy by the pound to the working folks and tourists who stumble off Euclid Avenue looking for a sugar fix.

Baraniuk's Sweet Shoppe is inside Cleveland's famed Arcade Building, built in 1890 as the first indoor shopping mall in America. (It's true; the Target wrote a school report on it last year.) The Arcade is one of her favorite things about the city—well, when she isn't running late. Five stories of Victorian splendor, with four balconies and a skylight that makes you stop and stare. It's one of the most beautiful places in Cleveland.

The only problem with this century-old marvel is that there are only two entrances: one on Euclid, and the other on Superior.

And right this second—55 seconds before she's officially late and officially fired—the Target is equidistant from both entrances.

And screwed.

If by some miracle, everything on the block ceased to exist *except* for the Target and the Sweet Shoppe, then she could make it to work with enough time to strap on her red-and-white checked apron and force out a smile.

But between her location and the Sweet Shoppe there are a series of empty storefronts, victims of the economic downturn. Dusty mannequins, nicked wooden counters, forgotten signs about sales that happened years ago. Try plowing through that. You'd need a sledgehammer, a blowtorch, and a bulldozer.

The thing is, the Target knows she *can* pull off a miracle. At least, a miracle by most people's definition.

But she promised herself a while back, after all of the stuff about Evos went public: no more miracles.

Right now, though, does she have a choice?

So the Target runs straight for the wall… and goes straight through it. To the outside observer, it would look like someone running into a shadow and disappearing. Only, this shadow is made of solid brick.

There's more to it than that, to be sure. But the Target

doesn't know how to explain it, or even the basic mechanics of *how* she does it. Last year, she cautiously asked her science teacher, Ms. Procaccia, about the physics, of, you know, *stuff going through stuff*.

Ms. Procaccia explained that no object is truly solid. In fact, everything you see is mostly empty space between atoms. That said, the way those atoms are arranged prevents objects from flowing through each other. "Otherwise," her teacher said with a smirk, "our bodies would fall right through the classroom floor and into the basement."

Oh, how the Target was tempted to plunge her fists through Ms. Procaccia's desk and say, *You mean like this?*

How *does* the Target not fall through the floor? She doesn't know that, either. Her body seems perfectly normal and solid most of the time. But when she means it, when her mind is focused on it—just like you focus when you want to pick up a paper clip—she can pass through things like a wall or a door or even a concrete slab with ease.

What does she feel? Butterflies in her stomach and a slight tingling all over her body. But nothing nasty or unpleasant. Rollercoasters are far worse in comparison.

But here's the thing.

And it's an important thing.

(There's always a thing, isn't there?)

The Target can't pass through a living person—or any living thing, for that matter. No humans, no animals, no plant life. Once she walked through a tree in the wood, just to see what would happen. (Wood happen, ha ha.) Nothing at first. But when she visited the same spot a week later, the tree was dead and in the process of falling over. Sorry, tree.

No living things—check.

The Target does everything in her power to avoid them

when phasing (that's what she calls it) through objects. She may be an Evo, but she's no killer.

So when she emerges from a wall in a part of the Arcade that's always empty—it's a little alcove that used to lead to another store, but has been abandoned for years—she's utterly horrified to find someone *standing in the way.*

Oh, shit!

She doesn't have the time to register *who* might be standing there. All she can do is contort her body like crazy to avoid them.

And for the most part, she does. (Chalk it up to another miracle.)

Except…

Except part of her elbow passes through the stranger's wrist. There's a horrible crunching noise as the intricate arrangement of bones are rudely snapped out of place. The man—now she sees that it's a man standing there, an older man—howls in agony, looking down at his hand, and then up at The Target. His mouth is screaming, but his eyes are questioning, as if to ask, *Now where in the hell did you come from?*

The Target can only skid to an awkward halt and mouth, *I'm so sorry!*

But the older man is already in shock by this point, collapsing to the ground in a messy heap.

A crowd quickly gathers around to see what the fuss is about. There are cell phones aloft, taking video, just in case this is the start of some disaster or outbreak. Or because it's fun to post human misery online. Nothing ever really happens unless it appears on YouTube.

The Target is so shaken up that she walks into the Sweet Shoppe a full two minutes late. Her boss is true to his word. She gets fired.

JOANNE and Luke settle on a reasonable chain hotel in Knoxville for the night, enduring the withering stare of the proprietor. Yeah, I'm black. I know that's a crime these days, especially around these parts, but all I want is a place to crash with my husband. I've had a long day, which included the double-murder of a nice suburban couple back in Atlanta, so why don't you give me a bloody break?

Joanne's dead tired; she admits that.

Plus her jaw is killing her. Ordinarily she's stoic about things like this. If women have double the pain threshold of men, then Joanne has the pain threshold of a half-dozen women. Even natural childbirth left her wondering—is *this* what all the fuss is about?

But mouth pain, that's something else entirely.

Especially when she tries to chew a lousy Caesar salad in a diner near their hotel. With every bite, the pain centers in her brain light up like a carnival display.

"You should let me take a look at that," Luke finally says.

"I'll be fine," she says. "Just let me eat."

"You can hardly eat, and you haven't had anything all day."

"I hate killing on a full stomach."

Luke looks like he wants to shush her, but then smiles instead. Gallows humor is the only kind they share these days.

Back at the room Luke finally convinces her to let him take a look. This is what he does for a living, after all. He pulls out his black dental kit and takes out a mouth mirror. Shows it to her to reassure her.

"See, nothing else, no picks, no probes, just a mirror. Let me have a look."

Joanne still can't believe she fell in love with a dentist. To be sure, the stability of his profession was an attraction— she'd been with too many mooches and layabouts, so a guy who picked up the tab was a refreshing change. Let alone a guy who paid his taxes and laundered his own clothing on a regular basis. It felt good.

"Open wide," he says.

The very act of opening her jaw even a *little*, however, sends paroxysms of pain throughout her entire face.

"AHHHHH."

"Hold still."

"AHHHHHHHHH."

"Shhhh now... Ah, I see what happened. One of your crowns was knocked loose. Hold on a second. This won't take long at all."

"AHHHHHHHHHHHHHHHHH."

"This might hurt a bit..."

Anyone messing with her teeth, even when it's her husband, takes Joanne back to when she was a frightened little girl at the mercy of a dental surgeon with the DTs. To her, there is no worse pain than what can be inflicted on the teeth. (She couldn't even bring herself to finish *Marathon Man*—one of Luke's favorite movies, naturally. All dentists love that movie.)

"AHHHHHHHHHHHHHHHHHHHHHHHHHH."

"There."

And like that, Luke has worked his magic, set things right, and she feels the pain recede with every breath. She reaches up and grabs his wrist, squeezes it. Luke smiles, puts down his tools, caresses her face. She closes her eyes and smiles back, then holds his hand tighter against her face, as if it's a heating compress. He sighs.

But Luke, as usual, is mistaking her touch for affection, and the truth is, she can't bear to look at him right now. Joanne would clench her teeth if they didn't still hurt. She wants to scream and lash out, sending all her deep reserves of pain out into the world. She can't do that, because she'd end up seriously hurting her husband.

So instead she decides to vent her rage another way.

She rips off his belt, pops a button before he finally understands what she's doing. He's about to ask, *Are you sure?*, so she pulls his face closer, as if to tell him, *Yes, I'm sure*. Luke blindly fumbles at her clothes, but she's already ahead of him. This is no time for a striptease. This is about shedding garments as quickly as possible.

She feels his skin under her nails and tears at it as if she were digging her nails into her own flesh.

LUKE doesn't know what the hell that was all about.

When's the last time we acted like drunk teenagers? Luke can't remember. The mission is everything. They've become like the worst kind of married couple, where everything fades away except for the business at the end. For most people, that means grappling with mortgages and credit-card debt and children's schedules. Luke and Joanne have no debt; their only child no longer has a schedule. So all that's left are the executions. That's their business now.

Luke sees the whole thing as a weird extension of his previous career. Dentists are widely feared—even more than cardiac surgeons who can crank open your ribcage to screw around with your heart, or neurosurgeons who can saw through your skull to play with your gray matter. Think about it: what those butchers do is far more ghastly. Yet, dentists are seen as the sadists.

It isn't about sadism, though. Not for Luke. His career as a dentist has been all about removing the unhealthy parts of a system so that the whole can thrive. No different than a diseased tooth. Evos are abscesses—infections at the root of humanity. Left unattended, the disease could spread until the whole mouth is at risk. Why would you forfeit the whole, when a little fix could save everything?

What happened to their boy, Dennis, made that painfully, horribly clear.

Now Luke and Joanne are resting in bed with the TV on. A mindless distraction so they don't have to deal with the sudden silence in the room. There are no fancy channels; just the usual network fare. Supernatural shows, edgy sit-coms, procedurals, reality shows.

But as the reality shows give way to the national news, one of the top stories turns out to be the Shelby double-murder. Just as Luke feared.

"Oh, shit."

"What is it?" Joanne asks, half-mumbling. The brutal sex has made her sleepy.

Oh, it all makes sense. Affluent couple, "savagely butchered" in their own home. But neighbors talk. Rumors about Mr. Shelby, claiming he was not quite what he appeared to be.

"Shit," Luke says again. "They're going to connect the dots. I told you this couldn't last forever. Sooner or later someone's going to—"

"Shhh," Joanne says, fully awake now, "I'm trying to listen."

A neighbor of the Shelbys from the down the street dares to speak the word out loud. "I think he was an Evo."

"Wonderful," Luke says.

The reporter continues:

"And sources close to the investigation believe this double-murder could be the work of…"

Luke stops breathing and waits for it. Waits for the

reporter to say that some kind of forensic evidence has been left behind, which in turn has led the police to other similar crimes throughout the southeastern U.S. Maybe they've gone so far as to capture some of their movements on surveillance cameras. Or even discover their identities. Hell, maybe right now they're breaking down the front door of their home in Buffalo…

"…the terrorist Mohinder Suresh."

Wait.

What?

Luke knows he should be relieved that their identities haven't been revealed. But something about it bothers him.

Mohinder Suresh hasn't driven around for hundreds of miles. Mohinder Suresh hasn't spent endless nights doing surveillance. Mohinder Suresh hasn't kicked down those doors, or pulled the triggers.

Mohinder Suresh. *Please.*

And forget worrying about this stuff. He's been driving himself crazy for nothing.

"Why should we even bother cleaning up after ourselves?" Luke asks. "They're going to credit it all to this Suresh guy anyway. In fact, we should start leaving notes. 'You're welcome, world. Love, Mohinder.'"

"Forget it," Joanne says. "How is this not a good thing? We're not looking for fame. Have you forgotten why we're doing this?"

Of course Luke hasn't forgotten.

"Meanwhile," Joanne continues, "we need to find a new target."

"What about L.A.? That El Vengador idiot is all but begging for someone to show up and put the barrel of a shotgun between the eye holes on his stupid mask."

"All the way out west for one Evo?" Joanne asks. "A waste

of time. Plenty of them to deal with here. There are probably a dozen right here in Knoxville we don't know about."

"Sure. But you know how hard it is to flush them out. They're all frightened and have battened down the hatches."

Which makes their mission all the more difficult. It's tough hunting monsters who look like ordinary people. Their hunt is based on Internet rumors and clues on social media, followed by laborious detective work.

Before June 13th, plenty of people posted videos of their alleged powers. But after that horrible day, everything was pulled down. Real leads are few and far between.

"We'll find more," Joanne says. "We always do."

"I wish we could get our hands on some of those swab kits. Sure would save us a lot of trouble."

Joanne pours herself a second nightcap, offers Luke one. He declines—booze is the last thing he needs right now—and climbs out of bed. He's still too keyed-up to sleep. Besides, before long it'll be 3 a.m. and he'll be staring the ceiling, thinking about ways to find their next target, hoping to give Joanne something to look forward to. Without a target in their sights, she tends to get morose. Conversation withers. It's like being married to a zombie. So why put it off?

Joanne puts herself to bed with whiskey. Lucky her. Luke ends up staying awake all night, furiously tapping on their laptop.

THE TARGET realizes that her life as she knows it is totally over.

Oh, God, is it *over*.

Being fired on the spot—after a lengthy and humiliating interlude of begging, all with the sickly scent of chocolate in the air—was bad enough. The Target had prided herself on being gainfully employed, just like her older brothers before her. They were able to maintain decent grade-point averages and sock away cash for community college. Her mother and grandmother expect the same from her.

So having to explain to her mom why she was home early will be spectacularly shitty. *I can't afford to support you, too!* her mother will yell. *Why are you doing this to me?* Mom rarely considers anything outside of her own needs to be important; she's a narcissist supreme. (The Target had learned the term this year in psychology class; it's the most useful thing she's ever learned in school.)

And then there's the mountain of homework she has to plow through. (Though she has to admit, she's kind of digging this week's assigned reading—Agatha Christie's *And Then There Were None*.) Teachers never seem to care about how much work their colleagues assign; they act as if they were the only teachers in the universe. The Target supposes that they're world-class narcissists, too.

This day has sucked hard.

She can't stop thinking about that poor old man. Hopefully someone got him to a hospital, set his wrist.

The tree's on her mind, too. She's murdered a tree and an old man's wrist. Maybe the TV news is right. Maybe Evos should be stopped.

To give herself a little mental break, she pushes her assignments aside and checks out YouTube for a while, mindlessly surfing from one video to the next. Some Lana Del Rey—her personal idol, and the only person who seems to get how truly dark it is out there. This, of course, leads to Lana Del Rey tribute videos featuring girls who fancy themselves decent singers (um, no). Which leads to kids goofing around, taking a "yoga challenge" in their parents' living room with predictably destructive results. Kids unboxing electronic gadgets. Kids eating giant bowls of ramen noodles. Kids doing homework, just like the Target is supposed to be doing. Kids with normal lives, who probably hadn't assaulted a senior citizen this afternoon.

Then she sees her friends on Twitter buzzing about a certain video filmed that day in Cleveland, so of course she clicks over to check it out.

And oh, God, is she sorry the moment she clicks the play button.

Her entire soul goes numb. It's like someone filmed her most secret, most intimate thoughts and then projected them on giant screens all over the planet.

She can't believe she was stupid enough to use her powers in public again.

And she can't believe someone just happened to be recording when she did.

Shit!

So now she's barricaded herself in the half-bathroom downstairs near the mud room, cell phone in hand. She doesn't want to watch it again, but she presses the little triangle anyway. Maybe if she plays it again, she'll wake up and realize that this was all a bad dream, that a new school day was ahead of her and she still had her stupid job at the Sweet Shoppe.

No such luck.

The video plays.

The grainy, jittery clip had been shot with a cell-phone camera. It's super-shaky, in fact, and the quality isn't too good. There's a sweep of the first level of the Cleveland Arcade.

And boom, there she goes, popping out of the wall. She sees the instant shock on her own face as she realizes she's about to collide with the old man. Look how her body contorts to avoid that collision! (See, at least she was trying to do the right thing.) And then, finally, the awful moment where the man's wrist breaks and she spins around, horrified, but keeps on running because she doesn't know what else to do except try to make it to work on time.

The Target can't believe it's up there for the whole city (the whole world!) to see. Who was the person holding that cell phone? No idea, because he or she didn't turn it around for a reaction shot. Not even a little selfie moment. The action was focused on the Target and that old man.

The account appears to be new (almost zero subscribers, and no other videos), and the handle is completely unfamiliar—COFFIN77. The one reassuring thing is that it can't be somebody the Target knows—otherwise, they would have posted her name, right?

The not-so-reassuring thing is that handle. COFFIN. One of her favorite movies of all time is David Fincher's *Zodiac*. She absolutely loves the cat-and-mouse aspect of it. The letters, the clues, the manhunt... but most of all, the name the killer chose for himself, which is so deliciously *creepy*.

Now, though, it feels weird, being on the other side of the equation. COFFIN. Ugh. Who would call themselves COFFIN?

Did that mean they wanted to put her inside one?

JOANNE hears a voice shouting at her, as if from the bottom of a deep, dark well:

"Holy shit, honey, you've got to see this!"

Joanne doesn't know who's speaking to her, but she knows the owner of that voice will soon be dead. No one would be stupid enough to wake her up like this, by shouting at her.

"Joanne, come here."

Oh. Her husband. That's who's speaking to her. Luke Collins is extremely lucky that he's married to her; otherwise, she'd be forced to blow his brains out.

As Joanne rubs the haze out of her eyes, she sees that her husband is on the laptop, still wearing the same clothes as last night—ripped shirt and all.

"You been up all night on that thing?" Joanne asks. "What, were you surfing porn?"

"You've got to see this. It was posted online just a few hours ago. I think it's legit."

Luke brings the laptop over to the bed, props it up on her belly, and then presses play on a YouTube clip. One minute, it's just an ordinary mall. The next, a teenager materializes out of the wall, bumping into an elderly shopper who starts howling in agony.

"Eh?" Luke asks.

"What the hell is that supposed to be?"

"Here, watch it again."

"No, what I'm saying is that it could be a fake," Joanne says. "We've seen plenty of those before—kids looking for attention. Remember that little jerk who pretended he could defy gravity, but it turned out he was just using special effects? I wanted to wring his neck, even if he wasn't an Evo."

"I thought the same thing, too. But look at the guy, the one she bumps into. For one thing, he's in his 70s. Does he seem like the type to join a bunch of teenagers in pulling a prank?"

"Could be. Lots of bored adults out there. But even if it is real, it's an anonymous post. Impossible for us to track down whoever made it. Or where it was filmed."

"But that's what I've been doing all night. Pinning down the location. It was killing me, but then it finally clicked."

"And…?"

"It's Cleveland."

"How can you possibly know that?"

Luke reminds her that he attended a dental convention there back in 2012, and the convention hotel was part of something called the Arcade.

"It's the fanciest mall I've ever seen—right out of the Victorian era. So when I saw that clip, I knew I recognized the place. I just had to wrack my brains until I remembered."

Joanne feels that tingle again. The thrill of the hunt. She put herself to bed with booze last night because there was nothing to look forward to—not after the Shelby killings. Part of her wouldn't have minded if she never woke up again.

But she has to admit, this sounds good. Though she doesn't want her husband to know she can be won over that easily.

"You should get some sleep," she says.

"Cleveland is only six hours away. We can be there by mid-afternoon if we hurry up, shower, and leave soon."

"You want to go to Cleveland and what, hope to run into this girl? That's ludicrous."

"This video was posted just last night. It's the best chance we have. You know I'm good at this stuff."

Joanne has to admit, in his own nerdy, determined way, Luke is kind of good at this stuff.

Still, a wife should never let her husband enjoy an easy victory.

"I don't know," Joanne says. "I was sort of coming

around to the idea of a long drive to L.A."

"Come on," Luke says. "The rust belt is lovely this time of year."

THE TARGET wants to gag because breakfast is pan-fried greasy pork sausage. Fried eggs, sunny-side up (sort of). Hard toast, with Great Lake-sized pools of butter floating on the surface.

If this world doesn't kill her first, her grandmother's cooking will.

As usual, the Target politely begs off and searches the fridge for orange juice. Something that won't instantly clog her veins.

"That can't be all you're having," her grandma says.

"Grandma, for real?"

"You need a good breakfast before school."

The Target sighs. This is all she ever has, first thing in the morning. Her grandmother knows that. But every morning, she tries to feed her fried meat and carbs anyway. The old grande dame is used to cooking for a house full of hungry people. But with Mom working nights and her brothers in their own places now, the Target is the only person at the breakfast table most mornings.

Her grandmother is now faced with more food than she knows what to do with. As usual, she'll pack it up and take it over to their next-door neighbors, who have a gaggle of hungry kids. But the trip over there can wait. Grandma sits down and turns on the morning news.

Which stops the Target's heart all over again. That's because the lead story is about a double-murder in Atlanta—a suspected Evo hate crime. And the likely assassin, "authorities say": Mohinder Suresh, the genetics professor-turned-terrorist.

A.k.a. the Boogeyman.

The whole thing with Mohinder Suresh confuses the Target. At first, he was supposed to be on the Evos' side—right? But now he's supposedly hunting them down? Whatever. You can't trust the media; it's just one more lie heaped on a mountain of them. The only thing you can trust, the Target believes, is seeing something with your own eyes.

Anyway, the Target knows that the idea of Mohinder Suresh coming after her personally is unlikely. There are hundreds, probably thousands of Evos hiding out across the country. And like anyone who's about to take a plane right after news of a horrific airline crash, she's probably suffering from crazy-irrational fears.

But…

But…

But what if this Mohinder Suresh sees the clip online and comes looking for her? Sure, there are hundreds—probably—thousands of Evos out there… but how many have been stupid enough to let someone catch them using their powers in public?

There are some things you can't fix. Like the way you're born. Your genetic makeup. Your gender. Whether or not you have powers.

But there are some things you can control.

The Target finishes her orange juice and walks the glass over to the sink. She looks down at the steaming breakfast she isn't going to eat and makes up her mind.

She needs to find out who posted the clip—and force them to take it down, no matter what.

LUKE thinks Cleveland is ugly, dirty, and dying. It's a classic Rust-Belt town where the boom is two full generations in the past and the outlook for the future is bleak at best. People stay because they can't imagine a life anywhere else.

Which, of course, reminds him of home.

Luke does the navigation thing while Joanne drives. He's been here before, but never in a car. They arrive just before rush hour, but end up caught in traffic anyway. Which is frustrating. Many of the Arcade shops close at 6 p.m., so if they don't make it there soon, their hunt will be delayed until tomorrow. Luke knows Joanne doesn't want to waste another night in a local hotel. She's not even fully convinced the online clip is real.

"There has to be a better way," she says, glaring at the traffic through the windshield.

"No, I-79 will get us downtown fairly quick," Luke says. "Trust me, when the traffic starts moving…"

"No, not that. I mean finding Evos. What if we *did* manage to steal a bunch of those swabs the cops had at the checkpoint? It would make our hunt a lot simpler."

"How? I know I said we should steal those kits, but I don't see how we could use them. Unless we walk up to random strangers and ask if they wouldn't mind us poking around in their mouths."

"You're a dentist, duh. We could set up a free clinic."

"Sure," Luke says. "And after maybe a thousand free teeth cleanings, we'll run across the one dude who can fly."

"His mouth's already open," Joanne says. "Wouldn't take much to kill him. The right amount of nitrous oxide, and—"

She makes a POOF sound with her mouth that Luke finds strangely erotic. This is the freakish state of their marriage: snuffing out a life has become a turn-on. More gallows humor.

* * *

"Well," Luke says, "until we track down a truckload of Evo swabs, I say we stick to the plan at hand."

Joanne repeats the POOF noise, as if she can somehow sense this gets a rise out of him. She doesn't smile much these days, but he knows this is her version of kidding around.

They make it to the Cleveland Arcade by 5:35. The hallways are bustling with the after-work crowd, people running last-minute errands before the commute home. Luke glances around at the couples, feelings alternating between envy and pity. Envy because maybe they have kids waiting for them at home, and there will be dinner and video games to play and jokes to be had.

Pity because they don't know the real threat out there—the monsters that could bring civilization to a crashing halt.

They pose as grief-stricken parents looking for their missing daughter. All they have is the best still from the YouTube clip, zoomed in on the Target's pixelated face. The good news is that the race of the girl is somewhat indeterminate. Luke and Joanne could very well be her parents, even though they're different races.

The bad news is that the race of the girl is somewhat indeterminate, so they really don't know much about who they're hunting. If someone asks, "Is she light-skinned?", they'll have to fake it.

Nobody seems to recognize the girl. Some people don't even bother looking—they're too wrapped up in their own personal dramas, or are worried about being the victim of some kind of sales pitch or scam. (Luke can't blame them. He was the same way, back when he had a normal life.)

But they know from experience that older Americans are more open to such questions. At the very least, the elderly like to have someone paying attention to them.

At about five minutes until six, they finally strike minor pay dirt.

An old woman, liver spots all over her face and hands, looks at the photo, looks at Luke and Joanne, looks at the photo, then finally says, "Doesn't she work at the candy shop?"

THE TARGET types a frantic message:

I am a friend of the person in that video. Please take it down right away, it's very important.

She types this on a computer at the school library a minute after it opens. This is the only place where she's (reasonably) sure she can keep things anonymous. A school IP, paired with an email anonymizer service (she likes Hide Me), should be enough. Chances are, this creep with the cell phone is just some anonymous dude who doesn't know her name. She doesn't want to inadvertently out herself.

The only problem is, she needs to keep making excuses to go visit the library to see if there's any response from COFFIN77.

After first period, she run-walks back to the library, which is in the opposite direction of her next class. But she can log on quick, see if there's a reply, then double back to class—and who cares if she's a little late? It's not as if she's going to get fired from school.

But all the computers are occupied, and the same goes after second period. This is so. Damn. Frustrating!

So the Target decides to take a chance and check Hide

Me from her phone. He won't be able to track her through her phone, will he?

She's just going to have to take that chance.

And after signing in…

Nothing.

Maybe the guy (or girl!) has already forwarded the clip to Mohinder Suresh. For all she knows, there's a national tip line to rat out suspected Evos. There could be a S.W.A.T. team scrambling for Cleveland right now, looking for that silly girl who broke an old man's wrist after walking straight through a wall.

School drags on… forevvvvverrrrrr.

When the end of the day finally arrives, however, the Target feels weird about heading straight home, where her Mom will probably take the opportunity to tell her how much she's ruining her life. Usually, she's racing for the Arcade, running like hell for the bus that will take her to Euclid Avenue—a bus that's almost always behind schedule, leaving the Target behind schedule, too.

Then it occurs to her: why not go there anyway?

Think about it: the person she's looking for (this COFFIN77 asshole) was almost certainly there, shooting video on their cell phone. Maybe they're always at the Arcade, hanging out. Maybe they just got lucky while shooting random shit.

And maybe if COFFIN77 recognizes her, it'll show in their eyes. And then the Target will finally know their identity.

Or at least, their face. And then maybe she could force this person to take down the video immediately.

It's worth the risk…

* * *

JOANNE says the name to herself,

"Marylou Winawer."

That's their target? Seriously? She sounds like a bored Cleveland housewife, not an Evo who can walk through walls.

But the owner of the candy store confirmed her identity, and even seemed to be glad to rat her out. Apparently she worked at the store until yesterday, when she arrived late ("for the goddamned last time," the cranky old bastard told them). Joanne knew their "worried parents" routine wouldn't fly with this guy, so instead they presented themselves as truant officers. The candy-shop owner didn't seem surprised. "I knew that kid was trouble." Even helpfully gave them Marylou's home address.

Back out in the car, they discuss strategy. This is always the part when Joanne starts to get excited. Thirty minutes ago, it was all just a fuzzy possibility. Now, it's official. They're on the hunt.

Every Evo, however, has to be handled differently. There is no one-size-fits-all method of taking them out.

"So, we're dealing with an Evo who can walk through walls," Luke says.

"Hard to pin her down in a corner, I guess."

"Our best bet will be to get her out in the open. Maybe on her way to school?"

"But then she could just dart into any building, right?"

"Our handicap is that we don't know Cleveland. And we're on her home turf."

"You said you attended a convention here."

"I'll be honest—I didn't do much exploring. Especially not in the residential neighborhoods. Buffalo is depressing enough."

"Let's at least go and take a look at where she lives. Maybe the right way will present itself."

Where Marylou Winawer lives turns out to be a neighborhood called Slavic Village. Luke does some of his usual nerdy online research and comes up with a plethora of facts that Joanne doesn't give a shit about—but she feels compelled to humor him anyway.

"Huh," Luke says, reading from his phone. "This neighborhood used to be its own township, Newburgh, dating back to 1799. How crazy is that."

"Absolutely insane," Joanne says.

"Lots of Czech and Polish immigrants settled here in the late 1800s, but they didn't start calling it Slavic Village until the 1970s. Is 'Winawer' Polish?"

Does it even matter?

Sometimes Joanne is astounded by Luke's ability to geek out about the most random things. Who gives a high holy hoot about the history of Cleveland and its myriad peoples? Luke does, now that they're here. While this comes in handy once in a while—like when he was able to identify the Cleveland Arcade from a random YouTube clip—it does get a little old.

Joanne doesn't to want to learn anything about this "vibrant yet struggling" neighborhood. She just wants to drive by the girl's house to see what they're up against.

Pin down the best way to kill this freak, and then do it.

Joanne says, "Hey. Can you get her phone number on that thing?"

MARYLOU, A.K.A. THE TARGET went back to the scene of the crime, thinking, *this is soooo stupid*.

And it was.

Not only did she have the weird feeling that hundreds of eyes were on her, but she was afraid to look directly at anyone, fearful she'd find her tormentor. Because if she did—what would be her next move? Threaten to kick their ass until they took down the clip?

Marylou was especially freaked out by the sight of any tourist holding a cell phone. At any moment they might spin around, aim the thing at her, and scream *Gotcha, sucker!*

What had she been thinking? Oh, right—*I don't want to go home.*

While she was in the Arcade, Marylou thought about maybe slinking back to the candy shop and begging for her old job all over again. At least that way, maybe her mom would crawl down out of her ass.

But as she approached the Sweet Shoppe, she saw that old man Baraniuk was talking to a couple—a white man, a black woman. They had the mannerisms of cops, and they were showing her ex-boss a photo.

Oh, no.

She told herself: Get a grip, girlfriend—these aren't government agents looking for Evos. They're probably just tourists looking for directions or something.

But then why are they showing Baraniuk a photo?

This had been a spectacularly shitty idea, Marylou decided, then hightailed it out of there. She didn't even bother waiting for a bus. She wanted to walk all the way back to Slavic Village to clear her head, give herself time to think.

So that's what she's doing now. Walking.

She knows she'll be late for dinner—but that's part of the plan. Mom leaves at 7 for her 8 p.m.-to-8 a.m. shift at the hospital (it's brutal, but the pay is better for the dehumanizing hours). If Marylou can waltz in the door after that, she'll at least be able to avoid that drama. Her grandma will probably try to convince her to eat something meat-laden and greasy, but that happened every night.

She's almost home when she receives a text on her cell:

I know who you are. I can help.

Oh, God, she thinks. Who is this? How did this person get my number?

She texts back:

Do I know you?

There's no response for the longest time. Which is extremely disconcerting. In fact, she's already at home and upstairs in her bedroom considering curling up into the fetal position for the rest of the night when her phone buzzes.

Please wait for further instructions.

LUKE drives them through Slavic Village to the address supplied by the guy at the Sweet Shoppe. He pulls into an empty space across the street.

The houses on this block are hodge-podge, from all different time periods. The Winawer house, for instance, is one half of a duplex that was probably built over a hundred years ago. To the right is a newer Craftsman-style home that looks only 50 or 60 years old. In front of the house is a small yard, not exactly manicured. Clean enough, Luke supposes, but he wouldn't want to raise a family there.

I wonder what it looked like when it was Newburgh, circa 1799, he thinks.

"This looks like a dump," Joanne says. "We're not dealing with suburban types like the Shelbys."

"No, I don't think so."

"Probably no alarm system. And this doesn't look like a Town Watch kind of neighborhood."

"I don't see bars on the windows," Luke says, "like some of the other houses on this block. Family can't afford them?"

"So she's a lower-middle-class girl," Joanne says.

"And she was using her powers in public. So she's probably not very bright."

They continue checking out the house, playing detective.

"So what now?" Luke asks. He knows that his wife likes to take the lead when planning these things.

"We need a look inside that house," Joanne says. "We can't see much through the windows, bars or not."

It's true. This place is nothing like the modern Shelby home, with its generously wide windows and those sliding doors out back by the pool. The windows are small (probably because it's easier to trap heat that way), and even if they weren't, the shades are drawn.

"We need a ruse," Luke says.

Joanne looks around the car at their supplies. All of the weapons are in the trunk, for obvious reasons. Not much here except for some luggage, their laptop, bottles of water, snack wrappers, and Luke's dental kit.

Which Joanne pulls from the backseat and drops into his lap. Not exactly gently, either.

"Huh," he says. "What am I supposed to do with this? Pretend to be an itinerant dentist looking for stray cavities?"

"No," Joanne says. Then she proceeds to tell him *exactly*

what he's supposed to do with his dentist kit.

A few minutes later he's knocking on the front door of the Winawer home, trying to work up the right kind of patter. How many dozens of times have traveling salesmen knocked on their door at home? Luke should be an old pro at this. The thing is, both he and Joanne are kind of hard-asses when it comes to solicitations, and practically nobody makes it past the vestibule. Just once, Luke opened their door to an overheated young woman who was hawking a new energy provider; he gave her a cold glass of water. (She didn't want to be knocking on his door anymore than Luke wanted to be answering it.)

But now Luke has to get inside the house long enough to formulate an attack plan. That means his sales patter has to be convincing and confident.

The door opens a few inches. There's a thick chain connecting the door to the frame. Two pale, tired eyes peer out at him. The old lady behind the door is short, that's for sure.

"Yes? Can I help you?"

"Good evening, ma'am, I'm Donny Sliwinski with Home Vanguard Services," Luke says.

The name Sliwinski came from the Slavic Village Wikipedia page about a 70s-era developer, and the business name was pulled directly out of his ass.

The older woman, who looks Polish, doesn't respond to the name at all. If she knows any Sliwinskis, she's not letting on. Great.

"I see you've got a chain lock, which is good," Luke says. "But it's nowhere near enough."

"What do you want? I'm not buying anything."

"My company is in Slavic Village tonight offering an amazing deal—over $2,000 worth of state-of-the-art home security equipment for free. In just five minutes, I can show you how to make your home more secure. And ma'am, no offense intended, but you could use something a bit more formidable than this chain. Do you know that crime is on the rise in this area?"

Or it's about to be, Luke thinks.

MARYLOU can hear her grandmother talking to someone downstairs, but she can't see who. A male voice. Official-sounding, like he's here on Very Important Business. But she doesn't dare step out of her room to find out who it might be.

What if it's a government agent—one of the people she saw at the Sweet Shoppe?

She's tempted to crawl out of her window and sneak away into the night. Go to a friend's house until she can figure out her next move. The problem is, none of her friends know her secret. Even back when Evos were a thing you could be in public, Marylou kept her powers to herself. She was already awkward and geeky. She didn't want the *freak* label applied on top of that.

So while it would be amazing to be somewhere else right now, how can she burden one of her friends with the horrible truth? Because sooner or later she'll have to tell them what's going on, and she doesn't know if she can withstand the looks of withering judgment, the social banishment. Marylou can always hold on to the hope that at least one of her friends will accept her for who she is. To have that taken away… No, that would be too much.

As she strains to hear the conversation downstairs, her cell phone beeps.

A text message.

JOANNE is watching as the old lady slams the door in her husband's face.

Nice.

But when he turns to look back, their eyes lock as they hear the noise at the same time.

The wail of police sirens—heading their way.

What the hell?

Okay, maybe the police are headed somewhere else. After all, as Luke noted (from his quickie Internet research), Slavic Village is a crime-ridden neighborhood.

But Joanne knows better. There's a tingling in her gut, an almost sixth sense she's had since adolescence, a feeling that tells her: *The coppers are coming for you.*

Luke knows it, too—but the hesitant look on his face tells her that he's hoping for the best, that he believes the police are headed someplace else. That he can knock again and somehow salvage this outing.

No, they're headed this way—come on! Joanne screams in her mind.

But Luke still hesitates. Even as Joanne waves him forward to cross the street and climb into the car so they can get the hell out of here. By the time he gets the message, the first Cleveland PD squad car has rounded the corner. Joanne can see it in her rearview mirror. Shit!

Luke sees it, too. But now it's his turn to wave her on, urging her to go, go, go.

If she could scream in this split second, she'd be screaming: *LUKE COLLINS, GET YOUR ASS IN THIS CAR RIGHT NOW!*

But instead he bolts across the porch, over the fence, then up the narrow space between the semi-detached Winawer home and that of its next-door neighbor. He leaps over a four-foot cyclone fence and disappears.

Well. That's something she didn't expect.

Joanne shifts into drive and slams a boot onto the accelerator, rocketing down the street. If the cops decide to pursue her, then fine. She's been in car chases before, and she's always prevailed.

What worries her is Luke. What the hell is he thinking?

MARYLOU is startled as she reads the text message at the same time she hears the sirens:

You're welcome.

It takes a moment to unpack the meaning of that message. Thank you—for what? Are you the guy knocking at my door? Or are you a cop?

She types:

Who are you?

More tomorrow. But don't go to school. Pretend you're sick.

Why?

The person at your door was here to kill you. The police scared him away.

How do you know this?

Because I'm the one who called the police.

Well. That sort of brings it all into focus, doesn't it?

Either her mystery texter is on her side and is genuinely trying to protect her from government agents, or it's Mohinder Suresh or whoever it is who likes to hunt down Evos for a living…

…or maybe he's messing with her mind just to get his (or her) jollies.

None of these possibilities is appealing in the least.

But when the cops knock on the front door and start to question her poor grandma, Marylou finally feels brave enough to venture downstairs. She sees her grandma, confused, trying to explain things to the cops. "He was selling home security systems," she says, still troubled by the sight of badges and guns in her living room. "I told him I wasn't interested and closed the door."

A few minutes earlier, one of the cops says, a dispatcher received an anonymous call that an old lady was being knifed to death at this address. "Why would someone say that?"

Sadly, Marylou thinks she knows why.

And she's pretty sure that this "anonymous tipster" might go by the online handle COFFIN77.

LUKE had only been thinking of his wife, of course.

But now he's seriously wondering: *What the hell was I thinking?*

The narrow gap between the houses led to a backyard, and beyond that (over another fence) a small alley overgrown with weeds. On instinct, Luke bolted right, swatting plant stalks and broad leaves out of his path as he ran. He crossed a street and ducked down another alley, then decided to change it up and go left this time. Keep it random, in case there were a pack of uniforms on his trail.

As it turned out, there were no cops in pursuit. And his trail was so random that Luke ended up behind a brick church with no earthly idea of where he was.

So now he pulls out his phone, taps a mapping app, then calls his wife and asks her to pick him up.

Not exactly the way he saw this night ending. However, he has learned something useful about the neighborhood: there are ways out if you need to split in a hurry.

Back at a chain motel on the fringes of Cleveland, Joanne opens a fresh bottle of scotch. Luke has a tumbler, too.

"We pushed it too hard," Luke says.

"You should have kicked your way in there," Joanne says. "Taken her out while you could."

"Yeah, right. I think it was just the grandmother at home. I didn't see the girl."

"I'm sure she was in there. And I think she saw us— because who else would have called the police?"

Fair point.

"Do you think she'll run?" Luke asks.

"I would," Joanne says. "Absolutely. She might even be on the road right now."

"Ugh."

"But," Joanne continues, "I think she's young and scared and probably not willing to make a bold move like that. I say we go back to the house early tomorrow morning and see if she shows her face."

Luke notes the depth of scotch in his wife's tumbler. At least four, maybe even five fingers' worth. He wants to say: *Maybe we should make this an early night, then.* But he knows better. And he doesn't want to get into an argument about it.

Instead Luke dumps out the rest of his scotch and

washes his own tumbler in the bathroom sink, then brushes his teeth. He fantasizes a little about what would have happened if he had kicked in the door, knocked down the old lady, and gone hunting. Sometimes he suspects Joanne wishes she were married to a bad-ass. More than the bad-ass he pretends to be.

Luke takes out his laptop and does more research on the neighborhood. Calls up a map of the streets so he'll know them better next time.

Joanne drinks her scotch, pours herself another, then finally turns in. Which is Luke's cue.

He crawls into bed, spooning himself up against his wife, wondering if they could maybe go for a repeat of the previous night. He tucks his right arm under her pillow, then places his left hand on her hip.

But Joanne's body is stiff, unresponsive. Luke is tempted to glide his hand up her belly toward her breasts, but thinks better of it. There's no reward tonight. Not for a job not-well-done.

Tomorrow he'll have to do better.

JOANNE watches from across the street.

It's painfully early the next morning. The house is quiet. No sign of the Evo yet—not even in the upper windows. This is a school day; she should be heading for class in about an hour. Joanne's head aches. She saw the judgment in her husband's eyes the previous night: *Why don't you put down that drink and go to bed.* It annoyed her that he could be confrontational with his eyes, but not his mouth. Come on, say it. Don't be a pussy.

So she ended up polishing off a good part of the bottle before finally turning in. *You don't understand, sweetheart,* she wanted to tell his sleeping form. *This is how I put myself to bed. Otherwise, I sit up all night thinking about* him.

Apparently, Luke was able to sleep just fine—which was also annoying.

"Here," he says now, handing her a cup of black coffee. They had bought four large cups at a fast-food drive-through. Anticipating a rough morning.

"No, I'm fine."

"Drink it," he insists. "It'll make you more alert."

"If I drink another, I'll have to find somewhere to pee."

"Hey, I'm standing guard, too."

"Then what happens if she walks out her front door—you come get me while I'm peeing in an alley somewhere? Meanwhile, she gets away."

"We don't even know she's here."

"No, we don't."

They continue to watch the house. No one exits. No one enters.

"I think it's just her and the grandmother," Luke says.

"Yeah? How do you know?"

"Why else would an old lady answer the door if, say, a mom or a dad were home? Also didn't see any toys in the living room, so I'm ruling out little kids. I think she's an only child or the youngest."

Joanne stares at the Winawer house with something like white-hot hate. If she could choose an Evo power, she'd pick one that could make things spontaneously combust.

(Of course, that would be beside the point, wouldn't it? She'd have to ask Luke to kill her, put her out of her own super-powered misery.)

More minutes tick by. The neighborhood is sleepy. Some blue-collar workers shuffle past, headed for their white vans, but none of them pays much attention to Luke and Joanne. Probably think they're a suburban couple here to buy drugs.

Still nothing.

"I say we kick in the door and drag this girl out of bed," Joanne says. "Enough time-wasting. Every day we're watching her house, it's another day when hundreds of Evos walk around unpunished."

"What if she's not inside?" Luke asks. "Then we've tipped our hand, and we really will have wasted our time."

As if we didn't tip our hand last night, Joanne thinks.

Then, across the street, the front door opens…

MARYLOU would stay in her small bedroom forever if she could.

No school

No work.

No social life.

Nothing.

Just meals sent up on a tray and electricity, and she'd be fine.

On second thought: don't even bother with the electricity.

Because now she's even too afraid to use her laptop. What if the people watching her have gotten hold of her IP address? They could theoretically track everything she types. She knew a boy in school, Iain, who was big on conspiracy theories. Even if only half the crap Iain talked about was true ("They put tracking devices in the water supply!"), then the world was a far scarier place than she had ever realized.

But Marylou cannot stay in her room forever, of course. She needs help from the outside world.

Last night someone tried to convince her that he (or she)

could provide that help. But what did her would-be savior really do? Pick up a phone and file an anonymous tip? Hell, anyone could do that. It doesn't mean she's got a guardian angel out there.

If she's going to trust anyone, she needs to start trusting in herself.

She can't be the only Evo in this kind of situation. What do they do? Where do they hide? How do they go about their daily lives?

Marylou knows the answers won't come to her out of thin air, so she decides to risk it. She opens her laptop and starts searching. Better to do something than just sit here, scared out of her mind.

She types into a search field:

EVO ESCAPE

There are a lot of hate sites out there, on top of the usual social-media postings with threats of violence and truly hideous memes—I LIKE EVOS JUST FINE / ESPECIALLY THE ONES POWERING MY FURNACE over photos of tortured and burned human bodies. Maybe they're genuine Evos who have been scarified along the way, maybe they're just random victims of unspeakable violence. Does it matter, either way?

But there are other kinds of sites.

One being a Hero Truther site, complete with positive stories about Evos—there's a lot of love for The Cheerleader on this site—along with… yes! Discussion boards. Marylou has to cycle through seemingly endless topics until she finds the one she needs: TRAVELER'S AID, it's called. She has to scroll down quite a bit until she understands what this is all about.

Apparently, there's an Evo "Underground Railroad." Modes of travel, complete with safe houses, that can transport Evos around the country, avoiding known roadblocks and Evo-swabbing checkpoints. Nobody links to these places directly, of course, but the site tells you how to leave a message so that someone will get back to you with instructions.

Marylou isn't sure at first. The whole thing could be an elaborate trap, meant to ensnare naïve Evos such as herself.

But what other choice does she have?

She's typing a message when there's a quick knock at her door, which causes her to jump out of her skin.

"Mary Louise?"

Oh, thank goodness. It's only her grandmother. Calling her by her two first names, which she hates—everyone else calls her Marylou, which she doesn't hate quite as much.

"Yes, Grandma?"

"I know you're not feeling well, so I'm going to run to the market for a few things. Will you be okay by yourself?"

For a moment, Marylou thinks: *Wait. I'll just go with Grandma! The government hit men after me wouldn't dare take out an innocent senior citizen, would they?*

But then she realizes: government hit men probably don't give a shit. They might suspect that Marylou comes from a long line of super-powered people. They might track down and kill her whole family, just to be sure!

Besides, she's supposed to be sick.

"I'll be fine, Grandma," she says as she types the words:

I don't know if this is real, but I could really, really use your help.

LUKE watches as the old lady goes tottering out of the front door and down the stairs, a reusable shopping bag hanging from her forearm. Grandmother Winawer, headed to the market. He wants to call out to her to pick up some toothpaste for them. (They're out.)

"See?" Luke says. "I told you. Grandma's the only one home."

Joanne says, "But you said the house was owned by an Elizabeth Winawer, 38 years old." That was according to a real-estate website. It's shocking, the kinds of records you can pull up just by entering a street address. "I think that one's a little older."

"Okay, so the mom's probably working nights."

"Which means she could be home at any moment."

"Right."

Joanne says, "Okay, here's what we do."

Luke is glad to hear Joanne sounding positive. It's the first time in days, the first time since Atlanta.

"Go on."

"We split up. I take the front, you take the back."

"This plan is sounding familiar."

"Right," Joanne says. "Just like the Shelbys. Difference is, this time, we set the house on fire *first*."

"What?"

Joanne smiles. Makes that POOF sound with her lips again.

"How does that help us?" Luke asks. "And don't forget, we're back to risking innocent lives. I thought we had agreed on that—no collateral damage."

"No risk to the innocent. We torch the place, then scream and yell to get their attention. When they come out, we make our move. I'll stay in the front, you cover the back. If I see little Marylou come out with her family, I'll play the

51

role of concerned passerby and get her alone, then blam, a bullet in the brain when she least expects it."

"And if she comes out of the back, then it's on me."

"Exactly. But remember—if she can walk through walls, you've got to cover the entire back of the house, not just the door."

Luke considers this. "The timing is tricky. What if the firemen arrive before we've killed her?"

"We do some research. Find out the response time in this neighborhood. Maybe that means calling in a false report or two."

"Or maybe even test out our incendiary device."

"You want to start another fire? That's so rock-and-roll of you."

Luke smiles. She likes it when he changes roles, becomes the proactive one. But he's been giving it some thought ever since she said the word "fire." They can't approach this like they're just trying to ignite the coals at a family barbecue. They need something with enough firepower to really attract attention.

"Do you know how to make a Molotov cocktail?" Luke asks his wife.

"Why would I?"

"Hey, you used to run with a rough crowd. Who knows what kind of mischief you got up to with your mates."

She punches him. "You're the bloody firebug."

No, I'm not, Luke thinks. Molotov cocktails are a little out of his area of expertise. Any recipe found online would be suspect. And even if he did find a reliable set of instructions, procuring the ingredients might raise some red flags. He's sure the government has all sorts of silent alarms set for anyone foolish enough to go shopping for bomb parts. *I'm not a terrorist. I'm a goddamned dentist.*

But wait...

That's it.

He has his dental license. He has access to all the gear they need.

"Come on, let's go before Mom gets home," Joanne says. "We take this bitch out tonight."

MARYLOU spends the day pretending to be sick.

Mom comes home and gives her the third degree— checking her temperature, looking into her eyes, appraising the quality of her (admittedly fake) coughs. She doesn't do this out of motherly concern for her youngest child. She's thinking about much how this could possibly screw up *her own* schedule, especially if she has to take time off from the hospital.

But Marylou assures her that she'll be fine, she just needs a day of rest.

Mom considers this, then narrows her eyes. "Someone bothering you at school?"

God, I wish it were that simple.

"No, nothing like that."

"Boy trouble?"

Good question, Mom! I have no idea if it's a boy or a girl who wants to murder me in cold blood.

But instead she just says,

"No!"

Mom backs off, leaving Marylou to herself. Only after she departs does Marylou realize she would have preferred her mother to stay around a little bit longer. In case, you know, this is her last day alive.

Before long it's evening, and Mom heads back to the hospital. Grandma heads out, too, to an activity night at the senior center. Which is good, because if anything's going to happen, she'd rather not have her family involved.

Marylou starts when—at long last—a text arrives:

Finally you're thinking straight.

She responds:

Who is this?

The reply:

You asked for help. I'm here to give it.

Do I know you?

No. But you will soon.

Yeah, Marylou thinks, but you could be anyone. Maybe the whole "Underground Railroad" is a honeypot. (Her conspiracy theorist pal Iain told her about those, too.) This could be a government agency trying to lure clueless Evos into a trap!

I need to know who you are.

Consider me a friend.

A friend would tell me more.

Okay, here's more: I need some money to get you on the railroad.

Money? This is something that honestly hadn't occurred to her. But of course, if you're going to ride the train, you need to pay for a ticket.

How much?

At least $10,000. Can you do that?

Hell no, she can't do that. That's about $8,500 more than she has in her savings account—which is earmarked for college. (All of her Sweet Shoppe earnings to date, minus helping out with some bills around the house.)

That's a little expensive.

Doesn't have to be cash. A lot of us work on the barter system. Look around the house.

For what? Marylou thinks. Something to steal? But instead just she thumbs,

OK.

Meet me in 30 minutes at Terminal City Tower. I know what you look like, so I'll approach you.

She hesitates, thumbs hovering over her phone. Thirty minutes? That's not nearly enough time. And if she does go to meet this mysterious person, then what? Is she supposed to run away with him?

(And the $10,000 she doesn't have?)

Yes, Marylou, that's what he's talking about. You've badly wanted to avoid this topic, but there's no squirming around it now. You're talking about leaving your family—possibly forever. Your grandma. Your mother. And even your stupid older brothers (who you will miss, even if they probably won't even notice you're gone). Your school. Your friends. Bye-bye to everybody and everything you've ever known here in Cleveland.

The person on the other end of the text exchange can sense her hesitation.

You don't have much time. There are bad people closing in on you.

What? Who!?

Pack light and leave now.

How do I know you're not one of those bad people?

Stay in your house and find out. But believe me—I want to help. I was just like you once, and I know exactly what you're going through.

She very badly wants to believe him. She needs a savior—a guardian angel.

What do I call you?

For now, call me COFFIN77.

In other words, the one who posted the video in the first place. Outed her to the world.

COFFIN77 works for the Evo Underground Railroad?

JOANNE thinks: forget Molotov cocktails.

When bad-ass dentists want to go on a rampage of mass destruction, they opt for the tools at hand. Namely, medical grade nitrous oxide—99.0% pure, and available at chemical-supply houses and gas companies everywhere. *If* you have a dental permit. Which Luke, of course, does.

And you need a way to make it volatile enough to explode, which is easy—because Luke had to go through training sessions to ensure that his tanks wouldn't explode, say, during a root canal, sending both D.D.S. and patient up in flames.

The nerve-wracking part is carrying their improvised explosives up to the front porch. The tank isn't heavy, but it feels unstable, like a loaded pistol with a hair trigger. No, it's even more precarious than that. The jerry-rigged bomb in her hands feels like it has a quantum trigger. Look at it the wrong way, and two molecules will decide to collide. BOOM.

Not that she doesn't trust Luke's scientific expertise. He was always the nerd of the family, the model of stability and rationality. But still… If what she's carrying goes off prematurely, it's goodbye revenge spree, goodbye husband, goodbye everything.

Would that be so bad, she wonders? The past year has felt like a kind of limbo anyway. Her life with Luke and Dennis, that all made sense to her once. Even with Dennis's condition. Even with the fantastical stories that Luke would tell their son—that felt like *real life*, the one she always thought she deserved.

Then one day, it was all taken away from her. BOOM. Just like that.

And the only thing that makes her feel better is this. Settling the score, one dead Evo at a time.

Joanne quietly makes her way up the wooden porch

steps, hoping no one is looking at her from inside the house. She places the tank next to a thick post that supports the wooden roof above the porch. This is an old house, built around the turn of the century during far more optimistic times. It'll go up quick, with the wooden porch as the perfect kindling.

Which means there can be no more hiding inside.

Joanne nods from the porch. Luke makes his way around to the back of the house to take his position. The yards here are small, but there's that central alley overgrown with weeds the size of small trees. Plenty of places to hide. Don't screw this up, Luke, she thinks to herself. If the Evo gets away this time, they'll never find her.

She leans against their car and pulls out her cell phone. Yeah, Luke rigged the tank with a simple app. Press the button, the device wirelessly triggers a spark.

Now Joanne hesitates. Not because she's concerned about taking a human life. Forget that. This isn't a human life we're talking about here; this is an Evo. If those sons of bitches hadn't come out, hadn't decided to terrorize the world, then Dennis would still be alive. This would be an entirely different sort of family road trip.

No, Joanne Collins hesitates because this is the only high she can feel now—the snuffing out of an Evo life. She prays that the little bitch will come out the front door, maybe partially on fire. She'll savor every step the freak takes toward her, the time it takes to pull the trigger, and— most of all—the look on her face when the Evo realizes this is the end, and all the powers in the world can't save her from her fate.

She pushes the button.

MARYLOU jumps at the sound of the explosion.

At first she doesn't want to believe it. It's just a car backfiring. A kid playing around with fireworks. Happens all the time in this neighborhood.

But then she makes her way to her mother's bedroom at the front of the house, parts the curtains, and peers down toward the lawn. There's a glow down there, as if someone has turned on a spotlight. Then sparks shooting through the air. And finally a full-on raging fire, consuming the porch like it's a starving beast.

Oh. Her mystery texter was right. She doesn't have any time left, not even to pack! She has to leave right freakin' *now*.

All she can think to do is grab her phone (without a phone, she's totally lost). She glances at the screen as she runs through the house. COFFIN77 has sent another text:

Think smart. They have you surrounded.

Marylou reaches the ground floor, sees the flames raging out by the front door. (Thank God Grandma and Mom aren't here to see this, she thinks). She has no idea how big the fire might be—the entire porch might already be ablaze! Sure, she's seen movies where people go leaping through a wall of flame, but those are just special effects, right? With her luck, she'd catch fire and burn to a crisp before she reached the end of the block.

No, with her luck—she'd catch fire *and* get shot in the back as she tried to run.

The only other way out is through the back door. But if COFFIN77 is to be believed, there's already someone there waiting for her to run outside, guns most likely trained on the door itself. The moment she steps outside, she's a sitting duck.

And the longer she stays inside, the more she risks

choking or burning to death in her own home.

Which means Marylou has *no choice* but to use her powers.

Where, though? She could phase through to the homes on either side. But if one of her neighbors happened to be standing in the way, she might kill them.

The front porch isn't an option, either. She can phase through brick and concrete; she's not sure if the same applies to fire.

Only once choice remains, and it's probably the riskiest of them all.

LUKE is reminded of the video games he and Dennis used to play.

The two of them, standing in front of the TV with plastic controllers in their hands that were designed to feel like crossbows, waiting for something to emerge from the deep, dark woods.

Step aside, Old Man, Dennis would say. *I'll take it from here.*

We'll see about that, punk.

Dennis laughing, because their banter was half the fun.

The trick with that video game was to quickly determine whether the thing emerging from the woods was a fellow hero or a foul, evil, life-ending foe. (You only had three arrows, at best, before the EVIL THING would come at you and eat you.) So there had to be a split-second moment of evaluation and judgment before you pulled the plastic trigger. You were allowed three "hero kills" before you were ejected from the game.

How many heroes have you and Mom killed, Old Man?

And then, just like in the game, a figure emerges from

the deep, dark woods. Or in this case, the back of the Winawer house.

Luke knows he shouldn't think, he should just squeeze the trigger.

But he hesitates for a fraction of a second to get a closer look at the human being he's about to gun down. *Hero or evil monster?* Old habits die hard, and this is vastly more difficult than a video game. She's just a girl, maybe a few years older than Dennis would have been. The look on her face is one of extreme fear. The dad in Luke wants to scoop her up and tell her everything is going to be okay.

Then Luke remembers why they're doing this—she's not a little girl, she's THE TARGET—and finally he squeezes the trigger.

But she's taken advantage of his moment of hesitation and hurled herself away from the door, screaming. Luke's bullet smacks against the back of the house, burying itself in the wall. He fires again, but the bullet intended for her chest instead slams into cement and wood—her body has already disappeared through the wall.

If Luke weren't so disappointed in himself for *missing*, he'd probably be awestruck. Deep down, he's still that comic book geek who almost can't believe his eyes when he sees an Evo use a power.

"Joanne!" he yells. "She's headed your way!"

MARYLOU thinks to herself, *COFFIN77 wasn't lying holy shit there are people with guns setting my house on fire and trying to kill me what am I supposed to do—I have nowhere to run, no one to trust...*

And then she forces herself to take a deep breath—her

grandmother always says that oxygen is the best way to feel a little smarter right quick—and take stock of her situation.

If she can get out of the house and run fast enough—using her powers, because at this point, why the hell not?—she can make her way to the Terminal City Tower, where COFFIN77 said he'd meet her.

Wait—why can't he come rescue her, if he's some big bad Underground Railroad guy with (presumably) Evo powers?

Marylou pulls out her cell phone and crouches down as she thumbs a message:

They're shooting at me please help!

The flames are now licking at the door. She doesn't know how long she can stay here before the fire and smoke get real bad. Or the people with guns decide to come in after her.

A reply arrives:

I can only help you if you make it to Terminal City Tower.

Gah! This is not much help at all.

Please!

I've done all I can. You have to RUN.

Shit shit shit.

Marylou steels herself. There's no doubt someone (or a whole bunch of someones) is out front, waiting for her to come out. Guns at the ready.

Well, it's time to give them what they want…

JOANNE is locked and loaded and ready for this little bitch to come popping out of the front of the house. Her powers probably let her walk through flames.

But can she walk through a bullet?

No, the front exit *has* to be the Evo's next move. This is a street of semi-detached homes. She can't phase over to the house next door, since she has no way of knowing whether she'd slam straight into one of her neighbors or otherwise call attention to herself. And running in the opposite direction would lead her to a fenced yard. By the time she could scale the four-foot cyclone fence, Joanne would have closed in and gunned her down like a caged animal.

So no dice. The teenage Evo will no doubt try something dumb like rushing out the front door, leaping through the flaming porch, trying to use the element of surprise.

Sweetheart, plenty of Evos before you have tried the same thing. You can ask them how it turned out when you see them in the afterlife.

And sure enough, as Joanne watches, the front door slowwwwly creeks open.

If this is her stealth move, then the little Evo bitch is going to have to move a little quicker.

But then…

No one comes out.

The door stays open.

What the hell?

Joanne runs out from behind their car and clears the street within seconds. She keeps her gun down low—doing her best to keep it out of sight so as to maintain the ruse that she's just a concerned passerby who's stopped at a burning house to see if anyone needs help.

But she's prepared to lift it at a nanosecond's notice to

take out the Evo the moment she appears.

She doesn't, though. Is she hiding? Maybe that's her plan. Crouch down and wait for Joanne to enter the burning house, then blast past her and run like hell.

That's not gonna work, either, honey.

Joanne lifts her gun—screw the ruse—and starts firing into the living room.

LUKE is startled to hear the

POP POP POP POP POP POP

sound of gunfire from the front of the house.

"Joanne!" he yells after a moment, wondering what the hell is going on. Is it over? Should he run around to the front of the house so they can get the hell out of Cleveland?

But nothing. No response.

He wishes they had some kind of communication. Walkie-talkies are a pain in the ass when you're holding and aiming a gun. But maybe some kind of Bluetooth or cellular thing. Especially if they're not exactly worried about covering their tracks.

Because all he can think right now is the worst: that Joanne fired and missed, allowing the Evo to run straight through his wife, crushing her internal organs as easily as she broke the wrist of that poor bastard in the mall.

"JOANNE!"

MARYLOU is not hiding on the first floor, waiting to rush past her attackers. Such a thing didn't even occur to her.

She's not even on the second floor anymore.

Instead she's wriggled into the 24-inch crawlspace above their house—which, for the record, is incredibly freakin' hot. And gross, full of ancient cobwebs and dust and sharp strands of fiberglass installed years before she was even born.

But this is the only way out.

Halfway through the crawlspace she hears the loud cracks of gunfire—why the hell are they shooting? She presses her hands against the wooden floor, feeling tiny sharp objects bore their way into her palms. If she survives this, she's going to scrub her hands for a week.

Marylou takes a deep breath—another hit of oxygen. She's never tried this before. Whenever she's walked through an inanimate object, she's approached it like a diver slipping into a pool of water. Sometimes it's a graceful entrance. Sometimes, it's more like a belly flop. (Which might be how it works—part mental, part physical.) But the point is, whenever Marylou has used her power, she's been propelling herself *forward*.

What she's about to attempt is something new, possibly something crazy: going *backwards*, and then *upwards*.

She's going to launch herself up, leaping through the roof-praying to God she'll be able to jump with enough force to clear the entire roof, and not, like, get her foot caught in it or something. That would be a hell of a way to die: her foot wedged in the roof at the molecular level while the burning house below her cooks her alive.

Marylou feels the warmth through the wood. No more hesitating. This has to happen now.

"JOANNE!" a voice calls.

One of my pursuers is named Joanne? she thinks. That's oddly disappointing. If you have a pack of crazy killers on your trail, they should have names like Rex or Soulcrusher or Killer Joe or something. But Joanne? One of her friends' *moms* is named Joanne.

Enough procrastinating. Otherwise, Big Bad Joanne will figure out where she's gone—and good luck ducking a flying bullet in a crawlspace.

Marylou takes a deep breath, then pushes up as hard as she can. She feels that familiar, dizzying sensation of passing through a solid object. And now… yes! She's through the roof!

For a beautiful moment, she's suspended in mid-air above her childhood home, which is ablaze.

But then she starts to fall.

And for a moment, she is very concerned that she's going to phase right back through the roof and land in the crawlspace. Or worse—phase through the floor of the crawlspace, and then the second floor, and maybe even her living-room floor, all the way down into the basement.

Please let there be solid ground beneath my hands and knees.

And…

There is.

Her landing is hard, don't get her wrong. The tar feels tacky, and one of her knees collides with a small rock, which *kills*.

But at least she's still on the roof.

JOANNE leaps over the flames and enters the house, gun raised, wondering if she's playing right into the Evo's hands.

The house isn't large. She's able to check the living room, dining room, and small kitchen with quick efficient sweeps. Dumpy furniture, probably second-hand, though everything is neat and orderly. Not that it will matter for very long, once the fire spreads inside.

An empty first floor means the Evo has either gone down to the basement—which would be a very stupid move—or upstairs. Another stupid move. Basements are death traps, and smoke rises. Maybe she won't even have to use a bullet. If the bitch holes up in an upstairs closet, the fumes will do Joanne's job for her.

Either way, she needs Luke's eyes on this.

Cautiously, she moves to the back door. Grabs the knob. Opens it as she shouts, "Don't shoot!"

LUKE doesn't shoot.

But he's surprised to see Joanne standing there in the house, gun in hand. Did she finish off the Evo? If not, what the hell is she doing?

Which is when Joanne gestures with her weapon. *Up. Look up.*

Luke finally gets it, and complies, readying his own weapon in case he sees the Evo in one of the second-floor windows.

He doesn't. Not even when he moves around to the side of the house, where he has a decent view of the bedroom and bathroom windows. She could be crouching down behind them—but that's a weak-ass strategy if you're trapped in a burning house that will soon be full of smoke.

"Anything?" Joanne.

Luke is about to reply "No" when he sees it. A head, bobbing. Not on the second floor, but up on the roof.

MARYLOU stands up and looks at the neighbors' house across the way. There's too great a gap between the houses for her to leap roof-to-roof. That's not her kind of power, anyway, though she wishes she had it. In fact, she wishes she had the power to fly *and* turn invisible. No one would ever see her again.

No, she's going to have to do this the old-fashioned way—using gravity. And okay, her powers, too.

The good thing is, she doesn't have to leap blindly into her neighbors' house. She can see into their darkened windows. And, thank God, they're not home.

JOANNE follows her husband's line of sight and sees her, too—the teenager up on the roof, rocking back and forth, preparing to move.

She lifts her gun and fires at the same moment that

LUKE fires and

MARYLOU takes off running, which means Joanne's bullet sails through the space where Marylou's head had been a second ago, and Luke's shot is off, too, lodging itself in the metal gutter instead of the Evo.

But the twin shots unnerve her—and the last thing you want when you're about to make a difficult leap across a chasm and straight into a brick wall is to be unnerved.

She feels her feet stumble a bit even as she wills them to pick up speed. *Come on—you have to make this leap now, there are no do-overs like in grade school. The two people with guns (howya doing Joanne?) won't give you a time-out, let you regain your composure and try the leap again. It has to work now.*

So she pumps her legs like crazy and launches herself

from the edge of the roof, her body like an asteroid that's been caught by the Earth's atmosphere and is being drawn in for a brutal hug…

JOANNE thinks for a minute that maybe this Evo can walk through walls AND fly, just like that crazy politician from all those years ago. So she aims high, squeezing off three shots in quick succession, hoping to catch her as she ascends—because if she flies away, they've lost their chance forever. *And* they'll be spending the rest of their killing spree constantly checking the skies, wondering if she's about to descend on some super-powered revenge kick.

BLAM BLAM BLAM

LUKE squeezes off two shots as well. He doesn't think the Evo can fly—the thought doesn't even cross his mind. But he's also trying to anticipate what she's trying to do, and the most logical thing would be to leap down to the neighbors' lawn, landing as softly as possible so that her legs will still be able to carry her toward the street and far, far away.

But the thing is…

MARYLOU isn't trying to fly, nor is she aiming to land on the lawn below.

Her goal is to hurl herself toward her neighbors' house, then use her powers to pass harmlessly (oh, God, please let this be the case) through the brick wall and onto the carpeted floor of a second-story bedroom.

This, however, is not the case. Gravity is much too strong.

Gravity pulls her down much quicker than she had estimated, and the best she can do is shield her face with her arms as she plummets toward a set of kitchen windows.

So while the gravity factor is a good thing—her pursuers' bullets fly harmlessly around her falling body—Marylou is uncertain about what will happen when her body tries to pass through solid panes of glass, as well as the aluminum frames that hold them in place. She's never tried this before. In fact, she's made a point of sticking to one type of barrier (wood, brick, concrete) when using her powers. Maybe she's only good at phasing through one type of material at a time.

She grits her teeth and braces for impact...

BOTH JOANNE AND LUKE watch as their Target passes through the side of the house like smoke through a screen door. Effortlessly, easily. They don't even hear the impact on the other side.

The two look at each other, as if needing to confirm what they've both witnessed.

Then Joanne starts running for the neighbors' house, with Luke in close pursuit.

MARYLOU wakes up on the unfinished basement floor of her neighbors' home, heaving, trying to suck some air back into her lungs.

What the hell just happened?

It takes her a minute to figure it out—that she is indeed able to phase through different kinds of non-living material, such as glass and aluminum. But she also apparently phased through the linoleum and wood that comprised her neighbors' kitchen floor.

Only the concrete of the house's foundation stopped her descent. Most likely because her subconscious mind realized that it was time to put on the brakes; otherwise, her body would have continued to fall through the foundation and down into the Earth itself until it reached a pocket of magma, where it would have burst into flames, and that would have been the end of Marylou Winawer.

Of course, her present predicament is not much better.

That's because now she's in a basement with only one staircase leading up to the ground floor, as well as a few small windows through which she could (maybe) scramble through to get to the front yard.

Not the best place to be with two gunmen looking to off you.

So Marylou needs to find a way out, pronto. Just as soon as she can breathe again. And make sure she didn't break any important bones upon impact.

As she sits up experimentally, she hears something strangely familiar.

Once she realizes what she's hearing, she can breathe a lot easier.

LUKE hears the same loud wail. "Crap. The fire department."

Joanne is pissed. "You said we'd have a 10-minute window."

"Someone must have called it in right away. So what do we do?"

They don't even have to say the words. Either they break into the house, find the girl, kill her, then make their way out of the house before the trucks pull up… or they don't. They would risk arrest. And this whole trip would be over, and they'd be left to face some grim realities they've been avoiding for a good long while now.

"Shit," Joanne says, as she realizes they have to go.

"It's the only call," Luke says. "There's no other option."

"Goddamnit!"

They race through the narrow passage to the front yard and pull away from the Winawer house just as the fire truck comes into sight in their rearview mirror.

JOANNE is even more pissed now. Pissed at the Evo, pissed at the plan, pissed at Cleveland, pissed at themselves.

Pissed at this whole situation.

All of this build-up—the preparation, the plotting, the endless driving—it's all manageable *if* there's a pay-off at the end. A cathartic release. A *revengegasm*. The girl getting away after all that is like a case of blue balls for her soul.

They have to find her. Otherwise, this failure is going to nag at them for the long haul.

Not to mention that the girl must have been able to get a decent look at both of them. For the first time, Joanne is confronted with the awful idea that maybe this can't go on forever. That perhaps a sketch artist will plaster their faces all over the Internet, and it will only be a matter of time before they're brought to justice.

That's not an option. She didn't promise Dennis she'd *try* to avenge him. Goddamnit, she's not going to let her boy down again.

MARYLOU says a silent prayer, thanking whatever Higher Power that was responsible for the sirens, and then feels the buzz of her cell phone in her pocket. Somehow, her phone has survived the ordeal that she's just put her body through.

She moans a little as she twists herself around to pull out her cell, which has a new text waiting for her:

You're welcome. Now GO.

Huh.

So COFFIN77 really is looking out for her. He's been right this whole time. Looks like he's her only hope for a future longer than a few minutes.

Marylou climbs to her feet slowly and awkwardly, feeling a dozen different stabbing pains all over her torso and limbs. They say you should let your body go loose when you're falling from a great height. But that advice probably doesn't apply to situations in which you're phasing through two solid surfaces and landing on a concrete slab. She can almost forgive her body for not adjusting.

(She also wishes she had the powers of Claire Bennet, the infamous Cheerleader who seemed to be able to walk away from anything. Well, almost anything…)

She trots up the creaky wooden basement stairs. The door at the top is closed (and with her luck, locked). But that doesn't matter to a girl like her. She can slip through any door she wants to. When her neighbors, the Buchanskys, return home later, they're going to stare in shock at the smoldering ruins of the house next door, maybe feel a little guilty that their own home was spared. They'll never know that they could have returned home to a corpse in the basement.

Still, Marylou is careful as she leaves through the back wall and heads for the alley behind their houses. The fire trucks should have scared the gunmen away by now, but who knows.

They could be deranged and determined types who think they have nothing left to lose.

LUKE tries to stay rational about the whole thing.

They're a couple miles away from Slavic Village now, having peeled away right before the fire trucks turned onto the block. Looky-loos probably saw their car—probably saw the whole thing, but what does it matter? They'll just blame it on Mohinder Suresh.

Now they're on 9th Street near Progressive Field, after making a pit stop at a local convenience store for coffee (his) and a six-pack of Great Lakes Eliot Ness lager (hers). The name strikes Luke as funny, given their current outlaw status. Joanne doesn't seem to see the humor, though. She's gone to a dark place. The place they desperately try to avoid.

This whole road trip is about avoiding those dark places, and Luke refuses to surrender to them that easily.

"This isn't over yet," he says.

Joanne interrupts a long pull at her beer to give him a sideways death glance. "You've got to be kidding, right?"

"Seriously."

"She could be anywhere."

"Hear me out," Luke says. "She has no driver's license. She's desperately afraid of being outed, so she's not going to go to a friend's house—otherwise, she would have already been there, hiding. That means she's on foot, and has a limited number of options for leaving town."

"Who says she's leaving town?" Joanne asks.

"Wouldn't you? If there were two armed killers hunting you, dogging your every move?"

"If I were an Evo, I'd put a bloody gun to my head and end my suffering."

"Well," Luke says, "good thing you're not. But back to her options. She's got trains, buses, or planes. I doubt she has the cash on hand for a flight, so that leaves trains and buses. No matter what, she's going to have to make her way downtown to catch one of them."

"She's probably there already."

"Maybe. But we have a car. She's on foot—and probably taking a circuitous route. So let's drive around and see if we can pick up her trail."

Luke isn't sure he can bring her back from the abyss this time. So he's practically elated when his wife says,

"You drive. I'll look."

MARYLOU is exhausted by the time she approaches Terminal Tower, the tallest landmark in downtown Cleveland.

She's walked from home to the Tower a billion times, but never like tonight. Looking over her shoulder like her neck was on a pivot, she darted up and down blocks both familiar and strange, trying to make sure nobody was following her. Did she phase through wooden fences and brick walls to further obscure her path?

Hell yes, she did.

Marylou wishes she'd gotten a better look at the car. Because *any* car that comes within 50 yards of her instantly turns into The Death Car, and the pounding in her veins is almost unbearable.

She wouldn't even have time to react if they saw her first and opened fire.

Making matters worse is the ticking clock that COFFIN77 has given her. Every few minutes he's texted her:

Are you close?

And then:

I can't wait here forever.

And then:

You need to be here within five minutes or I can't help you.

You're not helping as it is, buddy.

But then, at long last, she's making her way across Public Square and past the Soldiers' and Sailors' Monument—figuring that the cast-iron boys might provide adequate cover if shots ring out.

She looks both ways before crossing the street, heading toward Terminal Tower. And her new life.

JOANNE spots her first.

Goddamnit, Luke was right.

There she is, looking both ways before crossing the street, just like a good little girl. Joanne remembers when she was that age, about 16 years old, back in Manchester. Back then she didn't give a damn about looking either way when she crossed a street. A car hit her? She'd get right back up and kick the driver's ass.

But go ahead, Marylou Winawer. Be cautious.

Caution's about to get you killed.

"Stop the car," she tells her husband.

Luke, to his credit, doesn't question her. He pulls over to the side of the square. "You see her?"

"Cover me," she says, without explaining exactly what

she means by that. Joanne pops open the passenger door and launches herself out of her seat in one fluid motion. She makes her way across the square in a kind of jogging-walk, her hand on the gun in her jacket pocket. She doesn't want to draw anyone's attention until it's absolutely necessary.

We can end this right here, she thinks. Outside, in the confusion of rush-hour traffic. One bullet to the brain, and everybody will think it's just a car backfiring. That is, until they see the corpse. And by that time, Luke will have swung back around for her and they'll be headed out of this depressing city.

Joanne clears the distance between them in a matter of seconds.

The Target, meanwhile, is waiting for a bus to finish passing through the yellow light so she can cross. She has no idea that she's about to die.

MARYLOU thinks this bus is slowing down on purpose, just to make her exit that much more excruciating. The whole city's turned against her. She's not going to miss Cleveland, she tells herself. Not one bit.

By reflex, she turns to take one last look at the town she's leaving behind—quite possibly forever. She's spent every day since her birth in this city. Cleveland is her entire world. So it's only natural to take one last mental snapshot to remind herself of her old life.

But instead of a snapshot, she gets a close-up.

Of the woman.

With the gun.

Oh, shit, it's—

JOANNE pulls the gun out of her pocket and aims, knowing the girl's run out of places to hide. Go to the left, boom. Go to the right, boom. Head toward the bus and it's El Squisho. (She can only walk through walls, right?)

So just stand there—yeah, just like that, frozen in shock. I'm coming for you, you Evo bitch.

But wouldn't you know it—

MARYLOU runs toward the bus in a kind of crouching sprint. She doesn't know if she can pull this off. But she's dead if she doesn't try.

Cleveland transit buses are like most city buses—the passenger seats are raised a bit above street level, so that you can look down at your fellow citizens while they're looking down at you (*look at that loser, riding the bus*).

The bus is packed—it's rush hour. So normally, phasing through the bus would mean a world of pain for all those passengers minding their own business. A matched set of broken legs, possibly worse, as she phases through them. Marylou can't do that to a bunch of innocent people.

What she can do is crouch low enough so that she passes through the engine and lower workings of the moving bus, praying that she's clear of the human beings inside.

On a good day, she would never try something this crazy. The innards of a bus are complex. Steel, plastic, chemicals, and God knows what else. For all she knows, her phasing body will get hung up on some random object, ripping into her, possibly killing her.

But this is not a good day.

This is the opposite of a good day, in fact.

So she runs.

Just as—

JOANNE opens fire, three times.

But the girl disappears at the exact moment her bullets strike the side of the bus, making a horrible clanging noise.

Everyone in the immediate vicinity looks around, wondering where that awful racket is coming from. Joanne curses and tucks the gun back into her pocket before someone can point at her and yell. She tries to look curious, too, as if she's just another Clevelander on the way home, trying to figure out the source of those three loud bangs.

Please let the bus pull away to reveal the Evo's broken, mangled corpse. Please let the bus pull away to reveal her broken, mangled corpse. Please let the bus pull—

The bus pulls away, but—

MARYLOU is confused by her surroundings—the sounds, the toxic smells, the rushing wind, the heat. For a brief moment she wonders if she's died and gone to hell because of how bad this all feels. There are no butterflies in her stomach; there are angry, rabid moths doing Kamikaze dives at her internal organs. She wants to crouch down, cover her head with her arms, and pray that this doesn't go on for an eternity.

And then—

—and then she's running into the street on the other side of the moving bus, alive and well, much to her surprise. She doesn't stop moving, but slowly realizes that wow, she somehow did that. A car horn angrily honks at her—get out of the way, you stupid kid! Marylou holds up her hands by way of apology, still stunned that she made it out of that thing alive. The car honks again. Marylou jogs to the sidewalk, feels the car speed angrily past her.

As the bus moves out of the way, Marylou can see that

crazy lady Joanne across the street, her hands stuffed in her pockets, acting all innocent. But the fury in her eyes is hot enough to light charcoal briquettes.

Marylou can't resist. She gives her buddy Joanne a double middle-finger salute, then runs through the front entrance of Terminal Tower.

LUKE catches up with Joanne by the time she's halfway across the street. He doesn't have to ask what happened. He saw the whole thing. And he still can't believe it.

"Did you see what she did?" Joanne says. "Holy hell!"

"Look, there's two of us," he says, "and one of her. No way is she leaving this city alive."

"Yeah, there's two of us," Joanne says, "but the one of her can walk through walls."

They burst through the doors and take a moment to orient themselves. The Terminal Tower mall is like the Cleveland Arcade on steroids. Multiple levels, jammed with people, stores, hallways, stairwells, the works. Coffee shops, fast-food outlets, clothing retailers, greeting-card stores. All designed to cater to the after-work crowd. At one time, this building was the fourth-largest skyscraper in the world—followed by three buildings in Manhattan you might have heard of. For decades it's been the focal point of the city, and it's where you go if you want to leave the city by rail.

Which is no doubt what Marylou Winawer has in mind. Somewhere in this massive, sprawling complex, their Target is about to board a train.

"I think I've figured out her weakness," Luke says. "I saw it, just now."

"What do you mean? What weakness?"

"Did you notice how she crouched down when she went through that bus?"

"Yeah?"

"Why would she do that, unless she were avoiding something? And remember in the original video, when she collided with the old man, and it looked like she broke his wrist?"

Joanne nods as she gets it. "She can't walk through people without hurting them."

"Or killing them. So she avoids it all costs."

"Great. An Evo with a conscience."

"But think about it. This mall is full of people right now. She'll be using her powers sparingly. If at all."

"And if she needs to catch a particular train, she can't just disappear. If we split up and search each floor quickly, we'll be able to nail her."

"Discreetly," Luke says.

"Yeah," Joanne replies. "I'll be discreet as hell. Right up until the moment she stops breathing."

"I mean it. If you have a shot, take it, of course. Just remember we have to get out of here alive—otherwise, our mission ends tonight. We can't turn this thing into the Wild West."

"Who knows? Maybe we'll get lucky and a stray bullet will hit another Evo."

"Joanne—seriously!?"

"Don't get your panties in a bunch. Now come on, or we'll lose her."

MARYLOU has a serious problem: There are people EVERYWHERE.

Every time she turns to make an escape—BAM. There

are people in her way. She can't pass through them without seriously messing them up. That poor tree and the old man in the Cleveland Arcade were enough. She doesn't want to add to her body count.

But she also knows that Crazy Joanne won't stop pursuing her.

Marylou is looking up at them now, on a level above her. Joanne and the other guy—the white guy who was hiding in her backyard. She wonders about them. What makes you take a job where you go around killing children? If it actually is a job. Maybe for these psychos, it's a hobby.

They look like such ordinary people, Marylou thinks. She studies their faces long enough to know them by sight—but then turns around and quickly walks away before they catch her staring. You don't have to be an Evo to have the kind of sixth sense that tells you someone is looking at you.

Which brings her to the other serious problem: she has no idea what COFFIN77, her would-be savior, looks like.

How can she hide from two killers in a crowded mall—while at the same time being conspicuous enough so that some random dude will be able to spot her? (She's sure it's a dude, because only a dude would be bone-headed enough to come up with this plan.)

Marylou descends one more level, moving toward the ticket booths for the various rail lines. It would make sense that he'd be down here. Beyond these gates, sets of stairs take you down to the train tracks, and from there, freedom.

She scans the crowd, looking for someone looking at her—any tiny sign of recognition.

And she finds it!

Unfortunately, it's—

JOANNE is pulling the gun out of her pocket, running now, trying to clear the distance between them, pushing people aside, pretending like she's a cop on a manhunt. Luke's words are still ringing in her ears—*don't make this the Wild West*. It's good and sensible advice. But the urge to kill is so strong and—

MARYLOU spins and runs toward the escalator, the one full of people coming down. She races upward, darting around them, ignoring the curses and yells (*you crazy kid!*), praying that Joanne wouldn't be reckless enough to shoot at her in a crowd of people—

(Are you forgetting, kid, that she opened fire on a bus not five minutes ago? That she burned down your poor mother's house just to get at you?)

—but she manages to reach the top of the escalator unharmed. As Marylou dashes to the other set of escalators, the one that will take her to the next level up, she catches a glimpse of Crazy Joanne tucking the gun back into her pocket, trying to stay in stealth mode.

Does anybody see this? This crazy woman trying to mow down a teenager? Now she knows how Sarah Connor felt in the *Terminator* movies. Everybody oblivious while the killing machines close in…

Which gives her an idea: find a cop. Tell him Crazy Joanne is after her, along with a white dude. She's not a killer robot from the future. She's a flesh-and-blood human being who's trying to execute an innocent Clevelander.

But then Marylou reconsiders. If Joanne and her buddy *are* with the government, then what's a cop going to do? A federal badge trumps a local one, right? For all she knows, maybe cops have been given carte blanche to kill Evos on sight, too. Nobody's walking around wearing EVO LIVES MATTER t-shirts.

No cops, Marylou thinks. The only sensible thing to do is keep moving. Look for COFFIN77 and pray he's experienced enough to get her out of here without getting either of them shot.

She reaches the next level and finds herself in the middle of a throng of commuters, none of them giving her a second glance. Why would they? They've got their own problems and worries to deal with.

Since there are so many people, Marylou takes a chance. She backs up against a support column—thick, marble—and pulls out her cell phone. Maybe COFFIN77 has left her a new message that she missed in all the excitement of almost getting shot and running through a moving bus.

And there is indeed a message waiting for her.

But she barely has time to register its meaning before she hears a shrill cry—

"LUKE!" who turns around at the sound of his wife's voice and sees the girl leaning against a marble column, looking at her cell phone.

Young people. Always looking at their phones. Oblivious to the world.

Luke is able to make it in four long strides, by which point he has the gun out of his pocket, not caring who might see. Because this is going to end right now. He'll be Joanne's hero again. Who knows what will happen when they get back to the hotel tonight.

And now the girl is looking up from her phone, staring straight at him, frozen in fear. Here we go.

And then—

MARYLOU pushes herself back into the marble column, phasing completely through it, protecting her from any bullet that might be headed her way.

It feels so solid and *cold*.

But this simple movement has two unintended consequences.

One: her cell phone, which is currently in her hand, doesn't phase through the marble with her. It slips from her fingertips and makes a clacking sound as it smacks into marble, then falls and clatters on the ground.

Marylou has no idea why it didn't go through with her—after all, her clothes and shoes and earrings and such always merrily accompany her through inanimate surfaces. Maybe because she was holding it, and her body has some kind of phasing force field around it that only protects what she's wearing and the contents of her pockets?

But she barely has time to consider the ramifications, because of the second unintended consequence:

Her, falling.

See, on the other side of the marble column is a metal guard rail, which she also phases through. But beyond that…

Nothing.

Marylou tumbles through the air for an eternity before she lands hard on her back, all of the air squeezed out of her lungs for the second time tonight. This is even worse than the crash-landing in her neighbor's basement because the floor is hard, unforgiving tile, and her leg has slammed right into an old lady's walker. The senior citizen herself was spared, but the pain in Marylou's leg is agonizing.

"Oh, my word," the old lady says, trying to help her up. "What happened to you?"

Lady, I wish I could tell you.

she wants to say, all hard-bitten and callous, but the truth is, the old Polish grandmother here reminds Marylou of her own grandma, who's probably just discovered that her home and all of her possessions have burned to the ground. All because of *her*.

But Marylou can't move, can't speak, can't even cry right now, the pain is that bad. The physical pain, but also the mental anguish—that she was so close, and now some dumb evil woman named—

JOANNE is going to finish her.

Just one level up. Joanne saw the Evo pop out of the marble column, phase through the gate and stumble into thin air. She heard the landing and the astonishment of the crowd around her.

Now all she has to do is take the stairs to the next level and pretend to be a first responder. She wouldn't even need the gun. She could pretend to check for head and neck damage, tell people to back away, then administer some serious damage of her own. She fantasizes about the kind of sound it'll make when the neck cracks. She imagines that the Evo will make one last-ditch escape attempt and try to melt through the floor, but Joanne won't let go, and the cracking will be all the more pleasurable because she'll be able to see the panicked look in her eyes.

LUKE picks up the Evo's cell phone, which now has a cracked screen but still appears to be functional. He knows he shouldn't bother, but the would-be detective in him can't resist taking a look.

There's a text message on the screen from someone named COFFIN77:

Meet me at Traveler's Aid on the lower level now

The Evo has help! Probably has had help this entire time. And then he thinks about the police showing up… just in time. The fire department showing up… way ahead of time.

"Damnit," Luke mutters to himself as he runs for the stairs. It's not two against one. It could be two of them versus an entire Evo network!

MARYLOU ignores the pain, rolls over, and starts to pull herself forward until she's crawling like a baby, much to the dismay and shock of the onlookers. *You shouldn't move, miss!* Yeah, well, you'd move your ass, too, if you were being hunted by Luke and Joanne.

She may not have her phone, but she remembers the last text message that came through.

Meet me at Traveler's Aid on the lower level now

Please let this guy have guns or backup or an Evo army or *something*—or failing that, a quick way out of here.

Marylou climbs to her feet just as—

JOANNE reaches the next level up and sees that the Evo has gone down a level.

Shit! How did she recover so quickly? But then again,

Joanne remembers being that age. Sixteen. You think you're invincible when you're that young. God knows she was in scrapes far worse than a fall when she was that age, and it's a minor miracle that she made it to adulthood.

Joanne is sorely tempted to take her shot now, but thinks better of it. Too many people. The gun stays in her pocket. She's about to go running after the Target when she hears Luke yelling for her.

"Wait—I know where she's going."

Joanne stares at her husband. "How could you possibly know that?"

He shows her the phone with the cracked screen. "I think we've stumbled onto something a lot bigger than we realized."

MARYLOU is limping. Her kneecap feels like someone's jabbing a steak knife into it with every step, but she finally reaches the Traveler's Aid kiosk near the entrance to the regional rail line. And sure enough, there's a stocky man standing there, staring at her, smirking at her.

"Miss Winawer, at long last?"

"You're Coff—"

"Shhhh," he says, cutting her off. "Not out in the open. Come on, hurry."

Marylou follows him, still limping. This guy isn't what she expected, not at all. COFFIN77 looks like any number of pasty, doughy white dudes she (used to) see at the Sweet Shoppe in the Cleveland Arcade. Pretending to pick up a pound of buttercreams for a girlfriend (hah) or a mother (maybe as payment for living in her basement). He smells musty, like he doesn't see much sunlight or fresh air on a regular basis. A ratty overcoat is draped over his burly frame, and it probably hasn't been laundered since he purchased it.

This is her savior? The man who's going to protect her and get her out of town?

Turns out he's leading her to a ticket booth—Amtrak. The national rail network.

"Do you have it on you?" he asks.

"What? My phone?"

"No," COFFIN77 says, exasperated. "The ten grand, kid."

Crap. Marylou has forgotten all about that. She thinks about how she should explain that she didn't exactly have time to root through her mother's jewelry box after her house was set on fire and Luke and Joanne started using her for target practice.

"Not in cash," she says, stalling for time.

"Well, gimme what you got. I'll front you the ticket to L.A."

"L.A.?"

COFFIN77 grins. "That's where you're headed. To the loving arms of El Vengador. He's the only who can protect you. I'm just here to point you in the right direction. Don't you know this is how the Underground Railroad works?"

This isn't what Marylou wants to hear, because she needs protection *now*.

Suddenly it becomes clear to Marylou what this is all about. This guy is no Evo activist. He's a con artist. He waits to catch an Evo stupid enough to use their powers in public (hello, ding ding ding, we have a winner), and then he outs them, forcing them to put their fate—and money—into his hands in the hopes of "safe passage." Basically, ten grand for an Amtrak ticket and a finger pointed westward… to El Vengador? Seriously? He's on the news all the time. Everybody knows about El Vengador!

But then how did this COFFIN77 become part of the Evo Underground Railroad?

This guy isn't from the Evo Underground Railroad, she realizes. *He just let you assume that he was.*

"Look, I hid my mother's engagement ring upstairs," she says. "I didn't know if you'd show up, and I didn't want to get mugged with it on me."

"Smart thinking," COFFIN77 says. "You're going to be fine if you keep your head on straight."

"Here's the thing, though," she says, leaning close to the creepazoid. "Those two people followed me here from the house. I need you to keep them busy while I go after the ring."

The man who calls himself—

COFFIN77 agrees. "With pleasure, kid. Now go! Your train leaves in 15 minutes."

COFFIN77 knows all about the hard-ass couple who have been stalking poor Marylou Winawer. At first, he thought they were cops, and that they were onto *him*.

Because sure, he's been keeping tabs on his investment. Following Miss Winawer home from the Arcade the day she was dumb enough to use her little powers in public. He's done this twice before, but was never lucky enough to catch anything on video. That made it easy.

But what interests him now are Miss Winawer's would-be killers.

He happened upon them the previous night when he was strolling through Slavic Village, hoping to find an inconspicuous place to watch the girl's house. Imagine his surprise when he saw someone else watching the house, too! Then they tried the con with the security company (a smart idea; he'd have to remember that one), which gave him an idea. A way to earn the Winawer girl's trust.

Even after the cops scared them off, they came back. Big time. They torched her house and opened fire like they were in Syria, not Cleveland. Then they tracked their quarry all the way here, to Terminal Tower. Clearly, they're desperate. For some reason, they want this Evo dead, and *now*.

To a guy like COFFIN77, there's nothing better than desperation. You can work with something like that.

JOANNE and Luke watch the unlikely pair from the next level up. From the Traveler's Aid station to the Amtrak ticket counter, and now they're… splitting up?

"What did he give her?" she asks. "A ticket?"

"No, nothing that I could see."

"So where is she going?"

They eyeball the pair as they go their separate ways. The burly man strolls around, hands in pockets, taking in the scene, la-dee-dah—which makes it painfully obvious he's doing some ham-fisted surveillance.

"The little bitch told him about us," Joanne says.

"Yeah—but look at where she's going," Luke says.

Marylou Winawer, taking great care to make sure that her burly friend isn't watching, slips through a turnstile. And not because she paid for a ticket and ran it through the scanner. No, her hips literally *melt through the metal spokes*, with no one the wiser. Luke supposes she never, ever pays to ride public transportation. Handy power, that.

"Damn, she's headed for the tracks!" Joanne snarls.

Husband and wife bolt down to the bottommost level, not caring who might be in their way. Women, children, the elderly—they don't give a shit. All that matters is reaching the Winawer girl before she boards one of those trains. Once she leaves the city, she'll be nearly impossible to track, unless they want to stay glued to YouTube for the next month, hoping that someone will post a video of her screwing up again. Not bloody likely.

As they run across the concourse, looking like a harried couple desperately trying to reach their train in time, a burly man approaches. He puts himself squarely in their path, trying to get them to slow down for a second.

"Excuse me, but I think I can help y—"

BAM—Joanne throws an elbow into the man's jaw, sending him spinning like a top until he collapses in a heap on the ground. Luke can't help but smile. He's seriously impressed.

"Not now," Joanne gasps as they head for the turnstiles and leap over them.

A transit cop sees them, shouts "Hey!", and darts after them. Great.

LUKE half-turns as he runs and pulls the gun from his jacket pocket, along with the photostat dental license he carries everywhere.

"Police!" he shouts at the transit cop, flashing his gun and "badge" before turning back around and following Joanne down to the track level.

Luke doesn't bother waiting to see if the transit cop has bought the ruse. Does it really matter? He's come to learn that all you need is a certain amount of confidence to pull off any charade, no matter how ludicrous. Everyone wants to trust and believe in authority figures. Even fellow authority figures.

"Let's split up," Joanne says. "Search each train if we have to."

Luke had been afraid she was going to say that. There are a dozen train lines down here, easy. He wishes he had

60 seconds to scan a schedule and figure out which one might be Marylou's.

Hold on—she had been lingering by the Amtrak booth. That makes sense. The girl wouldn't head to a nearby suburb. She would be headed far, far away from here.

So Luke searches for the familiar logo and starts down the length of a train, peering into the windows, hoping to catch a glimpse of the top of her head. He's got a good angle for it. The tops of the seats are clearly visible through the windows, and even if she were to crouch down, he'll still see her. And if she were crouching down that much, she'd draw attention to herself on the train.

And his hunch is right. Because about six feet away—

MARYLOU emerges from within the guts of an Amtrak locomotive to realize she's *right behind Luke*—with his back to her.

Holy shit.

She watches as he steadily makes his way down the length of the train, looking into the windows, then checking his footing, then back to the windows, then back to his footing. Methodical. Careful. Relentless.

Marylou finds herself following along in his wake, fearful of disturbing the strange equilibrium between them. As long as she stays behind him, he can't see her and shoot her, right? He thinks she's already on the train.

But then another thought occurs to her:

She could phase through him right now and kill him if she wanted.

Why wouldn't she? This jerk and his pal Crazy Joanne have been trying to kill her all day. Who would blame her for taking him out?

All it would take is a running start, then BOOM, blast right through his body and enjoy the cracking sound of dozens of broken bones upon impact, piercing and slashing away at his internal organs. He'd bleed out before his partner Joanne could reach him.

Even if she did—Marylou would run straight through her, too. And enjoy it even more. Imagine the look on her face.

But no.

That's not the kind of girl she is.

The tree and the old man's wrist—that was enough.

Marylou Winawer is a good guy—an Evo who can help people. Maybe she's not a hero, because right now she's trying to save her own skin. But who knows? Maybe one day she'll be in a position to help. At the very least, she knows she's not a killer. She'll never stoop to their level, no matter how desperate things look.

As if the heavens have decided to put in their two cents, there is the sudden loud hiss of a train preparing to depart. Right on the next track. A local train. Almost fully packed with commuters.

Marylou turns to see it moving.

So does—

LUKE who is startled by the noise at first, but then realizes what it is.

And then he realizes that their Target is standing just a few feet behind him. They lock eyes.

Luke lifts his gun and opens fire. The echo of the shots through the train tunnels makes each one sound like a cannon blast.

But—

MARYLOU does not run.

She stands her ground, as they say in the media these days.

And though she's not moving, she imagines that she's moving forward at great velocity. The bullets Luke fired are standing still, just hanging in the air. In fact, they're not even bullets. They're tiny, oddly-shaped walls. And Marylou can walk through walls of any size, right? Hell, she was able to phase through a moving bus. What are bullets to her?

While she doesn't know how her powers work, if it's the space between atoms that she's subconsciously exploiting, one thing is clear:

Bullets can't hurt her.

Not if she doesn't want them to.

They sail through her body and smack into the moving train behind her, and nothing's more exhilarating.

The moving train…

LUKE knows that Dennis would not be proud. (*Nice shooting, old man!*) But he doesn't understand. How could he have missed at such close range? With the Target not even moving?

The Target smiles and tells him, "You missed."

Luke takes a step forward, raises his gun, and fires again—and this time he sees what's happening.

The bullet, sailing right through her not-quite-solid body.

Joanne runs down the track firing her gun before Luke has the chance to tell her not to bother. He wants to stop and explain, but he has the feeling Joanne won't be interested. Let her figure it out just as he did.

Not one of her bullets hits home, no matter how close Joanne gets, even though she fires until she starts dry-clicking.

When the gun smoke clears a little, the Evo is just standing there, staring at both of them.

"Listen to me," the Target says. "If I see either of you two on my trail again, I won't hold back. Bullets can't hurt me. But I can seriously mess you up. You don't want a demonstration, do you?"

Luke and Joanne look at each other, both at a loss for words. This is something they hadn't considered. A bulletproof Evo. How do you kill something you can't shoot?

They turn their attention back just in time to see their Target, Marylou Winawer, leap through the moving train, carefully choosing a seat with no passengers. They feel like parents seeing their kid off to college, wondering if she'll look back at them. She does, in fact. She gives them a double middle-finger salute before settling down into a seat, her back to them.

The train roars down the track, picking up speed, whisking its passengers away from Terminal Tower.

"Okay, that just happened," Luke says.

"Yes, it did."

All of that chasing, that planning... It's a crushing letdown. Luke is worried about how Joanne's going to take it. They've encountered powerful Evos before, and no doubt they'll find others with more serious powers—but this means that they'll have to rethink their entire strategy.

Joanne surprises him, though, by nudging his shoulder. She's not depressed. She's too busy plotting something.

"How about we take care of some unfinished business upstairs?"

It takes Luke an embarrassingly long time to realize she's not talking about sex. She means Marylou's burly helper.

MARYLOU eases back into her seat and takes a quick inventory of what she has.

It doesn't take long. In fact, it would be easier to list the things she doesn't have:

Cell phone.

Jacket.

House keys.

Money.

A destination in mind.

Her 16-year-old life has been pared down to the bare essentials: the clothes on her back, the shoes on her feet, and nothing else.

Well, there's her powers.

Luke and Joanne didn't manage to take those away from her.

Everything else? Well, yeah.

Even if her house hasn't been burned to the ground, it's not going to be livable for a long while. Fortunately, Marylou's older brothers have places elsewhere in the city. Mom and Grandma won't be homeless. All of their possessions might be gone, but how important are they? What matters is that they're safe and alive.

And maybe someday they'll understand. Maybe even be proud of Marylou for what she did tonight.

The ticket-taker comes ambling down the aisle, punching holes in his ticket pad, making change and saying "good evening" to the regulars. Marylou stands up and heads for the back of the train, nervous at first... but then she realizes how she can pull this off. Because she has her powers. She can easily slip into maintenance closets and other hidden compartments and hide for as long as necessary. She can slip onto other trains undetected—if she's smart about it. She can sneak into the dining car and take whatever she likes.

She can do this all the way to L.A.

Maybe COFFIN77 wasn't so useless, after all.

And maybe El Vengador could use an Evo like her.

COFFIN77 is applying a cup of ice to his (surely) bruised jaw, realizing that the girl isn't coming back with that ring.

Damn.

Gotta remember, next time—get the payment as early as possible. Don't give them the wiggle room. Maybe even insist on payment before the train station. He used to like to run this con at airports—that is, until the government started swabbing at check-in. Trains were the only way now. But as this little girl showed him, it was far too easy to give him the slip in a train station.

He's about to go home when he sees the killers approach him. The black chick who cold-cocked him in the face. The white dude, looking like he's lost a puppy.

For a minute, he thinks he should run. Maybe even call for the cops.

But wait...

They're clearly not happy. Which means the Evo got away. And COFFIN77—whose real name is Bobby Ayres—sees a way to make a nice payday after all.

"That was a nice one, with the transit cop," he tells the white guy when's he's close enough. "What, did you get that from a Cracker Jack box?"

The white guy just nods. But his partner says,

"Sorry about the crack on the face. Thought you were trying to stop us from catching her."

"Stop you? Hey, I was only trying to help."

"Oh, yeah? So you're not one of those Evo activists?"

"Hell no," Ayers says. "I hate the freaky bastards. No, I like to take them for everything they've got before running them out of my town. But I'm guessing you two have a different way of handling them."

The black chick smiles. "You might say that."

"Well, I like your style."

"Hey, I'm Luke," the white guy says. "This is my wife, Joanne."

Oh, Ayres thinks. One of those liberal couples, huh? Then it'll be even sweeter to fleece these obnoxious pricks.

"Call me COFFIN77," Ayres says.

"That your code name?"

"Of sorts. More like an online handle. Took it from an abolitionist, Levi Coffin, who died back in 1877. Makes the Evos trust me—like I'm serious about their cause. It's even better if they do a little digging and figure it out for themselves."

"Nice one," Luke says, and Ayres isn't sure if he's mocking him or not.

"You know a lot about this Evo Underground Railroad?" Joanne asks.

"More than anyone in this city."

Luke smiles. "Can we buy you a cup of coffee? Maybe a bite to eat?"

"Not sure how much biting I'm going to be doing tonight," Ayres says. "You nailed me pretty good, Joanne."

"Well, then, today's your lucky day," Joanne says.

"How's that?"

Luke claps him on the shoulder. "Because I'm a dentist."

The husband and wife lead him upstairs and across the street to Public Square. As they round the Soldiers' and Sailors' Monument, Ayres starts doing some mental calculations. How much should he ask per Evo name? He can't make it sound like he has dozens. He can reliably fake three or four—at least long enough for him to cash out and move on. Maybe five grand a head? That would mean 15 or 20 large, which would be a nice cushion for a long while.

Bobby Ayres is mentally depositing the cash into his savings account when the world, inexplicably, goes black.

JOANNE says, "What an asshole."

Together, they quickly bind and gag him and shove him into the trunk of their car. It's is still parked on the square— no tickets, even. Maybe it's their lucky night, too.

"If this guy knows even a little about the underground Evo network, it's worth the risk. Who knows? Maybe he'll be able to finger an entire nest of the bastards."

"Smart thinking," Luke says.

"We've got to stop working piecemeal," she says. "It's a waste of our time."

"Agreed. So I'm guessing you want to steal some swab kits from a checkpoint somewhere?"

"Not exactly. I think we have everything we need in this car."

"Yeah?"

Luke starts to slam down the lid, but Joanne stops him.

"Wait—isn't your dental kit back there?"

LUKE finds them another motel room, this one on the western outskirts of Cleveland. Part of a national chain. Totally anonymous. Free breakfast included, with premium cable and in-room refrigerators. This time, Luke books two adjoining rooms. And requests that they be on the far side of the building, near the constant thrum of the interstate.

"Don't tell anybody," he tells the college-age front-desk manager, "but my wife snores like a chainsaw trying to cut through a brick wall. So I give her one room, and I take the other, near the highway, which helps drown out the noise."

The manager smiles, probably thinking to himself, Man, marriage sucks.

They drag a punch-drunk Bobby Ayres into the room at the far end, then securely fasten him to a study desk chair with zip ties. The only other things in the room: a fresh bucket of ice and Luke's dental kit.

Luke tells Joanne he can handle this. He knows what to look for, after all.

"I may suck at moving targets," he says, "but I'm still the best dentist in the family."

Joanne fishes the guy's driver's license out of his wallet and reads the name. "Do you really think Bobby Ayres here needs a good dentist?"

Luke sees her point.

Soon, his wife is alone in the room with Bobby. Luke stands outside to keep watch, making sure that nobody wandering by in search of a cold soda pop at midnight hears the horrible whimpering—and then, the bloodcurdling screams—coming from the room at the end of the row.

After a while, the punishment begins.

And oh, is it horrible. Luke can only imagine what she's doing in there. He gave her a few basic pointers, but she was impatient. I want to learn on the job, she said.

They agreed, though, on a tag-team approach. Joanne would do the damage; Luke would do his best to patch it up. Just like in Marathon Man. You dip a man in hell for a while, then you yank him out and give him a few minutes on the beaches of heaven.

Luke can't help but wonder what hell will be like for the burly man. Which tooth Joanne's selected, and how she's planning on digging it loose. How far she'll go.

He wonders how far he'll follow. And if it will ever be far enough.

HEROES

REBORN

EVENT SERIES

BOOK TWO

SAVE THE CHEERLEADER, DESTROY THE WORLD

KEITH R. A. DECANDIDO

For Stan, Jack, and Steve

CHAPTER ONE

12 JUNE 2014
A LETTER WRITTEN BY CLAIRE BENNET ON HER LAPTOP

Dear Hammer:

I'm writing this on my laptop while I'm 30,000 feet in the air in a private jet. Yes, it's Angela's jet. And no, I still won't call her "Grandma." Mom's Mom is "Grandma." Angela is "Angela." I don't care if her son was my biological father. Dad is Dad, my biological father was Nathan, my biological mother was Meredith, and Angela is Angela. And, of course, you're Hammer, because of that stupid trench coat you always wear.

God, you're not even here, and I feel like we're having the same stupid arguments about what to call family.

I have no idea when you'll see this letter, or even if you'll care if and when you do. I'm going to upload it to Micah's secure server. Hopefully you'll see it there. Either way, though, I don't know what's going to happen in Odessa.

It's supposed to be a big summit about all of us who have powers or gifts or special genes or whatever the latest buzzword is. "Evos" seems to have stuck. I've hated that word ever since the President first used it, but I hate "gifted" even more. So I guess "Evos" it is.

This summit is supposed to change everything, to make everything better, to give Evos a chance to make their voices heard. I want to be hopeful about it. When I jumped off that Ferris wheel four years ago, this was exactly the kind of thing I was hoping for.

The reasons for it, though? Not so much. Honestly, if I knew then what I know now, I never would have jumped off that Ferris wheel. I would've let Hiro take me away along with everyone else. I wish I could just get Hiro to take me back in time and let me change it, stop myself from talking to the press that day.

But even if I knew where Hiro was right now, he wouldn't do it. He's scared to death of stepping on butterflies. He says he's given up time travel, because there are always side effects nobody expects.

It's funny, I never got that butterfly line of Hiro's until the barge. Just before you and I met, I started reading. Before I was on the barge, I never read anything more complicated than a web page for fun. Books were just something I read for school. But Mohinder and Micah had stocked the barge with so many books, and I started reading them. Ray Bradbury. Ursula Le Guin. Sarah Orne Jewett. J.K. Rowling. Agatha Christie. And Mickey Spillane.

Anyhow, there are times when I wish I could go back. But if I change the past, I don't meet you—and in a lot of ways, I'd be okay with that. But if we don't meet, then the twins don't happen. I can't risk that.

They're due soon. The twins, I mean. Muffin and

Squeaker. Batman and Robin. Brad and Angelina. Hiro and Ando. One of these days, I'll pick actual names for them.

God, I hope my water doesn't break during the summit, that would just be *perfect*.

Anyhow, the main reason why I'm writing you this letter is because I need to tell you everything. Back on the barge, you always said you wanted to know about my life *before* Central Park. You kept telling me that I was a public figure after that, so you didn't need to know about that.

So I told you all about my life growing up in Odessa— the very same town I'm going to now—and then discovering my powers and going on the run and living in California and going to college and Sylar and Hiro and the Petrelli family and the Sullivan Carnival.

You told me not to tell you anything about after that, because you said you knew it all.

But you didn't. You really, really didn't.

So I'm going to tell you. Maybe you'll understand, then. Maybe you won't. I don't care, but I need you to know.

CHAPTER TWO

Noah Bennet watched as a couple of uniforms put Samuel Sullivan in the back of a blue-and-white. He'd be taken to the NYPD's Central Park Precinct on the 86th Street Transverse to be held until he was released into federal custody. Lauren Ambrose would use her pull at the CIA to take care of that.

He looked down at his daughter, Claire. "Is everyone safe?"

Claire nodded as they walked through the Sullivan Brothers Carnival, which had somehow materialized in the middle of the Great Lawn. "Yeah, Hiro's taking care of them, they'll be fine."

Hiro Nakamura had used his teleportation powers to get the carnival's customers and other employees out of harm's way when Samuel had tried to start an earthquake.

"Who's taking Samuel?" Claire asked as the cop closed the blue-and-white's door on a handcuffed Samuel. "Is it a new Company?"

That prompted a smile from Noah. As far as he

knew, the Company he worked for—under the guise of Primatech Paper—was defunct. Though he supposed the lone surviving founder, Angela Petrelli, would have kept the corporate entity intact just in case. Aloud, he just said, "An old one," riffing on the CIA's longstanding nickname. "Lauren called in some favors."

Noah noticed that Lauren was giving a formal statement to the press, the only civilians who were still around at this point.

"What's she telling them?" Claire sounded dubious.

"There was a gas main rupture."

Rolling her eyes, Claire said, "Of *course* there was."

"And all the other stuff—the flying, the rumbling—all just special effects put on by a *very* gifted showman."

"You still can't see it, can you?"

That took Noah back. Claire had the patented teenager you-just-don't-understand-Dad look on her face, but the tone of her words carried a seriousness that surprised him.

No. That wasn't fair. Claire had been through more than any twelve people and had not only survived, but thrived. She was one of the strongest people Noah had ever known, even discounting the regenerative powers that rendered her effectively invulnerable. It made Noah both incredibly proud to be her father and incredibly scared for what more she might have to go through.

But he would protect her. That was what he had done from the moment Kaito Nakamura had handed the infant over to him on the roof of the Devaux Building in this very city eighteen years ago.

He asked her, "See what?"

"The future—one where we all get to live out in the open."

"Claire, you know how I feel about this." He started

to walk away. They'd had variations on this argument practically since the moment they were forced out of Odessa.

But Claire was insistent. "How long can we keep this under wraps?"

Before Noah could answer, he heard a gaggle of journalists approaching them. Lauren was strolling away, having apparently finished her prepared statement, but as usual that wasn't enough for the media. Suddenly, Noah found a bevy of microphones shoved in his face, and he had to hold up his hand to avoid the glare reflecting off his horn-rimmed glasses from the camera lights. He blinked spots out of his eyes as the questions started coming.

"Excuse me!"

"You were witnesses. What happened?"

One of the first things that Eric Thompson had drilled into Noah when he recruited him for the Company all those years ago was that, if by some strange happenstance he wound up speaking to members of the fourth estate, there were only four words he should ever say. And he said them now: "I have no comment."

Undaunted, another reporter turned to Claire. "Can you tell us what you saw here tonight?"

Noah shot Claire a look, suddenly wishing he had Matt Parkman's telepathy so he could transmit the words, *Don't say anything!*

Luckily, it seemed he only needed the look, as she just muttered, "What he said."

Proudly, Noah smiled and started to walk away.

Of course, the reporters kept at it.

"Miss, please, you have to have seen *something*."

"Are you sure, Miss?"

"You look like you want to say something."

Noah turned around. Not only had Claire not moved, but that last reporter was right. She *did* look like she had something to say.

Don't say anything!

"Actually, I do have something to say."

Noah winced. His mind immediately started weighing exit strategies—absolutely none of which would work in a huge public park while at least a dozen cameras, both video and still, were pointed right at him and Claire.

So he tried a simple fatherly warning. "Claire."

She turned to look at him. "You're right. People don't change." Then she walked over to the press. "You want to know what really happened here tonight? Keep the cameras on me."

And Noah watched in horror as his daughter ran over to the giant Ferris wheel—and started to climb it.

Noah had seen the videos that Claire and her friend Zach had made of her testing her powers. One of them was of her jumping from a tremendous height and then getting up and walking away like it was nothing.

It seemed she was re-creating that little experiment for a much wider audience.

Lauren had noticed that the press hadn't dispersed after her statement and saw what Claire was doing. She approached Noah. "What's she doing?"

"Breaking my heart," was all Noah could say in reply.

All eyes were riveted on Claire as she reached the top. Once she clambered to the very highest point of the wheel, she looked down. Noah wasn't sure if she was looking right at him, but he certainly felt the power of her gaze.

Every discussion, every argument, every disagreement, every talk they'd had—it had all been theoretical, academic. There was no question in Noah's mind that the general public would need to be sheltered from the gifted people in their midst, as they had been for decades.

His daughter was about to change that.

The reporters all gasped audibly as Claire jumped off the wheel. She plummeted to the ground like a rocket, yet the fall seemed to be in slow-motion to Noah.

With that one leap, Claire finally did the one thing that Sylar, the Company, Danko and his mercenaries, Ted Sprague, Arthur Petrelli, and Samuel and his carnies hadn't managed to accomplish.

Noah could no longer protect her.

She landed on the grass and dirt with a sickening crunch. The journalists all looked horrified—but they all ran closer as well, and Noah wondered how many of them were concerned for Claire's safety and how many just wanted to look at the body.

But Claire was standing upright before any of them reached her. The act of standing shoved her dislocated left leg back into place, and then she grabbed her misshapen right arm with her left and snapped it into shape with a crack that echoed off the trees and carnival attractions.

The reporters were openly gaping. All eyes were on Claire.

Including, Noah realized, those of the other gifted people who had come to stop Samuel: Hiro and his friend Ando Masahashi, who were right behind Noah and Lauren, and Peter Petrelli, who was standing by one of the game booths—with Sylar. Noah almost gaped, wondering what the hell *he* was doing here, standing with Peter like they were old buddies.

For her part, Claire was staring right into the cameras, unblinking as the lights shone in her face, already fully healed from the fall, her visage marred only by leftover blood.

"My name is Claire Bennet, and this is attempt number…" She trailed off and chuckled. "I guess I've kind of lost count."

Noah sighed and then whispered to Lauren, "Come on."

"Don't you—"

"I know what she's going to say. And I can't stop her, not now. But I can minimize the damage."

He walked over to Hiro and Ando and spoke to them in Japanese. "We have to get out of here."

Ando actually replied in English. "What is she doing?"

Somehow, Noah didn't feel right giving Ando the same non-answer he'd given Lauren. "Falling on her sword. No sense in the rest of you being impaled alongside her. She's made her choice to go public, but that doesn't mean you have to."

Ando nodded, but Hiro was raptly watching Claire.

"Hiro," Ando prompted.

Shaking his head, Hiro said in Japanese, "Yes, Mr. Bennet is correct—for now. But all those people I teleported to safety will not remain quiet about how they escaped the carnival."

Noah sighed. He hadn't even considered that. The important thing had been to get the other carnies from Sullivan Brothers and the innocent attendees to safety. In the past, he'd been able to contain such sightings with help from Rene, but even the powerful Haitian couldn't erase the memories of so many hundreds of people, assuming he could even find them all in a city this large.

Peter and Sylar came over to them.

Before Noah or anyone else could speak, Peter held up both hands. "I know what you're gonna say, but Sylar's— well, he's changed. He saved a woman's life today."

"Ando and I saved many hundreds of lives." Hiro sounded almost petulant.

Lauren finally jumped in. "We can argue over who saved who later. Right now, all eyes are on Claire, and she seems to want it that way. The rest of you need to get far away from here."

Sylar nodded. "She's right. It may be a brave new world out there, but I for one would rather face it on my terms, not the media's."

"If Claire's family tree comes out, it's gonna be a mess," Peter said.

"It's a mess for later," Noah said. "For now, we need to join hands so Hiro can take us far away from here."

As everyone did as he had advised, Noah heard his daughter say, "I can't tell you where we came from, but I can tell you where we are: here. Most of us are just people trying to live normal lives, no different from anyone else. I was a cheerleader in high school. And I've gotten to help save the world. It's about time people knew that I did that. And also—"

Whatever else Claire was going to say was lost as Hiro grimaced and Central Park disappeared…

CHAPTER THREE

On the one hand, Claire's heart was beating so hard inside her chest that she felt like her ribcage would explode. Here she was, a simple girl from Texas, standing in the Oval Office, meeting the President of the United States.

On the other hand, after being killed during an attempted rape and waking up on an autopsy table with her entire chest cut open, running *into* a burning building, getting shot, having her brain sliced open, and watching more people than she cared to think about die, from Jackie to her birth mother to her first college roommate, this kind of felt anticlimactic.

The large oval-shaped room sported two couches facing each other perpendicular to a large easy chair, with two more chairs facing it. Behind the easy chair was the President's desk, where the commander-in-chief was sitting as Claire entered, surrounded by a half-dozen Secret Service agents and several men and women in suits. The only one of them she recognized was the Vice President.

The President got up from his chair and smiled. "So—

you're the young woman who changed the world."

Claire glanced nervously from side to side. "I guess?"

Walking around to the other side of the desk, the President approached Claire, who was standing behind one of the couches. He was even taller in person than he seemed on camera, and he practically loomed over her now. "It's a pleasure to finally meet you, Ms. Bennet. You've created quite a stir. Luckily, it's one we were prepared for."

"Actually," she said very quietly—she felt weird correcting the President, but this was important—"it's Ms. Petrelli. I'm going by Claire Petrelli now."

"Well, the late Senator Petrelli is the reason *why* we were so well prepared for this."

Claire nodded. "Building 26."

"Yes." The President frowned. "How much do you know about that, Ms. B—er, Ms. Petrelli?"

"I know everything about it. My father worked for it, and my biological father was Senator Petrelli."

One of the men in suits stepped forward. "The President is asking because your name wasn't in the files that the senator provided. And they were quite comprehensive."

"My father—" Claire smiled. "*Both* my fathers—have been very protective of me. Especially my adopted father. It's to protect him—as well as my mother and brother— that I changed my name. If the press wants to go after my family, let them go after the Petrellis. They can handle it."

The President nodded. "No doubt. In any case, I'm glad you're here to be one of my Lenny Skutniks for the State of the Union."

Claire blinked. "I'm sorry?"

One of the women came to Claire's rescue. "Lenny Skutnik was the first special guest in the gallery back in '82. He rescued a woman from the Potomac—dove right in and swam after her and kept her from drowning."

Nodding, Claire smiled. "A real hero."

The Vice President said, "President Reagan invited him to sit up in the box, and since then, every State of the Union's had a guest. Including, now, you, Ms. Petrelli."

"I'm honored."

"You should be," the President said. "What you did took tremendous courage. I know it hasn't been easy, answering the same questions over and over again. Not to mention all the medical tests."

"Actually, those have been fine." She smiled. "It's always kind of fun to watch another doctor stare in surprise every time I heal right in front of them."

"You can rest assured, Ms. Petrelli, that your bravery hasn't gone unnoticed. The reason why I invited you here today to be my guest at the State of the Union is because you and people like you are a big part of my speech."

That made Claire more than a little nervous. *Are they opening Building 26 for business again? Something worse?*

"Don't worry," the President added quickly. "It's nothing you need to be afraid of. I pride myself on not making the same mistake twice."

The Vice President grinned. "We prefer to make newer, more interesting mistakes."

Several in the room chuckled at that. Claire, though, was not one of them.

The Vice President continued. "Besides, the cover-ups aren't really tenable anymore, you know?"

"Not that I think you're wrong or anything, sir," Claire said slowly, "but why do you say that?"

"Central Park is built on a very large swamp. There *are* no gas lines under it."

Claire winced. Lauren had probably had no idea of

that when she came up with the cover story—which, to be fair, she had had to do on the fly. But it was just another indicator to Claire that she had done the right thing.

A short young man walked into the office. "Sir, it's time."

The President nodded and moved toward the door. "Who's the designated survivor this year?"

One of the women said, "The Housing Secretary."

Smiling, the President said, "Lucky him."

This much Claire did remember from school: one member of the Cabinet was left in the White House during the State of the Union in case something happened to the House Chamber, since pretty much the entire government would be together in one building. She also knew that, since 2001, certain members of Congress spent the evening in undisclosed locations for similar reasons.

At the time she'd learned about the practice, Claire had thought it to be absurdly paranoid. Now, though, she realized it seemed like something her father would have come up with...

Ten more Secret Service agents met them outside the Oval Office, and they all moved swiftly through the corridors of the White House.

The President was talking to one of the women. "Did we get the final notes on the budget section?"

"Amazingly, they said it was fine as is."

"Really?"

"No one was more surprised than me, Mr. President."

Claire realized that, of the sixteen Secret Service agents that were surrounding this group of people, four of them were *very* close to her.

Are they here to protect me? Or to protect everyone else from me?

She was pretty sure it was the latter.

The four agents maneuvered her toward a long line of limousines parked outside the White House, and guided her into one of them. She was seated across from a man in a suit and a man dressed like an airline pilot. One of the agents took the seat next to her.

The man in the suit said, "You're the indestructible girl."

"I guess so, yeah."

"So you're *real*."

Claire rolled her eyes. "Please don't ask me to cut myself."

He held up both hands. "No, no, I believe you. I mean, if you're sitting in the President's box for the State of the Union, then this isn't just a crazy gag. I figured it was some stunt for a new movie or something."

The airline pilot was just staring out the window as the limo slowly pulled out. Sirens blared through the air and red-white-and-blue lights strobed across the car's windows as they drove down 15th Street. Claire found it almost hypnotic.

She reached into her purse and pulled out her phone, hoping there might be a text from Gretchen Berg.

There was nothing new. There hadn't been anything new since the two texts her former best friend had sent on the 14th of December. The first was a picture she'd taken of some tabloid or other on a supermarket rack. A picture of Claire and Gretchen on the campus of Arlington University was splashed across the front page with the headline, "INDESTRUCTIBLE GIRL IN LOVE NEST WITH CO-ED."

The second text read, "How could you do this to me Claire? They won't leave me alone! I never want to see you again!"

Under that were about thirty texts from Claire, all trying to get Gretchen to relent and respond.

Still no reply.

She sent another: "Please text me, Gretch, let me know you're okay? PLEASE?"

It only took a few minutes to arrive at the Capitol. Five more Secret Service agents joined the one in the car to escort the three of them inside to the President's box, which overlooked the House Chamber. The room was huge, all wood paneling, and quite lovely. Watching the speech on a computer monitor—which Claire had only done once, and then just because of a homework assignment—didn't give one an appreciation for how *big* the chamber was.

Two sections of seats were empty, and of the three seats on the main dais, only one was occupied—by the Speaker of the House. The President would sit in front of her, with the Vice President on her right.

The airline pilot and the other guy sat to Claire's right. To her left were the First Lady and the President's children. The First Lady smiled at her and said, "Welcome."

"Thank you."

"You look nervous."

"Really?" She chuckled. "I don't feel nervous. I feel—" She shook her head. "I don't know what I feel. This is *really* not what I expected my life to be like."

Raising an eyebrow, the First Lady asked, "You mean before or after you realized you couldn't be hurt?"

"Both." Claire looked away. "And I can get hurt—just not physically."

A voice from below cried out, "Madame Speaker, the Vice President of the United States, and the United States Senate!"

The Vice President entered and sat down next to the Speaker as about a hundred people filed in to sit in one of the unoccupied sections. Claire figured that it wouldn't be quite all one hundred senators, and sure enough, four seats were empty.

After that, the Dean of the Diplomatic Corps was announced, followed by the Chief Justice, the rest of the Supreme Court, and the Cabinet. The one time Claire had watched the State of the Union, it had been on YouTube, and it had started with the President's actual speech, so she'd never seen the preliminaries before.

It took about a half hour for everyone to be introduced and seated, and then finally came the words they'd all been waiting for: "Madame Speaker, the President of the United States."

It took quite a while for the President to make his way down the aisle, shaking hands and smiling and thanking people amidst thunderous applause.

When he finally made it to the dais, the Speaker formally introduced him, which led to *more* applause, and then at last the President began to speak.

The speech started with a litany of clichés and platitudes that Claire found herself utterly incapable of paying attention to. She briefly considered checking her phone to see if she'd heard from Gretchen, then decided against it. *It's not like today's going to be any different.* Gretchen had been her best friend, and Claire probably wouldn't have made it through the early days of college without her. But Claire had also gone public without consulting her—or even warning her.

Now the President was talking about the airline pilot, who had apparently rescued several passengers after an emergency landing in the Atlantic Ocean. After the applause for him had died down, he glanced at her. Claire squirmed in her seat.

"Also with us is Ms. Claire Petrelli."

Claire noticed that the President paused before saying her last name. No doubt the notes in front of him and the teleprompter both said "Bennet."

"I'm sure you've all seen the video of Claire's dramatic jump off of a Ferris wheel, and I'm sure you've seen the interviews she's done in the month and a half since. But Claire is not unique—and she is not a freak, either. Claire is one of hundreds, possibly thousands, of evolved humans who walk among us. These 'Evos' have kept themselves hidden because they live in fear. Now you might think they have little reason to be afraid. These are people who can fly, who can move at supersonic speeds, who can teleport from place to place, who can change the course of mighty rivers. But they're also people who are different.

"This country's history has been marred by an inability to accept that which is different, but it's also been blessed with an ability to move past that. People with skin the same color as me came here in bondage. The Constitution of the United States, as originally written, considered people who looked like me to be only three-fifths of a person. When immigrants from Western Europe, from Latin America, from Eastern Europe came over here, they were initially viewed with distrust and not considered 'real' Americans.

"But we've been able to move past that. I'm not three-fifths of a person anymore, I'm the President of the United States. Women can own property and vote. You don't see employment ads reading, 'Irish need not apply.' Not that we're all there—we still have a long way to go, and that is why these 'Evos' have felt the need to stay in the shadows. This administration was recently made aware of the existence of 'Evos,' thanks in part to the late Senator Nathan Petrelli. Mistakes were made, primarily by a rogue agent who has since passed away. I can assure you that the same mistakes will not be made twice. Evos are people, just like us—just like my ancestors who came to this country in chains, just like so many of your ancestors who came in boats or planes hoping for a better life. The American dream isn't just for white people, it isn't just for landowners, it isn't just for men, it isn't just for heterosexuals—and it isn't just for people who don't have strange powers. It's for *everyone*.

"Which is why I'm going to urge Congress to pass the Evo Registration Act. Let me emphasize that this is *not* going to be a mandatory registration. What the act will do, assuming it is passed, is empower the Department of Homeland Security to collect information. Any Evos out there who wish to register with the government may do so—but those who do not may choose not to, with no fear of reprisal. In addition, any Evos who are convicted of a crime will be compelled to register as well. It is our hope that law-enforcement agencies will be able to use this information to keep all Americans—Evo or not—safe."

Claire just stared straight ahead. She hadn't expected this, and wasn't sure how she felt about it.

She *had* wanted to live out in the open. At least the President had made it clear that they weren't going to do what Emil Danko—the rogue agent the President had referred to—did, making warrantless arrests followed by imprisonment without trial. If Danko had had his way, *all* the gifted people—*what did he call them, "Evos"?*—would be rounded up into prisons. Even the ones who hadn't done anything wrong.

But the President said that this new law would be voluntary. She hoped that would be the right thing.

The speech went on, but she barely noticed any of it. A small voice in her head that sounded a *lot* like her father said, *You wanted to go public, Claire-Bear—this is what happens.*

CHAPTER FOUR

Noah Bennet came home just before nine in the evening, his third twelve-hour day in a row. Thanks to a recommendation from Lauren, the Department of Homeland Security had hired him as a consultant. Ever since Congress had passed the Evo Registration Act, DHS had been setting up registration centers in major cities throughout the country. Noah had so much experience dealing with special people—or "Evos," since it seemed that the neologism of the President's speechwriters had caught on—that his advice had proven highly useful, both in terms of what to test for and how to defend against their powers if needed.

For now, Noah's work was strictly advisory, but his boss had promised that he would be sent out into the field to check out the registration centers in person.

On the one hand, it was good to be *doing* something. While Noah had no real money issues—whatever else one could say about the Company, they had a fantastic retirement plan, and Noah's two decades working for them had given him a nice big 401(K) he could easily live off of for the rest of his life.

But while he could survive without having to work, he hardly could call that living. He needed something to *do*.

Luckily, DHS needed his help. They had no idea what they were doing. Everyone Homeland had assigned to the project got their knowledge of Evos from comic books and movies—Noah was the only one with first-hand experience.

It would be strange, though, to go into the field and *not* bag-and-tag.

He fell more than sat on his couch and stabbed at the television remote.

The box was already set on one of the twenty-four-hour news stations. A woman in a maroon suit was, irony of ironies, discussing the Evo situation.

"—passed by Congress, and soon we'll be seeing registration centers opening up all over the country. So far, public opinion has been refreshingly positive, and a lot more Evos have been coming out of the closet—or, I guess maybe it'd be better to say coming out of the phone booth? Anyhow, ever since Claire Petrelli's big jump here in New York, we've seen a bunch more Evos be more public with their abilities. Not to mention a few old news stories that make a lot more sense now. But it still hasn't been determined who, exactly, the two Asian men were who apparently teleported the attendees of the Sullivan Brothers Carnival out of Central Park on that night in December. The Internet has taken to nicknaming them Tetsuo and Kineda, after the two main characters in *Akira*.

"But it's not all happy shiny news. The head of that carnival was a man named Samuel Sullivan, and even as Claire Petrelli has been appearing on TV and radio and YouTube, Sullivan has been languishing in a prison without trial."

Noah winced. How had they found out about that?

The camera switched to a two-shot, revealing that there was a wheelchair-bound guest sitting across from the newswoman. The guest was an older man with close-cropped salt-and-pepper hair, wearing a slightly rumpled suit. As she introduced him, he pushed his large, plastic-framed glasses up his nose.

"With me is the lawyer for the Sullivan Brothers Carnival, Jacob Kurtzberg."

And that answered Noah's question. For all the peculiarities surrounding it, the carnival was still a business, and that usually meant some manner of legal representation.

Kurtzberg said, "Thank you for having me."

"Jacob, can you tell us, please, what's happened to your client?"

"Well, technically, the carnival is my client, but Samuel Sullivan is the legal owner of the carnival, and he was detained on the 7th of December of last year. He was arrested and brought to the NYPD's Central Park Precinct, and then he was remanded into federal custody. He has not been arraigned, he has not been permitted to consult with his attorney, to wit, me. In fact, I can't even get a straight answer when I ask where he's being held."

"What was he charged with when he was arrested?"

"I don't even know that!" Kurtzberg had raised his voice but immediately got himself under control, clearing his throat. "Honestly? The only charge they can make stick is setting up the carnival without a permit, which is a misdemeanor. The carnival will happily pay the fine and make whatever other restitution the city of New York demands. But no such demands have been made. No such *anything* has been made."

Angrily, Noah stabbed at the MUTE button on the

remote. He took out his cell phone and contemplated calling the office.

No. You're just a consultant. And this isn't your problem.

Instead, he called Kojin Sushi and made a takeout order. He supposed he could have had it delivered, but considering that the Japanese restaurant in question was located on the ground floor of his very apartment building, such a request seemed the height of laziness.

Once he'd ordered the shrimp tempura appetizer and a sushi dinner, he got up and walked over to the refrigerator to pour himself a glass of water from the filtered pitcher he kept there.

Only after returning to the couch did he un-mute the TV, mostly because Kurtzberg was done talking and the camera was centered on the newswoman. To Noah's horror, there was an image of Claire behind her. *What now?*

When he hit the MUTE button once again, the woman's voice filled the room. "—which tonight aired some old video footage of Claire Petrelli testing out her powers while wearing, of all things, a cheerleader uniform."

His heart sinking, Noah watched as the screen cut to one of the videos that Claire and her friend Zach had made: her jumping off an abandoned refinery on the outskirts of Odessa.

The newswoman was talking over the video roll. "The source of the video has only been identified by his online handle of 'Hellbee,' and—"

Angrily, Noah turned the television off. He knew exactly who "Hellbee" was.

Snatching his phone out of his pocket, he called his ex-wife at home.

Naturally, Doug answered the phone. Because Noah's day hadn't been crappy enough.

"Douglas residence, go for Doug."

Noah forced himself to take a deep breath to center himself before responding. "Hi, Doug, it's Noah. Is Sandra around?"

"Oh, hey, Noah! Good to hear from you! Hey, that daughter of yours keeps showing up on my TV. She's made quite the stir, hasn't she? And to think, she's actually my step-daughter now. I gotta say, I've never been this close to anyone famous."

While imagining all the ways in which he could kill Doug and dispose of the body such that it would never be found, Noah very quietly said, "That's nice, Doug. May I please speak to Sandra?"

"Oh, of course, not a problem. Hang on a sec."

After the clunk of the receiver being put down, Noah waited several seconds, hearing distant, indistinct voices in the background.

"Yes, Noah?"

"Have you talked to Lyle lately?"

"Not since the semester started, why?"

"I just discovered that some gossip show aired Claire's old tapes that she and Zach made. The person who gave them the tapes has the Internet handle 'Hellbee.'"

At first, Sandra said nothing, but Noah could tell that she was turning it over in her mind, trying to figure out a way that it couldn't be Lyle. But she was probably also thinking of the bee with devil horns that Lyle had been doodling ever since he was eleven, when he realized that his initials were a homonym for the nickname. It was his go-to username on all social media.

Finally, Sandra said, "Let me talk to him."

"You sure? Because I'm perfectly happy to drive to his dorm and talk to him myself."

"Noah Bennet, you will do no such thing. Lyle's your son, not one of those Evos you like to bag and tag."

He sighed. "I'm not doing that anymore, Sandra, we're just—"

"I don't care, Noah. Really, I don't. The only people I care about are Doug, Claire, and Lyle. Doug's doing fine, I'll deal with Lyle, and as for Claire—well, I just need to turn on the TV to see how she's doing, don't I?"

"Believe me, that wasn't my idea," Noah said weakly. Sandra certainly was getting all her digs in tonight.

"Oh, I know that much, Noah. You've had plenty of stupid ideas in your time, but even you're not that crazy. And speaking of stupid ideas, why is Claire going by 'Petrelli' now?"

"It's for our protection." Noah tried very hard to sound like he believed that.

Sandra replied with the bitterest laugh he'd ever heard from her. "Right! Because lying to protect the Bennet family has *always* turned out *so* well!"

Noah took off his horn-rims and set them down on the end table, rubbing his eyes with his thumb and forefinger. "Sandra, I—"

"I'll talk to you later, Noah. As soon as I've talked to Lyle, I'll fill you in."

And then she hung up.

Noah took the phone away from his ear and just stared at it, as if it would provide answers to how, exactly, his life got so screwed up.

There were times when he wondered what would have happened if he had done as Kaito Nakamura had instructed and simply treated the child of Meredith Gordon and Nathan Petrelli as a Company asset. If he had reported her abilities to the Company when they manifested and given her back to them, just as Kaito had instructed all those years ago. If he had been a good Company man instead of a loving father.

Then he remembered Elle Bishop. Her father—one of the founders—had given his daughter over to be used by the Company, and she had grown up to become quite the sociopath.

No, he had made the right choice. Regardless of the consequences, Claire had grown into a brilliant, compassionate, amazing young woman, and twenty years in the Company told him that she never would have been allowed to do that under their thumb.

Shaking his head, he put the phone in his pocket and went downstairs to get his dinner.

CHAPTER FIVE

6 SEPTEMBER 2011
UNION WELLS HIGH SCHOOL, ODESSA, TX

Claire never thought she'd set foot in this school again. In fact, she never thought she'd set foot in her hometown again. The last time she had been there was when she confronted Sylar on Level 5 of the Company's headquarters located under Primatech Paper.

Yet here she was, stepping out of a town car that had parked right in front of her former high school. Hanging across the building's façade was a huge banner with her picture on it, which read: WELCOME TO UNION WELLS HIGH SCHOOL, THE SCHOOL OF CLAIRE PETRELLI.

She was met by the principal of the school, a very tall woman named Laurie Prichard. Claire looked up at her as they approached the entrance together. "You do know I didn't actually graduate from here, right?"

Ms. Prichard smiled, showing perfect white teeth. "Let's just keep that to ourselves, shall we? It's been a huge help for recruitment *and* alumni donations, both of which took a big hit after that homicide when you were here. We need all the help we can get."

"No, that's fine—I guess." It wasn't really Claire's concern, in any case. And she could understand how enrollment might be an issue on a campus where someone had been killed. Lots of students transferred out after Jackie Wilcox was killed by Sylar. Including, now that she thought about it, Claire herself.

The principal led her through the hallways, which were surprisingly empty. Noticing Claire's confusion, Ms. Prichard said, "Everyone's already out in the bleachers, waiting for you."

Claire nodded. After her starring role in the State of the Union address, she had been forced to hire a publicist, an intense young woman named Danielle Katz, as the requests for personal appearances were becoming overwhelming. Which was good, as Claire never would have heard from her former high school if Ms. Prichard hadn't been able to contact Danielle. Luckily, Danielle was on the ball enough to recognize Union Wells for what it was, and sent that particular request straight up the ladder to Claire herself.

As they turned toward the exit to the football field, Claire noticed a bulletin board filled with pictures of cheerleaders in the oh-so-familiar red-and-white uniform.

Peering closely, she saw a sign at the top of the bulletin board that read, JACKIE WILCOX MEMORIAL CHEER SQUAD. And the uniforms did have one new feature: a black band on the right arm.

Nodding appreciatively, she followed Ms. Prichard as the principal pushed the metal bar that unlatched the door leading out to the football field. Even before the door opened, she could hear the noise of the kids sitting in the bleachers.

Walking out to the hundred-yard expanse of grass, Claire saw that the bleachers were filled with students, and a podium had been set up in the home goal area just under the uprights. Behind the podium there were a bunch of assorted adults sitting in folding chairs. Claire recognized some of them as teachers she'd had when she was a student here.

A giant red ribbon stretched across the goal line, held up by poles that had been stuck into the ground.

And above the scoreboard in big black letters were the words, PETRELLI FIELD.

As Claire walked toward the home goal, a smattering of applause started somewhere in the bleachers. It slowly grew into a huge standing ovation.

She shook her head.

Ms. Prichard whisper-shouted over the din of the applause. "What's wrong?"

"I still don't get why they're applauding."

One person shouted, "We love you, Claire!"

There were two empty chairs next to the podium, and Claire sat in one of them while Ms. Prichard approached the microphone.

"Okay, settle down," she said into the mic. She could barely be heard over the crowd, but the noise level decreased quickly as the principal glared at the bleachers.

Claire couldn't help but smile. The really talented teachers had teenager-silencing abilities that to Claire seemed to be as much a super-power as her invulnerability, and obviously Ms. Prichard was one of those. The bleachers were dead quiet within ten seconds.

"Today, we're honoring one of our most distinguished alumni. Claire Petrelli has shown tremendous courage in revealing her abilities to the public. She's become the face of the Evo movement, and I am proud to have her here to inaugurate our newly remodeled football field. Claire was a cheerleader on the old field, and here she is to cut the ribbon for the new one. Ladies and gentlemen, boys and girls—Claire Petrelli."

The applause started again, with many of the kids standing up as well.

Claire smiled as she adjusted the microphone downward so it was closer to her face. "Thank you," she said, hoping it would make the crowd quiet down.

It didn't. She didn't have Ms. Prichard's power.

So she waited them out.

Eventually, they all stopped clapping and sat down, and she said, "Thank you" again. "I'm flattered by all this clapping, but I'm not really sure why you're doing it."

One person screamed, "'Cause you're awesome!"

Several kids cheered at that.

"The thing is, I'm not. I'm just a girl—I was a cheerleader here, just like lots of other girls. I went to class, I did my homework—mostly." She smiled, and several people laughed—even Ms. Prichard. "I had friends, I went to parties, I went to dances, and I cheered on the football team—just like lots of other girls."

She looked down at her notes, and took a deep breath.

"Last week, a woman in Hammond, Louisiana, who's able to stretch out parts of her body like a rubber band rescued a little girl and a cat from a tree. Two weeks ago, a man in Baskerville, Virginia, who can hear a lot better than most people heard a couple crying for help in an abandoned building and called 911. They'd been trapped for three days, but he was the only one who heard them. Last month, after a big rainstorm in Pueblo, Colorado, a man with tremendous speed cleaned out his neighbor's basement before the water damage got too bad. And just yesterday in Warren, Michigan, a woman stopped a purse snatcher by creating an oil slick out of nothing. All of these are also just normal people who happen to be Evos."

Claire looked up at the sign above the scoreboard and sighed.

"I know it's called Petrelli Field after me, but as far as I'm concerned, this field is named after my father, Senator Nathan Petrelli, and my uncle, Peter Petrelli. They were real heroes who tried to make the world a better place. My father died for it. Peter saved my life, more than once. I hope that this new field will be a symbol for the new hope that everyone can live in peace together."

Turning to look at Ms. Prichard, Claire saw the principal nod and get up from her folding chair. She joined Claire at the podium and brandished a large pair of scissors. One of the handles was red, the other white.

Claire shook her head. *Even the scissors are the school colors.*

Together, Claire and Ms. Prichard walked up to the big red ribbon that stretched across the goal line. The principal handed Claire the scissors, and Claire cut the ribbon with a flourish. The two ends slowly fluttered to the grass, and the crowd once again cheered.

After the ceremony, Claire was brought over to a small table in the sun where students could come and meet her and ask for her autograph and have pictures taken with her. It felt like it took forever, though it turned out to only be an hour. She kept answering the same questions over and over again.

The one she got asked the most was, of course, "Can you hurt yourself and then heal for us?" Or something like that. Someone *always* asked that—usually a lot of someones.

At this point, Claire's stock answer was, "There are, like, a million videos on YouTube. Just watch one of them."

"But it's not the same!" Which was what a lot of the someones said. But Claire was insistent.

Eventually, the kids all went back to class and Claire was free to go. Ms. Prichard walked her back to the town car, which was still parked in front of the school.

"Thank you again, Claire. This really meant a lot to the kids—and to the school."

Claire gave the woman her brightest smile. "It was my pleasure, Ms. Prichard." She even mostly meant it.

After shaking the principal's hand, she climbed into the car.

"Airport?" the driver asked.

Nodding, Claire said, "Please." She'd flown in the previous night and stayed overnight at one of the hotels near the airport. Now she was flying to New York to meet with some doctors who wanted to test her blood.

There'd been a lot of that. To Claire's mind, this whole insanity would be worth it if scientists could find a way to use her blood's healing properties to help people.

As the town car drove down the streets she grew up on, Claire found herself thinking about Peter. She hadn't heard hide nor hair from him since Central Park. In fact, she'd barely seen him then, as she had been busy trying to convince the other carnies of Samuel's true, nasty nature.

In fact, what really surprised her was how few of the Evos she actually knew had joined her in coming out. She would have thought that Hiro at the very least would embrace going public. But he and Ando had remained underground, as had Peter and his mother, Matt Parkman, Mohinder, Tracy, and the others. Claire wasn't really sure why—maybe just because they'd all been through so much.

Still and all, she figured she'd take another shot at calling Peter. It would probably do as much good as texting

Gretchen had—she had finally given up on that sometime in April—but she had to try. Peter was too important to her.

Naturally, she got his voicemail. "You've reached Peter's phone. Please leave a message."

"Hi, Peter, it's Claire. Again. Look, it's been nine months, and I haven't heard a word. I've tried asking your mother where you are, but you know how she is. For someone who can see the future, she *sucks* at giving straight answers. Anyhow, I just want—I just *need* to know you're okay. Look, you don't have to tell me where you are, just let me know that you're alive and okay. Please? Things really are better now that we're out in the open. I just spent an hour being told by a bunch of high school kids how cool I am. Just please? Call me?" She let out a long breath, said, "Bye," and ended the call.

CHAPTER SIX

12 SEPTEMBER 2011
EXCERPT FROM *NBC 5 NEWS AT 10*, CHICAGO, IL
"Breaking news, now, on the house fire on 43rd Street in Canaryville. NBC 5 has obtained exclusive footage from the security camera in Frankie's Pizza Shop, located across the street from the house in question. The image is a bit pixelated, but you can see that there is a human figure who suddenly—wait for it—there it is, he *catches fire*. The fire then spreads to the rest of the house, as you can see. There's also this segment where the same figure is seen running away from the building, still on fire. This is more and more looking like a case of arson caused by an Evo. Chicago Police Department spokeswoman Bethany Mazursky had this to say…"

"The arson investigation is ongoing, so we cannot comment specifically. However, the possibility of Evo involvement means we are in contact with the Department of Homeland Security—but right now, that's only a possibility. We are investigating *all* possibilities, just as we do for every case."

"Here now in our studio is Gregory Quaye, Alderman of

Ward 4. Alderman, thank you for joining us."

"Yes, thank you for having me."

"Alderman, you recently spoke out, along with the governor, both Illinois senators, half a dozen other aldermen, and four of Chicago's congressmen about the inadequacies of the Evo Registration Act."

"Yes, I did. And this incident in my ward speaks to why we're so concerned. And yes, that's just the latest incident. In Miami last week, there was an attempted drive-by—but the intended target instead killed the gunman by electrocuting him with his fingers. There's a couple of thieves in New York who can walk through walls and are robbing people blind. There's a man in Seattle who's walking up to people, telling them to give him their money, and they do, without remembering it a minute later. And right here in Chicago last month, a woman on Diversey touched a car and made it disintegrate, just so she could get a parking spot. For that matter, we still don't know what *really* happened in New York last year with that carnival that appeared out of nowhere. Yes, the Petrelli girl's done a nice job of distracting us from the questions that still haven't been answered, like the earthquake. But in light of these events, the federal government needs to take a harder tack with Evos before more harm is done. It's a small miracle that nobody died in that fire, but the Evo responsible for it is still out there and still dangerous. And yes, we need *more* than simple voluntary registration. Laws regarding firearms have always had to change to accommodate new guns appearing on the market, and this is no different. Evos are, for all intents and purposes, weapons, and we need to regulate the use of those weapons before more people get hurt."

"Thank you, Alderman. When we come back, sports with Steve, looking at what the Bears did yesterday, what the Cubs did tonight, and what the Sox hope to do tomorrow."

CHAPTER SEVEN

It was with a smile on his face that Jacob Kurtzberg wheeled himself out of the elevator and toward his hotel room. After months and months of being stonewalled, he had finally been able to make his case before a judge, across from an Assistant U.S. Attorney who tried and failed to argue that Samuel Sullivan was a national security risk.

Judge Ventura was having none of that. Even if Samuel was a terrorist, he had a right to counsel, not to mention a right to be charged, which he hadn't been. Jacob had also made it clear to the AUSA that he would continue to be very public on the subject—he'd been appearing on every television show that would have him, from national cable news to local network news and back again, trying to get justice for his client—and that the Supreme Court would be his next stop.

The truth of the matter was that Jacob knew that Samuel was guilty as sin. Samuel was indeed an Evo, and Jacob was morally certain that Samuel had killed his brother Joseph and also Lydia, not to mention destroying an entire town and trying to do the same to New York City.

But what Jacob was morally certain about didn't matter. You convict people based on moral certainty, you get the Salem Witch Trials. In a civilized society, what mattered was what you could prove in a court of law. And the only thing they could actually prove was that he had set up the carnival without a permit. For that, Samuel had been held in a hole somewhere here in D.C. for nine months.

Not for much longer, though. Judge Ventura had ordered the AUSA to produce Samuel for a meeting with counsel, to which he was entitled under the law. An hour after leaving the courthouse, Jacob got a text saying that Samuel would be in an interrogation room in the District 3 headquarters of Metro PD first thing in the morning. It meant he'd have to schlep over to V Street, but he'd just call a car service like usual. The carnival was paying for it, in any case…

He arrived at the door to his room, pulled out his keycard, and pushed it into the slot. After the light turned green and the lock clicked, Jacob pushed the handle downward, and the extra-wide door opened automatically.

Before he could wheel himself in, however, he felt a breeze and saw a blur shoot past him.

"What the—?"

He wheeled himself in to see Edgar standing in the middle of the hotel room, his trademark knives gripped in his hands.

"Edgar? What are you doing here?"

"Heard you were gettin' Samuel outta prison."

"Of course I am. That's my *job*." Jacob hadn't even seen Edgar since the mess in New York. Last he'd heard, Samuel had accused Edgar of killing Joseph.

"Well, you're doin' it too well to suit me."

Another blur, and Jacob looked down in shock to see

blood pouring from his throat, staining his suit, gushing onto the metal arms of his wheelchair. The pain didn't actually come for a second or two, but then it was everywhere, all over his body.

He fell forward, barely feeling it as he collapsed onto the carpeted floor, blood now pooling under him.

"I—" he managed to croak out.

The last words Jacob heard were: "Samuel's stayin' in his hole for's long as possible. Forever'd be best."

CHAPTER EIGHT

1 OCTOBER 2011
THE WHITE HOUSE, WASHINGTON, D.C.
Noah fidgeted as he sat outside the Oval Office.

Next to him, Angela Petrelli was smiling. "Is something wrong, Noah?"

He glanced over at the closed door on the curved wall. "Just not used to this level of—well, publicity. I'm more comfortable in the shadows. We always did things in secret, under the radar. That was the *point*. And we did it well. This…" He shook his head.

"Those days, I'm afraid, are long gone, thanks to Claire. The toothpaste is out of the tube."

The woman on the other side of Angela, whom Noah did not know, said, "It was always going to end up this way. It's a wonder you kept it under wraps as long as you did, but there are just too many Evos now. The Company was never big enough to handle so many."

Noah leaned forward to try to get a better look at the woman. "I'm sorry, you are…?"

Before she could answer, the door to the Oval Office opened, and a young man said, "The President's ready for you three now."

With a heavy sigh, Noah stood up. Angela and the other woman did the same.

As they walked toward the door, Noah whispered, "Do you have any idea what this is about?"

"Yes." That was all Angela would say.

Working for DHS had its issues, but one thing Noah did *not* miss from his Company days was Angela's tiresomely enigmatic nature.

Noah had only seen the Oval Office on television. Oddly, it seemed *smaller* in real life, with the furniture kind of crammed together.

The President was sitting in an easy chair, with the Vice President and the chief of staff seated to his left. The young man who'd brought them in indicated the couch on the President's right for the three of them. Noah sat farthest from the President, while Angela sat in the middle, leaving the other woman to sit nearest the commander-in-chief. That suited Noah fine.

Without any preamble, the President started talking. "Even as we speak, Congress is voting on an amendment to the Evo Act that will make registration mandatory."

Noah tensed. This was a game-changer, to say the least. Though given the reports they'd been getting, he couldn't bring himself to be surprised.

The Vice President said, "This changes how the registration centers will be operating. And since not registering will be a felony, it will also require a level of enforcement that was not previously necessary."

The President looked right at Angela. "Now, DHS could start from scratch on this. Mr. Bennet here has done excellent work to bring Homeland up to speed, but this will require an entirely new mandate. I think it'll be much easier on everyone if we outsource this to a company that already has extensive background and experience in these matters."

The chief of staff then spoke up. "We did our due diligence on 'Primatech Paper,' Ms. Petrelli. It was fascinating reading. Turns out that all twelve of you who founded the company had equal ownership shares. And when someone dies, all that person's shares go not to, say, their heirs, but instead to the surviving shareholders."

Noah turned to stare at Angela. He knew for a fact that the other eleven founders of the Company were deceased.

"Which means in real terms," the Vice President said, "that you're the sole owner of the company—lock, stock, and Level 5."

That caused Noah to wince. If the Vice President knew about Level 5, then their security was severely compromised. Either that, or Nathan had revealed a lot more to the President than Noah had realized.

Angela gave that irritating half-smile of hers, hands rested calmly on her lap. "Your intelligence with regard to the ownership structure of the Company is quite accurate, Mr. Vice President."

"Thanks," the Vice President said dryly.

The President leaned forward. "Ms. Petrelli, the U.S. government would like to contract Primatech Paper to enforce the amended Evo Act."

"The Company is inactive, Mr. President," Angela said. "The files and resources and personnel are all scattered to the nine winds. It would take tremendous time, effort, and capital to bring the Company back up to fighting strength, as it were. I'm not sure this is the best idea."

Noah frowned. Angela wasn't actually refusing. *What is she playing at?* That was a question he had often asked himself when dealing with Angela or her late husband.

The chief of staff leaned back on the couch. "Ms. Petrelli, a minute ago you remarked on how good our intelligence is with regard to your company. You were correct—in fact, it's so good that we're quite familiar with the overwhelming number of felonies committed by Primatech's personnel. Breaking and entering. Kidnapping. Attempted murder. Assault. Fraud."

"Fraud's a misdemeanor," the woman next to Angela said.

That got a smile out of the chief of staff, but it wasn't a particularly pleasant one. "The point, Ms. Petrelli, is that you can accept the President's offer, or I can walk over to my office and make a call to the Attorney General. I guarantee you'll spend the rest of your life in prison, and it will *not* be a minimum-security prison, either."

Angela turned to look at the President. "So it's blackmail?"

Noah managed not to snort. The President was up for reelection next year. If he didn't get a handle on the Evo situation soon, he wouldn't stand a chance in hell of winning a second term.

"It's you being offered a choice," the President said. "Make it now, please."

"Actually, I made it already nine days ago. Since you seem to know all about the Company, I assume you know what *my* particular 'Evo' ability is." Angela used air quotes and a tone of purest derision when she uttered the term "Evo." "You see, on the 21st of September, I woke up from a dream. In that dream, I saw this very meeting happening. And then I turned on the television to see a news story about the death of Jacob Kurtzberg, at which point I knew *why* this meeting would be happening. Given that Mr. Kurtzberg's murder has dominated the news for the past week and a half, it was inevitable that your little law was going to need changing. However, my interest in running the day-to-day of the Company is very close to nil. In the past, I had colleagues who were happy to be administrators, but they're all, as you know, quite dead. However, since I knew this meeting was coming, I took steps."

The chief of staff said, "You listed Ms. Kravid here as your business partner when you checked in with security, but she's not on Primatech's org chart. I assume she's one of the steps you took?"

"Yes. As I'm sure you all know, Erica Kravid is the head of Renautas. Just yesterday, I finalized the deal whereby Renautas bought the Company. *She* is now in charge."

"And," Kravid said quickly, "I'm more than happy to take on the contract. Renautas is very interested in the many possibilities inherent in these Evo powers. These people can change the world in so many ways, and they've been hiding—even after that blond girl made it possible for them to come out of the phone booth, so to speak. With this new law, we'll have unfettered access to them. We can cure diseases, we can make all manner of scientific breakthroughs, we can protect the environment—we can do *so* much. Mr. President, I relish this opportunity."

"Good." The President leaned back in his chair. "Mr. Bennet, you're probably wondering why you were invited to this meeting."

In fact, Noah had been hoping that his presence would go unnoticed. In response, he simply said, "Yes, sir."

"I want you to be a part of this. You worked for Primatech in the past, and you've been invaluable to Homeland. The Secretary's reports have been frankly gushing. Since you've done a great deal of the work setting up the registration centers, and since you have experience with field work of

the type that will be required, I want you to play a role."
He turned his gaze on Kravid. "I assume, Ms. Kravid, that
having Mr. Bennet on board will be acceptable."

Noah noted that the President had not phrased that as
a question. Which was one of the reasons why he didn't
object.

Kravid smiled. "Of course, Mr. President. I'd be a fool
not to make use of Mr. Bennet's experience."

"Good." The President stood up. "The vote should be
completed tonight, and I'll sign the bill in the morning.
Thank you all."

"Thank you, Mr. President," Kravid said as she rose to
her feet.

Once they had left the Oval Office and were standing
in one of the White House hallways, Kravid offered her
hand to Noah. "Mr. Bennet, I'm Erica Kravid. It's truly a
pleasure to meet you. I've read quite a bit about you, and
I'm looking forward to having you on my team."

"I'm looking forward to it as well. Consulting is nice,
but—I prefer to get my hands dirty. Field work is where
I'm at my best."

Kravid smiled. "That would explain why you didn't
object to the President all but ordering you to work for me."

"Oh," Angela said, "Noah's good at following
instructions."

The young man who'd brought them into the Oval
Office reappeared. "If you'll come this way, please?"

Noah nodded, recognizing that they were being escorted
out.

"Are you free this afternoon, Mr. Bennet?" Kravid
asked as they walked through the West Wing toward the
exit. "We have a lot to discuss, and I'd like to get started as
soon as possible."

"Absolutely," Noah said. "Besides, this law is the right way to go. Evos have been hiding for too long—it's become second nature to them. They need to be brought out into the open."

Angela shot Noah a look. "I'm surprised to hear you say that, Noah. You were always so gung-ho about keeping things secret."

He shrugged. "Like you said before, the toothpaste is out of the tube. There's nothing we can do about it now, so we have to make the best of the situation." Then he smiled ruefully. "Besides, I was only gung-ho because that's what I was told to be. Like you *also* said, I'm good at following instructions."

"Mostly." That damned half-smile again.

"Either way," Kravid said, "it's a brave new world out there, and Renautas is going to be at the forefront of it, I can promise you that."

CHAPTER NINE

17 OCTOBER 2011
TRANSCRIPT FROM *INSIDE THE BELTWAY WITH CHRISTINE HARBOUGH*

CHRISTINE HARBOUGH: Good evening, I'm Christine Harbough, coming to you live from Washington. Everyone's talking about Evos these days, especially with the new amendment to the Evo Act that means that all these people with strange powers beyond those of mortal men will have to register with the government. In the week since the amendment was passed in Congress, we've seen the capture of an Evo in Wilmington, Delaware, who nearly set fire to an entire city block. The question is, what does the most famous Evo have to say about all this, and we've got her here tonight. Claire Petrelli, welcome.

CLAIRE PETRELLI: Thank you, Christine.

CHRISTINE: So what do you think of this new wrinkle on the Evo Act?

CLAIRE: I gotta say, I'm not thrilled about it. The whole reason why I went public was so that we could all be who we are to everyone. So that people wouldn't have to hide who they are. But it goes both ways. I went public because I wanted to. I know plenty of Evos—some of whom are good friends of mine—who have not gone public. Now they have to, and that's totally not fair.

CHRISTINE: Well, I think the people who've been assaulted or had crimes committed against them by Evos would beg to differ.

CLAIRE: Look, I'm not saying that criminals shouldn't be prosecuted. What I *am* saying is that all Evos shouldn't be punished because of the actions of a few. That's the sort of attitude that led to putting Japanese-Americans in internment camps during World War II. Is that really what we want to do again?

CHRISTINE: That's not a bad point, Claire, but nobody's talking about internment camps, they're talking about registration. Same way you're supposed to register a handgun or a sniper rifle.

CLAIRE: I've heard that argument before, and it's totally bogus. Look, my power isn't a weapon. I can't hurt anybody, all I can do is not get permanently hurt by someone else. How's that a weapon? I met someone last month who's technically an Evo. You know what she can do? Turn things different colors. It's not even permanent— she can only change the color while she's concentrating. Why should she have to register *that* with the government if she doesn't want to?

CHRISTINE: Yeah, but where do you draw the line? Okay, it should just be Evos who have actual dangerous powers, like ones who can blow things up or set themselves on fire or move things with their mind. But who decides what's dangerous?

CLAIRE: Where you should draw the line is in forcing people to do it. Or, I guess, not forcing them. The act was fine the way it was originally written because it gave people the choice.

CHRISTINE: Speaking of choices, you're heading to Walter Reed tomorrow?

CLAIRE: Yeah, I've got another appointment with a geneticist, Dr. Deng Hsu. We've been trying to figure out ways to make my healing ability transferable. They've actually been able to use a transfusion of my blood to heal people, but it only works with people who have the same blood type as me, and even then it doesn't always do everything we hope for. But we're still trying, and Dr. Hsu is optimistic that we can figure it out.

CHRISTINE: So you don't mind being experimented on?

CLAIRE: It's my choice. I want to help people. Like I said, I can't use my power to do much—it's mostly defensive. But the one thing my power can fight is disease and injury. And since it's not a secret anymore, I can do what I can to try to save the world.

CHRISTINE: Well, I hope that works out for you. Claire Petrelli, the face of the Evos, thanks for coming on.

CLAIRE: Thanks for having me.

CHRISTINE: Up next, the President's reelection strategy, as well as the slew of candidates lining up to oppose him. You're watching *Inside the Beltway*.

CHAPTER TEN

Claire felt personally betrayed that, after everything the President had said in private to her in the Oval Office and in public to the whole world at the State of the Union, he had gone and changed the law. To be fair, there had been intense pressure to make the change even before the carnival's lawyer was killed, and it went into overdrive after that.

However, the day after the lawyer was killed, two Secret Service agents showed up at the house she was living in, saying that they were her new protection detail, by order of the President.

At the time, her response had been, "Um, okay, but if anyone shoots at us, I'm gonna come out of it better than you guys."

The agents hadn't laughed.

And so she accepted that two agents of the U.S. Treasury Department were going to be her constant companions. When she had let her father know via e-mail, his response had been: "That's the best news I've heard all year."

If nothing else, the number of paparazzi stalking her had

155

gone down a lot since the protection detail started.

She had just finished doing an interview with a local station that would air on their five o'clock news, and had returned to the house in the suburbs. The large house on Fox Rest Lane was owned by the Petrelli family. Nathan had used it as his D.C.-area residence when Congress was in session, but it had been unoccupied since his death.

Right now, Agents Ana Hopwood and Bekenya Uduwana were on duty. The former stayed outside on the front porch, while the latter came inside with Claire.

Uduwana checked through the entire house and declared it to be clear.

"I'm gonna go take a nap," Claire said. "You and Ana can help yourselves to the kitchen."

"Thanks, ma'am," Uduwana said as she took a seat in the large living room.

Claire knew that neither of them would take her up on the offer—they never ate or drank anything while on duty except during specific break times, and then only one of them did so at a time. And it was always food and drink they had brought themselves. That had been true of every pair of agents she'd encountered. It was especially hilarious given that Angela paid someone to keep the kitchen well stocked at all times, and the provisions in the house were a lot nicer than the junk the agents brought for themselves.

She poured herself a glass of water and brought it upstairs to the bedroom.

As soon as she closed the door behind her, a voice said, "Claire, please, don't scream."

Whirling around, she saw Peter Petrelli—and Sylar!

"What the hell are you—"

Sylar put a finger to his lips. "Shhh. We don't want to get the agents all upset now, do we?"

"How did—" She shook her head. "How'd you get in here? Agent Uduwana checked the house!"

Sylar turned to look at Peter. "How soon they forget." He looked back at Claire. "Come on, Claire, you know what we can do. Do you *really* think getting past a couple of Secret Service agents is much of a challenge?"

Claire glared at Sylar, unable to keep the disgust off her face. Not that she was particularly motivated to. "Let's find out."

Peter held up a hand. "Claire, wait! We just want to talk to you."

"Oh, 'we' do, do 'we'? I haven't heard from you for *months*, you ignore every text, every voice message, every e-mail, and when I do finally get to talk to you, you're with *him*?"

"Look, I know you and Sylar have a history, but—"

"'History'? That's what you call it?" Claire was livid, but kept her voice down only because alerting the agents would just make things worse. Ana and Bekenya were good, but they were no match for Sylar. "He *sliced my head open*. He's killed dozens of people, including your brother!"

Peter sighed. "I can explain it, and I will, I promise, but first you have to listen to me—do *not* let them experiment on you."

"Nobody's experimenting on me, they're doing tests on my blood."

Sylar snorted. "I'm sure they were *very* convincing when they told you that."

Peter shot Sylar a look. "Nothing good will come of this, Claire. You can't let them. It'll be Dad all over again."

Claire knew that Arthur Petrelli had funded Mohinder Suresh's experiments on Evos. "This isn't the same thing.

Your father's work was done in secret. Everybody knows what I'm doing—it makes it a lot harder to hide things."

"You really believe that?" Sylar asked in a patronizing tone.

"I'm telling you, this is a mistake, Claire." Peter moved closer and gave her his best sincere look.

But Claire wasn't buying it—not with that bastard standing right next to him like he was his bestie. "And I'm telling you both to get out of my house."

Peter smiled, arms raised, palms up. "It's a Petrelli house, Claire. I've got as much right to it as you do."

She shrugged. "Fine, I'll just let the agents know you snuck in. That'll go over *great*."

Now one of those hands was held up, palm toward Claire. "No! No, it's okay. Look, we just wanted to warn you that—"

"Fine. You warned me. You can leave now."

Claire tensed. She was sure that this was the point where Sylar would do something insane.

But instead, he simply put a hand on Peter's shoulder. "I told you this was a bad idea, Peter. Let's go."

With that, the two of them shot out the window—which Claire had only just realized was open.

That explains how they got in, anyhow.

At least now she knew why she hadn't heard from Peter. And as long as he was hanging out with Sylar, she was just as happy to keep it that way…

CHAPTER ELEVEN

25 OCTOBER 2011
EXCERPT FROM NEW YORK 1 BROADCAST, NEW YORK, NY

"I'm standing right now in front of the Petrelli for Congress offices on Third Avenue and 62nd Street. It was from this office that Nathan Petrelli made his run for Representative of New York's 14th Congressional District. The office was shuttered when Petrelli won the election but then withdrew for personal reasons. Petrelli was later appointed by Governor Malden to be the junior senator from New York to replace Senator Dickinson when he passed away. Petrelli himself died last year. For that entire time, these offices have been closed—but today members of the media were invited to a press conference being held by Peter Petrelli, the late senator's younger brother. The younger Petrelli has a history of depression that became tabloid fodder during his older brother's campaign, but lately he's been working as an EMT here in New York. And now someone's coming out of the front door—and it's Mr. Petrelli. Let's listen."

"Ladies and gentlemen of the press, thank you for coming. My brother, rest his soul, believed in the fundamental human rights of all people. He believed not only in the Constitution and the Bill of Rights, but also in Amnesty International's Universal Declaration of Human Rights. I know if he was alive today, he would have voted for the Evo Registration Act back in January—and he would've voted against it last week. As it's been rewritten, the Evo Act is wrong. The Universal Declaration states that every human being is entitled to basic human rights, such as equal protection and freedom from discrimination, without distinction *of any kind*, such as on the basis of race, color, sex, language, religion, political or other opinion, national or social origin, property, or other status. The Evo Act as it's been rewritten violates the Constitution and violates the Declaration. I will not be registering with the Department of Homeland Security. I have many friends who are also Evos, and they will not be registering with the Department of Homeland Security. We will not stand by and be discriminated against."

"Tell me you got that—ladies and gentlemen, Mr. Petrelli just grimaced for a second, and then he literally disappeared. I've never seen anything like it, though I guess it confirms that he's an Evo. Once again, Peter Petrelli, the younger brother of the late Senator Nathan Petrelli, is an Evo, and has just declared war on the rewritten Evo Act. He claims to speak for many Evos when he says he won't abide by it, and quoted Amnesty International's Universal Declaration of Human Rights to support his argument. It looks like the lines between Evos and us regular humans are being drawn."

CHAPTER TWELVE

4 NOVEMBER 2011
PLACE DE LA CONCORDE, PARIS, FRANCE

Antoine Mercier stood in front of the Rue Royale, right by the obelisk that was the centerpiece of the Place de la Concorde, chanting, "*Je ne vais pas déclarer!*" over and over again, together with several others. One of the people nearby was holding a sign with those words in French, another in Spanish, a third in German.

«*Je ne vais pas déclarer!*»

The plaza was filled with people protesting the European Union's passing of *Droit d'Évolué Déclarer*. Some were Evos openly displaying their powers, like the woman who was flying and the man who was setting off fireworks from the tips of his fingers. Others were normal people who had joined the group in solidarity. Antoine couldn't always tell, of course. His mentor—a secretive, but brilliant *Anglais* named Claude—had always told him that the reason why normal people feared Evos was because they generally looked just like normal people, until they used their powers.

«*Je ne vais pas déclarer!*»

In Antoine's case, he could manipulate light. Claude

had shown him how to make himself invisible by bending light waves around himself, a skill Claude himself had. However, Claude was limited to that invisibility (though it wasn't much of a limitation, truth be told). Antoine could also create light shows and make lasers and change the colors of things. It was actually fun, but totally harmless—well, except for the laser part. He saw no reason to tell the government about his private life.

«*Je ne vais pas déclarer!*»

And then the *gendarmes* showed up, dressed in riot gear.

In French, one of the police said into a megaphone: "This is an illegal gathering! Disperse immediately!"

"*Je ne vais pas déclarer!*"

Two women flew up into the air, arm in arm. Antoine figured that one of them could fly and was carrying the other.

One of the women spoke in German, her voice projecting louder than the megaphone. "We will not surrender! The Petrelli Movement will not be stopped!" Then in French, she repeated, "The Petrelli Movement will not be stopped!" Then in Italian, then in English. She also said something in a language he didn't recognize, though he could make out the word "Petrelli."

The people around them all started shouting, "The Petrelli Movement will not be stopped!"

Peter Petrelli's speech in New York had gotten billions of hits on YouTube and had become the rallying cry of Evos throughout Europe—and elsewhere, but Antoine didn't much care about what went on outside his home. Petrelli had galvanized Evos all over the world by quoting the Declaration of Human Rights. Americans usually just talked about their own country as if it were the only one in the world. Petrelli recognized that there was a world beyond the United States.

And then, when the EU fell into line behind the U.S., just like it always did, by passing a similar law, the Evos—and the other people—of the EU responded.

The *gendarmes* were unimpressed with the human amplifier. "Disperse immediately!"

Antoine used his powers to pull the light reflecting off of the parts of the Place he couldn't see into his own line of sight, so that he could observe the whole scene. There were snipers set up on the roofs of the buildings on the Rue Royale and other officers coming from all sides. They were being surrounded.

"Oh, this isn't good," he muttered to himself in French.

Next to him, a British girl asked in English, "What is it?"

"They're surrounding us," he said in her language. "This will end poorly."

"Let 'em try, yeah?" The girl held up her right hand, which started to glow.

In French, the *gendarme* with the megaphone said, "If you do not disperse, we will be forced to take action."

But he could barely be heard over the multilingual chant of, "The Petrelli Movement will not be stopped!"

«Disperse immediately!»

«*Je ne vais pas déclarer!*»

"The Petrelli Movement will not be stopped!"

"If you do not disperse *now*, we will open fire!"

"The Petrelli Movement will not be stopped!"

Thanks to his bending of the light, Antoine could see the sniper on the nearest rooftop, and he could also see the girl next to him.

So he knew that they both acted at the same time.

The sniper fired his rifle just as the British girl let loose with a stream of heat from her hand.

And then the girl right beside her fell over, and with a shock, Antoine realized that the sniper had seen the girl's glowing hand and had fired at her to keep her from using her powers.

Too late, as it happened. The stream of heat engulfed two of the *gendarmes*, who immediately caught fire and went screaming and running through the Place.

Chaos erupted a moment later as the police opened fire and several Evos used their powers.

Antoine was one of the latter. He reached out with his power and forced the light to bend around several of the weapons being held by the police. The guns were still there, just no longer visible, which at least got some of them to stop shooting for a moment.

Fireworks exploded under two of the policemen, and three of the *gendarmes* found their riot gear turned to stone, trapping them in their own clothes.

One of the things Claude had drilled into him from the get-go was that when things got bad, get out. Since Antoine could make himself invisible, he bent the light around himself so that no one could see him and then got far away from the Place de la Concorde as quickly as he could.

As he ran, he heard the sounds of gunfire and of various powers being used, and he heard the screams of the wounded on both sides.

He no longer heard any chants.

CHAPTER THIRTEEN

15 NOVEMBER 2011
A GUEST EDITORIAL IN *WASHINGTONIAN MAGAZINE* BY CLAIRE PETRELLI

The tragedy in Paris earlier this month was one of the worst events of recent history. And it never should have happened.

There are serious problems with human-Evo relations, not just in our country, but all over the world. Paris proved that. But violence is not the solution to the problem.

All the riot in the Place de la Concorde accomplished was to make things worse.

Ever since his speech in New York, my uncle, Peter Petrelli, has been the unofficial spokesman for what everyone now is calling "the Petrelli Movement." But this is one Petrelli who doesn't endorse it.

I love my uncle. I do. He's done a lot of good over the years, as a hospice nurse, as an EMT, and as an Evo. He's stayed under the radar until now. Very few people know how much good he's done, how many lives he's saved.

But what he's doing now is wrong, and it needs to stop.

It's not going to be easy. But Evos are here to stay, and everyone has to accept that. I agree with Peter on many things. The Evo Act as it was originally passed in January was perfect. The amendments are wrong, and I've said so, in public and in private. I've even been lucky enough to be able to express my reservations to the President himself. At the very least, I can attest that there's a dialogue going on.

This so-called "Petrelli Movement" isn't a dialogue. It's a screaming match. And then it's a fight. When Peter gave his speech in New York last month, it was like lighting the fuse on a stick of dynamite. And now it's blowing up in all our faces.

We need to live in peace with one another. The reason why I've been open about being an Evo is to show that it can work. But also it's important that people who want to stay hidden can do that, too.

The United States has been a leader in the world ever since the early twentieth century. And we need to be the leader now, and that means *not* treating Evos like second-class citizens. It means letting us live our lives like normal people, not forcing us to register, not forcing us to let the government keep track of us.

If we act like we care about the rights of *all* our citizens, the rest of the world will follow suit. The *Droit d'Évolué Déclarer* only passed in the European Union because of the amendments to the Evo Registration Act here.

A couple of years ago, my father, Senator Nathan Petrelli, started a program that was much worse than what's happening now. Evos were being rounded up and held without warrants and without due process. We just were kidnapped and locked away without anyone knowing what had happened to us or why.

Nobody really knows about this program, even now. There were some news stories, but they quieted down pretty quick because there was no evidence. And that's the worst thing. Because nobody knew we were even there in the first place, nobody knew we were being treated this way.

At the very least, *that* can't happen anymore. That's why I revealed myself last year, and why I've stayed in the public eye. The people who want us locked up, want us put away, can't treat us that way anymore.

But they can still treat us like second-class citizens. This has to stop.

And I believe it will. The history of our country is one in which people are gradually granted more rights than they had before. The Founding Fathers wanted more rights than they had under King George. After the Civil War, people with darker skin came to have the same rights as those with lighter skin, although the struggle was long and hard. In 1920, women won the right to vote. And now we're seeing homosexuals get the same rights as heterosexuals.

We have to do the same for Evos. We have to be treated like *people*. Not like non-humans. Peter was right about one other thing: whether it's the Constitution or the Declaration of Human Rights, we are still human and we still deserve the same rights as everyone else.

So today I'm asking—no, I'm begging. Please, stop the violence. If you're part of the Petrelli Movement, please don't use violence to resolve the problems you're having. And if you're a member of the government of any nation, from the President of the United States to the Council of the European Union to all other governments throughout the world, please do not make registration of Evos mandatory. Let us have our choice.

This article was written with the assistance of Washingtonian *reporter Sabrina Piazza.*

CHAPTER FOURTEEN

24 NOVEMBER 2011
THE FRENCH HOUSE, BRENTWOOD, MO

A year ago, Noah Bennet had hosted the world's most awkward Thanksgiving dinner. It had been, he knew, a pathetic attempt at normalcy in a life that had stopped being normal the moment his first wife was killed by an Evo while pregnant with their child. Even his second marriage had started out as a sham, a cover to make his life look more normal than it really was.

Hardly a surprise that Sandra left him. The only surprise was that it took her so long.

But he tried. He got Sandra and Doug and Claire and Claire's roommate, as well as Lauren (who had saved his ass with regard to food preparation), to all show up. It actually wasn't nearly as bad as it could have been, but it was still pretty dreadful, all things considered.

Noah had put the Thanksgiving dinner together because the Company had been disbanded, leaving him with nothing but his family. However, with Sandra gone, Lyle gone with her, and Claire off to college, he didn't even have that.

Now it was a year later, and he was back out in the field,

doing what he had believed a year ago to be impossible: bagging and tagging. Well, tagging, anyhow, and only bagging if they resisted. It was an interesting change.

Erica Kravid had not accepted all of Noah's recommendations. But Noah had to give her credit for at least listening to all of them and giving them a fair hearing. And one suggestion she embraced wholeheartedly was the Company's "one of us, one of them" policy for field work.

"If you're going after Evos," he had said to her in one of their many meetings following that fateful morning in the Oval Office, "you need to have an Evo around in case things get ugly. Some of these people are incredibly dangerous. They might be more compliant if they see one of their own helping out."

"One of us" were recruited from FBI, NSA, CIA, DHS, ICE, and various police departments. "One of them" were all registered Evos who had volunteered or, in some cases, been recruited. In fact, some of the latter came from the same pool as the former—Matt Parkman hadn't been the only law-enforcement type to develop powers. Indeed, Noah had suggested recruiting Parkman, but Erica had told him that he'd declined.

Lauren had also been tapped, but she, too, declined, saying that the whole nonsense with the Sullivan Brothers Carnival, culminating in Claire's coming-out in Central Park, had pretty much put her off of Evos. She was happy to stay in the CIA and gather intelligence on foreign nations "like a normal spook."

Noah envied her the choice. But as last Thanksgiving had shown him, he wasn't really good at anything else *but* this.

His partner was a very large and very intelligent man named Caspar Abraham. His powers related to memory, though unlike, say, Rene, he didn't eliminate them so much as transfer them to inanimate objects. He chose to use pennies as his repository, mostly so he could make "penny for your thoughts" jokes.

Noah expected to stop wincing at that any day now.

As Noah drove the rental car through the tree-lined streets of a St. Louis suburb, Caspar was finishing up a phone call. "Yes, of course. I'll be home tomorrow, and I've already made the reservations at Giovanni's. I'll make this up to you, sweetheart. Love you too. Bye."

Noah smiled. "Gladys is pissed, huh?"

Caspar shrugged. "I warned her when I took the job that the hours would be—inconsistent. That weekends and holidays were fair game. Guess she either didn't believe me or just didn't think it through."

Noah pulled up in front of the house of their target, a building that reminded Noah far too much of the house in Odessa. It was your standard two-level house of the type that had been built during the great suburban migration of the 1950s.

Looking up and down the street, Caspar said, "I hate suburbia."

Noah shot him a look. "Why?"

"Intellectually, I know I'm in Missouri, because we flew into Lambert. But if you'd put me into a coma back in D.C. and then woke me up here, I'd have absolutely no idea where I was. This looks just like every other suburban street in the country. Now, if you woke me in New York or San Francisco or Chicago or Dallas or in St. Louis proper, I'd know immediately where I was. Cities have personalities, they have character. This? It's like that Pete Seeger song, little boxes made of ticky-tack." Caspar shook his head and smiled beneath his salt-and-pepper goatee. "Sorry.

Arguments with Gladys always make me philosophical."

Frowning, Noah said, "That didn't sound like an argument to me."

"Gladys is very controlled. It's one of the things I love about her, honestly, that she doesn't fly off the handle. If you'd heard her side of the conversation, you'd have noticed how terse she was, how clipped. That's how I know she's pissed. Trust me, that was an argument, and I didn't win."

Remembering his own shouting matches with Sandra, particularly once she realized how many times Noah had had Rene alter her memories, Noah had to admit to himself that Caspar and Gladys's version of marital distress was a lot more civilized.

But he said nothing aloud. Sandra was the past, and he needed to focus on the present.

Caspar got out of the passenger side and then opened the back door to retrieve the briefcase in which he kept his penny supply. "So what's this one's name, again?"

"Alexander French." He retrieved the manila folder from the back seat. "This is the Company's file on him. We never got around to tagging him. As far as we could tell, his only ability was to see very far. Not a big priority."

"Well, let's just hope he isn't away visiting family for Thanksgiving." Caspar headed toward the front door.

Noah followed, hearing a susurrus of voices from inside. "Looks like our guy is the host."

"Lucky us." Caspar rang the doorbell.

After a moment, the door opened to reveal a white male in his thirties or forties with perfectly combed hair, wearing a polo shirt, Dockers, and white sneakers.

With a big smile on his face, the man said, "Happy Thanksgiving! What can I do for you folks?"

"Are you Alexander French?"

"Absolutely. And you are?"

Reaching into his jacket pocket, Caspar pulled out his ID. Belatedly, Noah did likewise. The hardest adjustment he had had to make in working as a government contractor as opposed to the Company was that he was now on official business and had actual legal authority.

"My name is Caspar Abraham, and this is Noah Bennet. We're with Renautas, a company that's been contracted by the U.S. government."

French's eyes went wide. "Wow. Well, I can't imagine what the government would need with me, but why don't you come in? We haven't sat down to dinner yet, but I'm sure Eleanor can scare you up some *hors d'oeuvres*." He pronounced the last two words closer to "horse's doovers" than the actual pronunciation.

Noah heard the clacking of claws on linoleum and recognized it instantly as the tread of a dog. This one was heavier and slower than Mr. Muggles, though. Peering over French's shoulder, he saw a big Golden Retriever ambling up toward the door.

French turned and said, "Scooter, sit!"

The dog whined softly and then sat on the foyer floor.

"Good dog!" He turned back to Noah and Caspar. "Sorry about that. Ol' Scooter-pie here always thinks that anyone who walks in the door is here to see him. Come on in."

Scooter raised his head when they entered, and he looked right at Noah.

Unable to resist, Noah knelt down and pet the dog. Scooter immediately lay down on the floor.

"He likes you, Mr. Bennet! But that's not surprising, Scooter likes everyone." French closed the door behind them. "Now then, what I can do for you boys?"

Noah actually smiled. Mr. Muggles had always been

Sandra's, to the point of obsession, but he had to admit that he missed the unconditional love that a dog would give a human in exchange for a simple belly rub.

Love—conditional or otherwise—had been in short supply in Noah's life.

From his kneeling position, Noah said, "Mr. French, are you familiar with the term 'Evolved Human,' or 'Evo'?"

"Oh sure, like those folks in Paris that went all crazy. Matter of fact, we had an Evo around here lately."

A woman walked into the foyer from the living room, which Noah could now see was filled with people of varying ages sitting on the couch, one of several chairs, or the floor. A large flat-screen TV was attached to the wall. Noah couldn't see the screen from this angle, but based on the brass-band noise coming from the living room, they were probably watching the Macy's Thanksgiving Day Parade.

The woman passed in front of a professionally taken photograph of French, her, Scooter, and a little boy. Noah guessed that this was Eleanor.

"What's going on, Alex?" she asked.

"Ellie, these gents are from the government, if you can believe that. They're asking about Evos. Who was that guy who broke into the Home Depot last week?"

"It wasn't a guy, it was old Karen Eriksen, and it wasn't the Home Depot, it was the church."

Noah winced. He knew that name from a report that had crossed his desk.

French snapped his fingers. "Right, right. Well, anyhow, Karen went and tore up the church. She didn't mean to, but she really didn't know her own strength. Come to think of it, I didn't see her this past Sunday."

Noah stood up, prompting a minor yelp from Scooter.

"I'm sorry to be the bearer of bad news, but I'm afraid Ms. Eriksen had to be hospitalized following the incident. She died of a heart attack a week ago."

"Oh, that's horrible!" French put his hand to his mouth.

But Eleanor was frowning. "Mind telling me how you know that?"

Caspar answered her. "Ms. Eriksen was registered with the Department of Homeland Security, ma'am, as all Evos are required by law to be."

"Which," Noah added, "is why we're here. Mr. French, I'm afraid that you're also an Evo, and you are as yet unregistered."

"I beg your pardon?" French sounded genuinely surprised.

"You haven't noticed yourself manifesting any strange powers?" Caspar asked.

Eleanor gave him a gentle slap on his arm. "Now, Alex, I *told* you that your vision was getting better."

"Well, sure, Ellie, but I thought that was just 'cause I eat so many carrots."

Caspar regarded French curiously. "How far can you see, Mr. French?"

"Er, well, I didn't want to say anything, but I'm guessing that's a rental car you're driving? You ought to let those fellas at the office know that there's a ding just below the gas tank."

Noah and Caspar exchanged glances. Noah had actually spotted that particular dent, but he'd had to peer very closely at the car to see it. He had asked the rental agent to make a note of it so they wouldn't be penalized for it when they returned the car.

"Look, I don't want to stop you boys from doing your job, and I certainly don't want to be doing anything illegal.

Believe you me, if I'd known I was one of those Evo people, I'd have signed right up—or whatever it is I'm supposed to do."

"You're not that far off," Caspar said. "We have some paperwork we'll need you to fill out, and you'll need to make an appointment at the nearest registration center. There's one in St. Louis you can go to."

"That shouldn't be a problem at all. Look, I've got a little den in the back of the house. Normally I'd say, let's do this in the dining room or the kitchen, but the dining room table's all nice and set up for dinner as soon as the parade's over, and I think Ellie'd kill me if we invaded her kitchen. So why not step this way and we can take care of business?"

Noah nodded. "Yes, thank you, Mr. French, that would be excellent."

French led them through the living room, stepping over children running around—one of whom was the boy in the picture, the others looking similar enough to obviously be related—and said, "Don't mind us, folks. These gents are here to take care of some paperwork. We'll be done in a jiff."

"Geez, who does paperwork on Thanksgiving?" an older man asked from the couch.

As they moved through the living room, Noah caught a glimpse of the TV screen and nearly stumbled in surprise.

Standing on one of the floats, waving at the crowd on Fifth Avenue, surrounded by people in full-body costumes that seemed to represent some manner of animated creature Noah didn't recognize, was Claire.

A chyron at the bottom of the screen read: CLAIRE PETRELLI, EVO ACTIVIST.

Noah also noticed that there was a man standing

unobtrusively in a corner of the float who had the unmistakable look of a bodyguard. He was grateful, at least, that she seemed to have some kind of security detail, and he wondered who was providing it. Knowing Angela, it was probably her.

The older man on the couch snorted again. "Dunno why *she* gets to be on a float. Lousy freak show."

Noah just stood and stared at the screen.

Caspar put a hand on his shoulder. "You okay, Noah?"

"Hmm?" He turned and stared at Caspar as if he had no idea who the man was. And for a second, he didn't. For a second, it was a year ago, and Claire was in his apartment, and they were eating a mediocre turkey, and…

He shook his head. "I'm fine. Sorry, just drifted away for a second. Let's go get this man signed up."

CHAPTER FIFTEEN

4 DECEMBER 2011
THE PETRELLI HOUSE, VIENNA, VA
Claire had started to take bets on the "second string" of her security detail.

Agents Hopwood and Uduwana remained the primary agents assigned to her, and they worked five eight-hour shifts a week, Tuesday through Saturday, ten to six. However, the agents working the six to two and overnight two to ten shifts rotated every week, as did those who worked the Sunday and Monday "weekend."

The bets took the form of what the new rotation would bring. Would the agents be tall or short? Male or female? Friendly or terse? What race? Most had been either white or black, with a few Latinos and one Asian woman, who had a weekend day shift.

The second-string shifts were staggered so that they changed at different times, but Sunday always meant a new weekend day-shift pair while Ana and Bekenya went off to do whatever Secret Service agents did on their weekends. Bekenya, she knew, would spend time with her wife and daughter, and also volunteer at a karate dojo. As for Ana, Claire had no idea—Agent Hopwood was one of the terse ones.

On this particular Sunday, she bet that it would be a new pair that she'd never seen before.

She lost. A black sedan pulled up to the house on Fox Rest Lane and out came Agents Arbucci and Rodriguez, who'd been her day-shift detail over Halloween weekend. They'd been kept pretty busy, as Claire had spent much of that weekend doing appearances and events for various children's charities.

After they formally relieved the overnight pair, Claire smiled at them. "Didn't think I'd see you two again after Halloween."

"You kidding?" Naomi Rodriguez said. "You were easy. Last year I had to do the President's kids trick-or-treating. *That's* a nightmare. Watching you talk to a buncha kids in a hospital is a cakewalk. Anyhow, you're clear today, right?"

"Yes," Claire said emphatically. "I've been going nonstop since Thanksgiving. And tomorrow I'm back with Dr. Hsu, and then it's more appearances through to New Year's. I want today to be a day of rest. Just me, the couch, and Netflix."

Rodriguez smiled. "Sounds like a plan."

However, Nick Arbucci was frowning. "Who's Dr. Shoe?"

Smacking Arbucci on the arm, Rodriguez said, "You remember, that geneticist who's checking out her blood?"

"Oh, yeah, right," Arbucci said weakly.

"You okay, Nicky?" Rodriguez sounded concerned.

"Nah, I'm fine. Not enough caffeine this morning."

"It's your own damn fault for not ordering the double latte like usual. Tell you what, you stay inside and caffeinate, I'll do the perimeter."

Arbucci nodded.

The rest of the morning went smoothly. Claire caught up on a romcom she'd been wanting to see, and Arbucci gamely pretended like he was interested in it, too.

At noon, Rodriguez took her lunch break. She actually took the car and went off somewhere to eat—not typical, but she'd done that last time, too. Arbucci took advantage of this to do the perimeter, a good excuse to get far away from any more chick flicks.

Then, just a few minutes into the next film, Arbucci came running in. "Change of plan."

Pausing the movie, Claire asked, "What's going on?"

"You need to pack, right now. There's a credible threat. We need to get you to Dulles."

Claire frowned. "The airport?" That was odd. The other times she'd been flown somewhere on the urging of the federal government, it had been on a military aircraft out of Andrews Air Force Base.

"Hurry, go!"

"Shouldn't we wait for Naomi?"

"There's no time, you have one minute to pack what you want. *Go!*"

Claire ran upstairs and threw about a week's worth of clothes into a suitcase, along with all her toiletries.

She paused long enough to shake her head ruefully. The last few years had taught her a bit too much about cutting down to the bare essentials. As a fourteen-year-old, she would have overstuffed three suitcases. Now, she still had plenty of room in her smallest overnight bag.

Running downstairs with the bag slung over her shoulder, she said, "I'm ready."

"Good." Arbucci led her to an SUV that was idling in front of the house. "Turn your phone off," he said as he opened the back door for her. "We can't risk it being tracked."

"It's already off." Another lesson Claire had learned from life as an Evo—not to mention as Noah Bennet's daughter—was to keep your phone off as much as possible. She also kept the GPS permanently disabled.

Arbucci hopped into the front passenger seat of the SUV and told the driver, "Go, go, go."

"Nick, what's going on?" Claire asked.

"That's need-to-know right now, ma'am."

"Okay." Claire wasn't satisfied, though. For one thing, that was the first time Arbucci had called her "ma'am" all day. The last time, he'd been formal to a fault, always referring to her as "ma'am" or "Ms. Petrelli."

Then again, the biggest crisis last time was a kid in a Thor costume hitting her with his *papier mâché* hammer.

Soon enough, they arrived at Dulles and were rushed over to a private jet parked on a runway far away from the commercial terminals.

Someone who looked like Secret Service was standing at the top of the small staircase that would fold up into the plane's door. Claire didn't recognize him, but it wasn't as if she knew every agent…

"Right this way, ma'am," the agent said, taking Claire's overnight bag. "We'll need to take your phone, also."

"It's off," she said as she climbed up the stairs and entered a very well-appointed private jet.

"We still need to confiscate it."

"Fine. Look," she said as she took her phone out of her purse and handed it to the agent, "will someone *please* tell me what's going on? Agent Arbucci said it was need-to-know, but—"

"Agent, uh, Agent Arbucci was absolutely correct,

ma'am," the agent said. "Buckle yourself in, please, we've got a long trip ahead of us."

"Where are we going?"

But the agent just turned and headed toward the cockpit. With a sigh, Claire sat down in a chair and buckled herself in.

The plane taxied down the runway for about twenty minutes before finally taking off. Claire spent that entire time staring out the window, as there was nothing to read, and most of her usual entertainment was on her phone.

Eventually, however, the plane took off. And only then did the agent come back, along with another man she didn't recognize. He was short, fat, and bald.

"We're heading to an aircraft carrier," the short, fat, bald man said. And his voice sounded familiar.

No, it wasn't his voice. It was his tone. It sounded a lot like how Nick Arbucci had been talking today.

"What aircraft carrier? What the *hell* is going on?"

Another man emerged from the cockpit, this one dressed in more casual clothes. "I'm sorry for this, Claire, but it was necessary. My name is Dr. Richard Schwenkman. I work for a company known as the Lamarck Project. And we're very interested in your genes."

Claire was not liking the sound of this. She unbuckled her seat belt and started to stand up. "Is the Lamarck Project part of the CIA, or Homeland, or—"

Schwenkman chuckled. "Hardly, Claire. I'm afraid that the government doesn't really pay well enough to be worth my time. And you've been a bit misled. You see, the Lamarck Project is run by a consortium of businesses, most, though not all, of which are headquartered in the European Union. Your blood is the holy grail of genetics research, Claire, and we need to study you more closely."

Cursing herself for not realizing it was a trick—although

she wasn't sure how she could have realized it, since Arbucci was the one in the lead, and she trusted him—Claire started to move toward the emergency exit. "So you tricked Agent Arbucci?"

Another chuckle. "Not exactly. Poor Mr. Arbucci is innocent of any wrongdoing, though I suspect he'll have a hard time proving that."

"I don't know what you're talking about, but I don't think you realize exactly who you're messing with."

"Oh, we're quite aware." Schwenkman sounded so incredibly smug, he reminded Claire of Sylar.

"Really?" Then she ran toward the hatch. She'd open it and jump out. The landing would hurt like hell, but she'd heal. And then she'd make her way back to D.C. and contact the *real* Secret Service—hell, she'd flag down a camera crew if she had to, it wouldn't be hard, she could just jump in front of a bus or something—and get to the bottom of this.

That, at least, was her plan.

However, before she took a second step, the short, fat, bald man suddenly disappeared from her peripheral vision. It was like watching Hiro teleport—one moment he was there, the next he wasn't.

Right after he disappeared, Claire stopped moving. She tried to continue walking forward, but she couldn't make her legs work.

Or anything else. She could feel her eyes blink, feel her lungs inhale and exhale, but she had no control over any of it—she couldn't even talk.

Then her voice said, "You're not going anywhere, Claire Bennet Petrelli. You're staying right here on this plane."

She felt her body walk back to her seat and watched as she buckled herself in. Then she felt herself put her hands on the armrests of the chair, at which point Schwenkman took the additional step of strapping down her wrists.

Then she found herself back in control, just as short, fat, and bald reappeared next to the obviously fake Secret Service agent.

Staring at him, she said, "You can possess people."

Bowing, the short, fat, bald man said, "Harold Esposito at your service. We knew you'd believe one of the Treasury agents. We just had to wait until you got a pair where one of them actually went *out* to lunch."

Claire shook her head. Looking back on it, it was impressively executed. And it only would have worked with Arbucci and Rodriguez; all the other agents stayed close by on their breaks.

"So what now?"

"Well," Schwenkman said, "if you try to escape again, Harold will possess you and he *won't* leave. In about four hours, we'll reach our carrier, which is in international waters, so the Coast Guard won't be able to interfere. I'm sure at this point, Agent Arbucci has checked in and is trying desperately to convince his superiors that he was possessed by an Evo."

"They'll probably believe him," Claire said defiantly.

"They might—but they won't be able to *prove* it." Schwenkman smiled. "I'm afraid Nick Arbucci's career is over. So, probably, is Naomi Rodriguez's."

"And this makes you *happy*?"

"Not as such," Schwenkman said. "It's just fascinating to me how important you Evos have become. My employers at Lamarck have spent a great deal of time, money, and effort to acquire you, and they were perfectly willing to ruin the lives of two people to do it." He moved toward the back of the plane. "That should let you know how important you are to us."

The fake agent went back to the cockpit, while Esposito sat in another seat near Claire.

As Esposito buckled himself in, Claire said, "I guess they paid you a lot of money, too."

"Enough, but that's not why I do it. I don't really *need* to work for money—I can just possess a random bank manager or someone else in charge of a lot of cash, walk out with a pile and then leave them to accept the consequences. But that got kinda boring, so I decided to hire myself out."

"So this is just a game to you?"

"It's *all* a game, Claire. Sooner you realize that, the happier you'll be."

"I *was* happy!"

"Really? Talking to morons on TV? Waving at idiots freezing their asses off on Fifth Avenue on Thanksgiving while standing next to people dressed like cartoon characters? Writing stupid editorials for the *Washingtonian*? Yeah, I read that, your ghost-writer did a pretty good job."

"I wrote that myself," she said defensively, which wasn't entirely true. It had actually been an interview with one of the magazine's reporters, who then transcribed it and cleaned it up. But it was still in Claire's words.

"Still, that wasn't a life. You were a figurehead for Evos, and you ask me, it was past time you retired from that job. It's a waste."

Unable to stand looking at him anymore, Claire turned away and looked out the window.

All she saw were clouds. They were obviously over water, which meant her plan would have involved a whole lot of swimming, if it had been successful.

Maybe she'd be lucky and Esposito would take a nap…

CHAPTER SIXTEEN

24 DECEMBER 2011
THE LAMARCK PROJECT CARRIER *CHARLES DARWIN*, SOMEWHERE IN THE ATLANTIC OCEAN

When he was a boy, Christmas Eve was Peter Petrelli's favorite day of the year.

There was always a big meal of fish and lasagna with family, and then they'd go to Midnight Mass. It was the only night he and his older brother Nathan were allowed to stay up so late. The pair of them would always go straight to bed after mass, hoping to fall sleep right away so that morning—and presents—would come sooner.

That never worked, of course. They'd stay up half the night giddy with anticipation, speculating about what they'd get for presents, before exhaustion eventually claimed them around three or four in the morning.

After a day of feasting and anticipation, Christmas Day itself was often a disappointment. The presents were never as good in reality as they had been in the boys' imaginations the night before.

He really hoped that he wouldn't be similarly disappointed today.

For the past three weeks, ever since Claire had disappeared from the Petrelli house, his mother had devoted every resource she could to finding out where she'd been taken. Through Noah, they'd also been kept abreast of the official investigation being handled by DHS, in conjunction with Secret Service, who'd failed in their protection duties rather spectacularly.

One of the first things Noah informed them was that Claire had been taken on board a privately owned jet that took off from Dulles. The aircraft was owned by a consortium based in Zurich, and they'd filed a flight plan that said they were headed to London, but the plane never showed up at its destination. DHS had hit a brick wall when investigating the plane, but luckily Peter's mother was not constrained by politics or borders or legalities. She quickly discovered the existence of a clandestine scientific endeavor called the Lamarck Project that was backed by the same Swiss consortium that owned the plane. They also had an aircraft carrier that was very carefully staying in international waters.

From the moment Noah had told them that Claire had been taken out of the country, Peter had started preparing. These days, he could only have one power at a time, so he had to choose wisely. The so-called "Petrelli Movement"—Peter *really* hated that name, but it had stuck—had been working to help Evos all over Europe, Africa, and Asia, and they were trying to make inroads into North and South America, though that had proven more difficult given the aggressive enforcement of registration in the U.S. Peter thus had a menu of powers to choose from among the Evos that he and the others had helped.

Ultimately, he decided that the most useful power to

have would be telekinesis. Sylar had that power, though he rarely used it to its fullest potential—given how many *other* things he could do, that wasn't a surprise—but Peter thought that if he took that power and spent some time practicing, he could really accomplish a lot.

And so, after stopping by Essex to visit Morgan Perdue, one of the people they'd rescued, he started honing his skills.

By Christmas Eve, his mother had located the Lamarck carrier, and Peter felt confident enough to try to rescue his niece.

As a result, his Christmas Eve in 2011 was spent flying over the Atlantic Ocean, wind blowing his hair back and roaring in his ears.

Before his father took that power away from him, Peter's Evo ability had been assuming the powers of anyone he was in close proximity to. As a result, the first two powers he got were those of his mother and brother: precognitive dreams and flight. He lost them when his father stole his powers, though he got a variant back when he injected himself with the genetic modification formula.

Of all the dozens of powers he'd had over the years, from invisibility to the ability to manipulate earth, the one he enjoyed most was flight. It gave him a wonderful unfettered feeling of joy. What he enjoyed most, though, were the unexpected aspects of it: being able to predict a shift in the wind by a change in its sound, for example.

When he had used Nathan's power of flight, it had been a lot different. There was almost no effort involved. Now, though, he was basically flying by telekinetically moving himself through the air, staying low to avoid being picked up by radar. It required a lot more concentration, so he couldn't lose himself in the joy of it.

Soon, the aircraft carrier came into view, and Peter breathed a sigh of relief. He'd worked hard to make sure that he took off from Gibraltar in the right direction to reach the coordinates his mother had supplied for the Lamarck carrier. The whole way over, he had been worried that he'd miss it, or that his mother's information was wrong, or that he'd be off course by a few degrees, or…

But no, there it was.

He set himself down on the stern of the carrier's flight deck, hoping that no one had picked up on his arrival.

That was a forlorn hope, as two large men with P90s came running down the deck toward him and started shooting.

Or, rather, tried to. They managed to fire a couple of rounds each, but Peter easily deflected them and then damaged the guns' firing mechanisms and ripped out their magazines.

Only then, as the two men stood there with suddenly useless P90s, did Peter realize that he recognized them. "You two used to work for Danko."

"Yeah," one of them said, "which means we know how to handle guys like you."

The other was reaching into one of the pouches on his all-black outfit. So Peter yanked all the items in that pouch out through the surrounding material with his mind.

Out came two grenades and two flash-bangs. Peter threw them overboard, followed by the two guards.

Peter had intended not to hurt anyone, but the mercenaries who worked for Danko had done a lot of harm to a lot of Evos as part of Nathan's little Building 26 project to round Evos up. Danko had been in charge of the people doing the rounding up. Peter had no compunction about making his hired guns take a swim.

Somehow, he wasn't surprised that the Lamarck Project had taken on Danko's old crew. He knew that Noah had advised DHS against hiring any of them, so that meant they'd have to go international to find similar work.

Three more mercenaries came onto the deck, but Peter dispatched two of them even more quickly than the first two. The third, however, he grabbed and turned upside down.

"Where's Claire?"

"Do your worst, freak. I ain't tellin' you where the other freak's bein' held."

Shaking his head, Peter tossed him overboard, too.

By this time, alarms were blaring all over the carrier, and people were coming to the rescue of the five men Peter had mentally thrown into the ocean.

While that was going on, he flew up to the bridge, tearing the door off with his mind—dramatic but necessary, as it had been sealed shut, probably as soon as the alarm went off.

There were four people on the bridge, and Peter asked them a simple question. "Where is Claire?"

One of the men replied in rapid-fire words in a foreign language that Peter didn't recognize.

Peter interrupted him. "Does anyone speak English?"

Another pulled out a pistol, which backfired right in his face when he tried to shoot Peter.

As the man fell to the deck, screaming in pain and clutching his right hand with his left, Peter asked, "Again, does anyone speak English?"

"I do!"

Peter whirled around to see a short, fat, bald man standing in the doorway he'd destroyed.

Then the man completely disappeared.

Peter tried to surreptitiously look around to figure out

where the man had gone—

—but he couldn't do it. Nor could he do anything else. He had no more control over his own body.

Or his own mind. He felt himself reaching out telekinetically, yanking the fire extinguisher from the wall and sending it flying into the rear window. It shattered rather loudly, and the bridge hands all ducked.

Peter then heard his own voice say, "This is *amazing*! I should start possessing Evos more often—I mean besides Claire, but that's boring, all I can do is cut my hand open or something stupid like that."

"Mr. Esposito!"

Peter felt his head turning around to face a man in a lab coat.

"Sorry, Dr. Schwenkman," Peter's voice said, "but this is fun!"

"You aren't being paid to have fun. You're being paid to keep this carrier safe."

"And I'm doing just that. Want me to kill this guy?"

Schwenkman shook his head, looking like he'd swallowed something he didn't like. "We're not *murderers*, Mr. Esposito, we're scientists. As for you, Mr. Petrelli—I know you can hear me, as Mr. Esposito's powers do not suppress his victim's thoughts, only their physical activity—do *not* return to this vessel. For one thing, we're going to figure out what leak lead you to us and eliminate it, and we're also going to change our location. It's a *big* ocean, and your niece is going to remain in it far away from everyone else so we can continue our work in peace. We're making amazing progress, actually." He leaned in close. "So go away and never come back, or I *will* let Mr. Esposito do as he pleases with you."

Peter wanted to cry out in anguish, but could do nothing.

This Esposito person had full control of his body.

They walked off the bridge and down the steep metal staircase to the flight deck. Peter was forced to follow Schwenkman.

"You may rest assured, Mr. Petrelli, that your niece is being well cared for. She's given three excellent meals per day—Chef Auerbach is quite talented—and our experiments aren't at all invasive." He chuckled. "Well, for her, is *anything* truly invasive?"

They arrived on the flight deck. Schwenkman gestured for a mercenary to come over. Peter recognized the man with the thick eyebrows as another of Danko's people, the one who had flown the plane that was supposed to take Peter, Claire, Tracy, Hiro, Matt, and Mohinder to Building 26 to be imprisoned. Peter had caused that plane to crash in Arkansas, and he hadn't been sure that the pilot had survived.

"Mr. Dougherty," Schwenkman said to the pilot, "I want you to fly Mr. Petrelli here to—" He paused, and then smiled. "Greenland. At that point, Mr. Esposito will release his hold and you'll fly Mr. Esposito back here."

A young woman ran up to Schwenkman. "You asked for this, Doctor?"

Nodding, Schwenkman took a small case from the woman, who dashed off.

He handed the case to Peter, who felt his arm raise as Esposito used his body to take it. "That's the sedative. When you land, use it—"

"—and then get out before it takes effect, yes, I know, Doc. This isn't my first rodeo."

"Good." Schwenkman moved off. "It's time for Claire's next blood draw."

Peter again tried to do something—anything—but he

could only watch helplessly as Esposito did whatever he felt like.

Luckily, all he was doing was walking over to one of the planes on the flight deck.

It was, Peter realized, going to take him a while to get back from Greenland…

CHAPTER SEVENTEEN

1 JANUARY 2012
THE LAMARCK PROJECT CARRIER *CHARLES DARWIN*, SOMEWHERE ELSE IN THE ATLANTIC OCEAN

Claire was pretty sure she had the plan all set in her head.

She'd been ready to give it a shot a week ago, but then Peter had gone and tried to rescue her. Mind you, she was all for that—being rescued by Peter would be just as good as escaping herself. But Peter had failed—thanks once again to Esposito, the creep—and security around Claire had gotten much tighter.

The first week or so, there had been armed guards around her at all times. However, they'd soon realized that the guards were pointless, since she could just run away from them. Even if they shot her, it wouldn't stop her.

No, the only one who could actually stop her was Esposito. And he had, every single time she'd tried to escape.

After that first week, she had finally given up the direct approach of running away from the guards, getting shot, being possessed by Esposito, and marching herself back to her cell.

(Sure, Schwenkman called it her "cabin," but it was a cell. No windows, only one way out, and that exit was locked from the outside and watched over by an armed guard. As far as Claire was concerned, if it walked like a duck, quacked like a duck, and tasted yummy with orange sauce like a duck, it was a duck.)

The first step in her new plan was talking to her guards. Nothing had worked at first—they were all pretty stone-faced—until one day when she was being taken back to her cell after an hour of stress tests. She'd run on a treadmill and lifted weights and some other stupid things, and when Schwenkman's assistant was done with her (these tests were so dumb Schwenkman himself didn't even bother to show up), a guard came to take her back. As they were leaving, he glanced over at the guard who was on duty in the lab and said, "Can you believe the damn Patriots?"

Seeing the opening, Claire had jumped in with: "What did Belichick's Bozos do *this* time?"

Both guards had stared at her. "You know football?"

She had actually smiled, one of the few times she'd even tried to do so since being kidnapped. "I'm a Texas girl—football's the state religion."

The guard who was taking her back to her cell had said, "Well, the Pats just beat the Skins—right after the stupid Jets beat 'em last week."

"Any word on the Cowboys?" she had asked hopefully.

That had gotten a grin out of the guard as they walked down the corridors of the carrier. "Cardinals won in OT."

"Damn." She had shaken her head. "I figured with the new coach they'd kick butt this year, and that Thanksgiving game was great, but..."

"Yeah, well, they ain't been worth watching without Aikman."

Over the next several weeks, Claire had kept talking to this particular guard—whose first name, she later learned, was Dion—about football, eventually getting him to start talking more about the aircraft carrier.

By the time Peter had taken his shot at rescuing her on Christmas Eve—which she'd heard about in gory, gloating detail from Esposito after he'd gotten back from dropping her uncle off in Greenland—Claire had learned that the carrier was called the *Charles Darwin*, that it had two pressurized water reactors and four turbines, and that the captain was a Belgian who was fluent in twelve languages but mostly only spoke Flemish, which Dion said was primarily in order to annoy everyone else. And also that neither her Cowboys nor Dion's Redskins had made the playoffs.

On the 30th of December, Dion had been talking about the New Year's Eve party, and how he wasn't going to get to go because he had guard duty.

"So I can't even go to the New Year's Eve party?"

Dion had frowned. "Actually, let me talk to Doc Schwenkman. He's really not that bad a guy. I mean, yeah, I know you think he's a jackass, but he's just doing what the bosses tell him. We all are."

Sure enough, Dion had convinced Schwenkman to let Claire attend the party, as long as Dion was with her the entire time.

Everyone was at the party, except for one person on the bridge. The mess hall had a satellite television set up, and they watched the celebrations taking place in Europe. Everyone drank *a lot*. To Claire's surprise, Schwenkman was the life of the party—he was a completely different person off duty, carousing and leading everyone in songs in French and German, and generally having a great time.

Claire didn't touch a drop of booze. Which was more than could be said for Esposito, who was passed out by the time London rang in the new year.

A couple of hours after that, the ones who were still conscious were waiting for it to be time for the ball to drop in Times Square.

Dion had been alternating between beer and soda, and at one point he looked at Claire and said, "I gotta pee. Where's Salkowitz?"

Claire pointed at the snoring Charlie Salkowitz, who was supposed to relieve Dion if he needed to leave Claire's side for any reason.

Chuckling, Dion said, "Figures. Never could hold his liquor. I'll be back in a minute."

As soon as Dion disappeared into the head, Claire turned and ran.

She had no idea if anyone noticed or if anyone was following her, but she also didn't care. All she thought about was putting one foot in front of the other.

And heading downward.

An alarm started blaring as Claire went down more and more ladders and steep metal staircases to get further and further belowdecks. She was hoping that whatever security responded to the alarm would head to the flight deck, since every other escape attempt she'd made had taken place there.

As she'd hoped, there was nobody guarding the reactor. Normally there was, but normally there wasn't a party. And it wasn't like this was a military vessel—though Dion had told her that it had been one, once, belonging to Russia—so they didn't have everyone on shift all the time. The guard here was more of a safety precaution so that nobody would enter the reactor and get boiled by the radiation.

Strictly speaking, Claire could get where she needed to go without having to go through one of the reactors, but this was the best way to guarantee that nobody would follow her.

She started to unlock the outer hatch, twirling the wheel.

"Don't move!" cried a voice from behind her.

She looked back and saw one of the guards whose name she didn't know. "Sorry, can't do that."

As she finished turning the wheel, the hatch making a satisfying *thunk* to indicate that it could be opened, the guard shot her.

The bullet ripped through her kneecap, and Claire stumbled for a moment, but she managed to hang onto the hatch and not fall to the deck. Since the bullet had gone straight through, the knee would be fine in a second or two.

Claire then pulled herself into the airlock, yanking the hatch shut behind her and locking it. Wincing in pain from her temporarily destroyed knee, she limped to the other side of the airlock and started opening the inner hatch. Once she did that, the outer hatch would be blocked shut in order to keep the ship safe from the radiation.

The wave of heat that blasted Claire was, oddly, not the worst heat she'd ever felt. She'd run into two fires within a year of learning about her powers, once on a train, once in her own house, and they had both been far more intense than this.

But it soon became apparent that this reactor made up in temperature what it lacked in fierceness. She was already drenched in sweat, and her clothes felt as if they were smoldering.

Quickly she moved to the other side of the reactor, climbing gingerly over the obstructions in her path. She had no idea what any of it did, but she went to great lengths not to disturb anything so as not to accidentally trigger a meltdown.

There was an emergency hatch on the other side, meant to be used only when the reactor was removed from the carrier for disposal. After several agonizing minutes, she reached it. Blisters had broken out all over her skin, and she screamed in pain as she grabbed the locking wheel on the hatch.

But she had come this far, and she'd felt worse pain. So she fought past it and turned the wheel.

Skin seared off, adhering itself to the wheel. Blood spilled and immediately boiled in the heat. Her grip kept slipping on the wheel as her flesh melted away, but she would not be stopped. She pulled and pulled until it finally opened.

Stumbling out, she found herself in a maintenance tube that would, if Dion had told her the truth, lead to the turbines.

As soon as she shut the emergency hatch behind her, she was plunged into total darkness. For a few seconds, she paused, catching her breath and waiting for herself to heal. Her hands and arms felt itchy as the skin repaired itself. She was still drenched in sweat—it was only cooler in this tube by comparison, it was still pretty stuffy—but once her skin was back to its old smooth, unblemished self, she started crawling forward in the tube, trying very hard not to think about how incredibly scary it was to be unable to see *anything* in front of or behind her.

Right, Claire, you just walked through an active nuclear reactor and survived, but this *scares you.*

She heard the turbines before she could see them. They were whirling at a great rate, keeping the boat steady and also generating the electricity used on board.

Closing her eyes put her back in darkness, so she didn't do that, but she did take several deep breaths.

Here we go.

Then she jumped through the turbine.

CHAPTER EIGHTEEN

Noah sat helplessly in front of the fireplace in the sitting room of Angela's mansion in the Hamptons, watching as the older woman poured herself another glass of Scotch with one hand while using an embroidered handkerchief to dab a tear-stained eye with the other.

"I can't handle another funeral, Noah," she was saying. "The whole point of this was to make the world a better place. We were supposed to live forever, helping a world become better than the one we were born into. I remember when we all got together, Adam was always talking long-term, about how if we worked quietly behind the scenes, we would do right by the world. We were so arrogant."

Noah glanced down at his smartphone again. Angela had forwarded the irritatingly clinical e-mail that the Lamarck Project had sent her as Claire's official next of kin.

"We regret to inform you that Claire Petrelli suffered a fatal accident while on board the Lamarck Project carrier *Charles Darwin* on the morning of 1 January 2012. She was accidentally caught in the turbines of the carrier and killed instantly. Claire was aiding us in our important research, but she was also a valuable part of the team and a friend to many on board. She will be sorely missed, and we offer our condolences to you for the loss of your family member."

Both Angela and Noah himself through his contacts at DHS and Renautas had confirmed the e-mail's claims, which Noah had initially dismissed as a ruse to prevent a second rescue attempt after Peter's failure on Christmas Eve. Indeed, Noah had been trying to convince Erica to authorize a more official rescue mission, but the jurisdictional issues were tricky. Instead, she'd been investigating an alternate angle, one that would involve Renautas acquiring the Lamarck Project or, failing that, hiring away their people.

Angela was still speaking. "I'm done with this, Noah. After all these years, I'm the only one still alive. We're like the ouroboros, eating our own tail. Half of us killed the other half—or we died of old age, or Sylar killed us." She shook her head. "Worst of all, I've had to watch my husband and my oldest son die. In fact, thanks to these *wonderful* powers of ours, I've gotten to watch them both die *twice*."

Noah decided against mentioning that the only reason she had seen Nathan die a second time was because she had insisted on trying to turn Sylar into Nathan after the former killed the latter. Instead, he tried to formulate something useless and clichéd to Angela in a feeble attempt to make her feel better. He still had his doubts—not that Lamarck was lying, they probably believed Claire was dead. But he knew his little girl. She wouldn't have just swum into the turbines of an aircraft carrier without a pretty strong belief that she could come out the other side alive.

Before he could say anything, though, he heard a creak from the French doors behind him, the ones that opened out onto the patio overlooking the beach.

Angela rose from her chair, Scotch still in hand, and Noah also stood up to gape as Claire entered the house.

"D—Dad?"

"Claire-Bear!" Noah ran to his daughter and clasped her in his arms. She was drenched and wearing only a few tiny scraps of clothing that had obviously been ripped to pieces.

Claire all but collapsed against Noah, breathless. "Didn't—didn't think anybody'd be—be home."

Angela said, "They told us you were killed."

"Good," Claire said weakly but emphatically. "Then it worked."

"Claire, that's amazing," Noah said, "but we have to get you into hiding. If they find out you're still alive, they'll come after you again."

Noah braced himself for an argument, but all she said was, "I know, Dad."

Letting out a long breath, Noah just held his daughter for several seconds.

Then he let her go so that Angela's staff could tend to her, getting her a change of clothes and some hot soup and tea. Angela explained that Claire had stayed at the mansion a few times when she was doing events out on Long Island, which was how she'd known to go there in the first place. She'd also left some clothes and toiletries behind for future visits. Noah nodded approvingly.

As the three of them sat around the small kitchen table, Noah with a mug of coffee, Angela with more Scotch, and Claire with her soup and tea, the bedraggled girl related the story of her journey.

"After I got through the turbines, I just floated while my body put itself back together. I waited for the sun to come up so I'd know which way was east—and which way was west. I started swimming that way and just kept going until I saw a cruise ship that was heading the same way."

"You didn't board it?" Noah asked.

Claire shook her head. "I didn't want to take the chance that Lamarck was monitoring radios. I just hung on to the underside of the boat until it got near land. I was lucky, it was going to New York, so I swam off when it came near Long Island."

Noah blinked in shock and then shook his head. The house was located right on the ocean, and earlier that day he'd seen several boats heading for New York Harbor pass by not too far away—certainly close enough for Claire to swim, in theory.

But in reality, that must have taken tremendous courage, strength, and presence of mind. "Claire, that's amazing."

"I guess." Claire mostly sounded exhausted, which didn't really surprise Noah. "I had a *lot* of time on my own to plan."

"Planning is one thing, executing quite another." Noah reached out and squeezed Claire's shoulder, giving her his warmest smile. "I'm proud of you, Claire-Bear."

She gave him a ragged smile back. "Thanks, Dad."

Angela said, "I'm proud, too, dear. And very impressed. Noah's right, that was truly amazing. And don't worry, I'll arrange passage for you to where Peter's running his underground movement."

Claire blinked. "He has a headquarters?"

"Him and the rest of the so-called 'Petrelli Movement.'" She shuddered. "Much as I agree with the movement's goals, I do wish they'd call it something else."

"I *don't* agree with the movement's methods." Claire spoke more forcefully now, the nourishment lending her strength. "All they've done is make things worse."

Noah said, "So did the Lamarck Project by kidnapping you. The President has given Renautas more autonomy, and our field agents have been encouraged to be more forceful. Riots are starting to happen here, too—on both sides."

Angela put a hand on Claire's wrist. "All being public has done is put a target on your back, dear. You can't go back to your public life."

"I can still help, though. You're right, I can't be the face of Evos anymore. If I show up in public now, the President will probably arrest me."

"Definitely. But don't worry, Claire." Angela smiled. "I'll keep you safe."

"We both will," Noah said.

"I don't *need* you to keep me safe, Dad!" Claire snapped. "You just want to hide me in a glass jar where no one can get at me. That was fine when I was a teenager, but I'm an adult now. I need to make my own way. I need to help our people. Maybe I can't do that the way I did before, but I *can* keep doing it."

Noah shook his head. "That'd be a mistake, Claire. You tried it your way, and—"

She held up a hand. "I don't want to hear it." She blew out a breath. "I'm exhausted."

Angela put an arm around Claire and led her toward the staircase. "I'll take you upstairs, dear."

Watching his daughter go off with Angela, Noah realized that she was right. She had to make her own choices. Besides, even if hers was the wrong way, it wasn't as if Noah's attempts to keep her safe had been howling successes. Either way, he'd done his part as her father.

Besides, she had escaped from that aircraft carrier without any help from him. Maybe it was time he recognized that his little girl had grown up.

CHAPTER NINETEEN

7 JANUARY 2012
PORT OF LE HAVRE, FRANCE

One of the cruise ship's crew, a nice woman named Laura Mayfield, greeted Claire as she approached the gangway to disembark.

"It's been a pleasure having you, Ms. Shaw, and we hope that you'll travel with us again."

"Thank you," Claire said. Angela had booked her a cabin under the name of "Alice Shaw," a private joke. It was the name of Angela's sister, whom she had abandoned at the Coyote Sands facility fifty years ago and who was still missing.

Laura handed her a stub of cardboard. "Your baggage is in Section D."

"Thanks again," Claire said with a smile. "This was certainly nicer than the last time I travelled by boat."

"Why, thank you!"

Claire walked down the gangway, watching as other passengers were greeted by assorted people.

Two dark-skinned men with curly dark hair approached her. One Claire recognized immediately as Dr. Mohinder

Suresh, and the other she realized was Micah Sanders, who was a lot taller than the last time Claire had seen him back in Kirby Plaza.

"Hello, Claire," Mohinder said in his amazing voice, a bright smile lighting up his face. "It's good to see you again."

"I should've known you two would be involved in this. Let me guess, you've got Matt, Hiro, and Ando along, too?"

Mohinder shook his head. "I'm afraid I've heard nothing from Matt in over a year, and Hiro and Ando returned to Japan after your little coming-out party in New York. I've heard very little from them beyond the occasional e-mail."

"The good news," Micah added, "is that those e-mails are encrypted and untraceable. I can do the same for you, too."

Claire nodded, remembering that Micah was, in essence, a cyberpath. He could mentally convince electronics and machines to do pretty much whatever he wanted.

Then she asked the question that Angela hadn't been able to answer: "What about Sylar?"

The two exchanged quick glances. "Sylar—does as he pleases."

"So nothing's changed, there."

"Well," Mohinder said bitterly, "Sylar has never been consistent about what he wants from one moment to the next. I wish my father had never contacted him. If he hadn't, he might have remained a watchmaker in Brooklyn, and all of our lives would have been considerably less complicated."

Jackie would be alive, was Claire's first thought. *So would Nathan.*

Mohinder indicated the port behind him. "We've got a barge moored in another dock. Come with us."

"I have to get my luggage first."

Nodding, Mohinder said, "Lead the way."

Claire nodded back. She wasn't looking forward to this, but at least Sylar wasn't there. It might actually be tolerable, and perhaps she could still do some good.

CHAPTER TWENTY

18 APRIL 2012
PORT OF VATHI, ITHAKI, GREECE

The chat server was one of Micah's own design, enabling him to make it secure in a way that Skype and other online chat programs weren't.

Claire sat cross-legged on the bunk of her cabin on the barge, a vessel called *Highland Dream* that was owned by MacLeod Shipping, a wholly fictional company secretly headed by Angela Petrelli. Her laptop was open in front of her.

On the screen before her were about twenty chat windows showing Evos from around the world who had either been rescued by the movement or had been contacted by them or had contacted the movement themselves. Some lived peacefully closeted, others had registered with their respective country's version of the Evo Act, and still others were on the run.

At this point, Claire had given the talk she was about to give dozens of times. The webcam showed only her face and the top of her T-shirt, and the only thing visible behind her was the Rihanna poster on the bulkhead. She was very careful not to let the porthole, with its view of the island of Ithaki, show on the cam. The image she needed to project was that of a normal nineteen-year-old, with no obvious clues as to where she was at present.

"The most important thing is that Renautas and Lamarck and the EU council and all the other government agencies can't keep an eye on *everyone*. There's too many people to do that practically. The trick? Be *incredibly* uninteresting." She shook her head and smiled. "It's funny, for years I wanted a normal life, and now I finally realized that that's the best camouflage."

One person, an older man, spoke up. "So you're not saying we should hide?"

"Hide in plain sight, is what I'm saying. Just do what everyone does. If you talk to a stranger, make sure you only talk about the weather or sports. Buy generic food, and keep it to simple stuff that everyone buys. Eat at popular restaurants—especially fast-food places. Only DVR really popular TV shows. Don't do anything that would make you stand out. Of course, the best way to do that is to *never*, under *any* circumstances, use your power in public."

A young woman said in heavily accented English, "That is not always possible."

"I know that, *believe* me. Sometimes you accidentally cut yourself and your family sees it heal. But try your best, and at the very least, try to keep it to people you trust. Definitely try not to let it happen in public. *Everybody*'s got a camera these days, and whatever you do on the street is gonna be on YouTube half an hour later.

"Also, we're working to get an underground railroad together for people in the States. Canada's version of the Evo Act is voluntary, like the U.S. one was originally. You've all got e-mail addresses on the 'Hero_truther' network, and we'll keep updating you that way. Any questions?"

One couple who appeared together in the same chat window asked, "What about our kids? We want to have them genetically tested to see if our powers got passed on."

"We're working on that. Some Planned Parenthood clinics are cooperating with us to do discreet genetic tests, and so are some private clinics. Micah will have the list up in the next week or two. Anything else?"

That was it, so Claire said her goodbyes to everyone and ended the call.

Then she looked up at Mohinder, who was standing in the door to her cabin. "Amazing."

"What is?" she asked.

"You're so much better at that. I'm an academic—I'm used to lecturing people, and they tend to tune me out. Micah's always talking in jargon about computers and electronics and security. We even had Sylar doing this for a while, and—well, the less said about that, the better. And Peter's the worst public speaker in the world."

"I don't know, he did okay in that press conference he gave at Nathan's old campaign HQ."

Mohinder grinned. "He practiced that for a week. Regardless, you've been a tremendous asset. It's good to have you."

"Thanks." She stared out the porthole at the sun shining down on the Greek island. "I just hope we're actually doing some good."

CHAPTER TWENTY-ONE

2 MAY 2012
E-MAIL SENT BY ABHAYA BHATNAGAR TO CLAIRE
BENNET PETRELLI

TO: claire@hero_truther.org
FROM: abhaya@hero_truther.org
SUBJECT: Incident in Bilund

Greetings, Claire. Thank you again for putting me in touch
with Claude. He has proven very useful in helping me not
be seen, even though my ability isn't invisibility as such.
But thanks to him, I can blend into the background even
more efficiently. I just wish he bathed more often...

I travelled to Denmark to follow rumors of a man who
could breathe fire. In fact, the first story I heard was that
there was a dragon in Bilund. And, given what has been
happening in the world, I was willing to believe it.

It turns out that an elderly man named Jamart Ærts has
breath that can BLOW OUT fires. A woman showed me a
cell phone video she made of him in a café putting out a
small oven fire by simply blowing on it.

The day after I arrived, the LEGO factory—the primary business in Bilund, which I learned is referred to as "Bricktown" in English—caught fire. Mr. Ærts literally blew the entire fire out. But, as I said, he is an elderly man. After putting the fire out, he collapsed right on Åstvej.

Paramedics arrived, but once they were told what had happened, they refused to treat him. The exact phrase used by one paramedic was translated for me by a local as saying that they only treat people, not mutants.

It wasn't Jamart Ærts's job to save lives, but he saved hundreds today. It was the paramedics' job to save lives, and they refused to do so.

I wonder what kind of world our children will inherit.

Best,
Abhaya

CHAPTER TWENTY-TWO

12 JUNE 2014
CONTINUING THE LETTER WRITTEN BY CLAIRE BENNET ON HER LAPTOP

So now, finally, we come to the part of the story where you and I meet, Hammer.

I used to love 4th of July when I was a kid. There was always a football game. In fact, there were always *dozens* of football games.

But the best 4th of July ever was in 2012.

Peter and Claude showed up on the barge when we were docked in Tarragona, Spain. You should remember that day pretty well: the 5th of June 2012, when you and seven other Evos were almost lynched in Monaco.

The first I heard of it was when Peter, Claude, and the eight of you all just appeared on the deck of the barge. Between them, Claude and Peter had been able to make everyone invisible, and then it was just a matter of getting from Monaco to Tarragona. Peter indicated that Sylar may have helped, but apparently he didn't stick around.

Peter has never been willing to talk about Sylar with me, ever since he broke into the house that time. And I haven't seen hide nor hair of him. Whatever—as long as he's not around, I'm happy.

Anyhow, Claude took off, while Peter stayed to help Mohinder take care of you all.

You were in such bad shape when you came in, wearing that stupid trench coat. I'd just finished one of Mickey Spillane's Mike Hammer books, and since you were unconscious, I started referring to you as "Hammer". Your head wound was pretty severe, and you had fractures in both your legs. Mohinder was worried at first that you'd never walk again, but you obviously proved *that* wrong.

By the time 4th of July rolled around, we were docked in Liverpool. Nobody in England was going to celebrate, of course. I remember Claude saying that morning, "Happy Illegal Secession of King George's Colonies Day!"

But we had Detlev. She was unconscious when Claude and Peter brought her over from Monaco with you and the others, but she'd made a full recovery, and she stuck around because she wasn't scared with us the way she had been out in the world.

That was your first day walking outside the infirmary, and you did so wonderfully. I remember being so proud of you and how well you walked around the deck of the barge.

And then Detlev created fireworks for us, because she's such a sweetie.

And we had our first kiss.

I never told you this, but I didn't date a lot. Most of the boys in high school were stupid, and I got asked out *all* the time—hello, blonde cheerleader?—but usually we only went to a movie or something and I never even kissed the boy.

I've kissed a few guys since I got my powers, including a really nice guy named West and a few others.

I'm being completely honest with you when I tell you that no kiss was as amazing as when you and I first kissed on the barge under Detlev's fireworks.

Too bad it all went into the toilet after that. You got all moody and annoying, and you kept saying we needed to be more proactive. You argued with me, you argued with Mohinder, you argued with Peter, you argued with Micah, you argued with Claude. Honestly, that one time, I thought you and Peter were going to kill each other.

And then you'd kiss me, and it was almost as good as that one on 4th of July, and everything would be okay for a little while.

But then you just up and left without a word. No note, nothing, you were just gone.

CHAPTER TWENTY-THREE

7 NOVEMBER 2012
PORT OF RAVENNA, RAVENNA, ITALY

Dion Cornwell stared at his tablet, which was playing a YouTube video of the President's reelection acceptance speech from late the previous night. His victory hadn't been as decisive as his first, and that was mainly due to his opponent hitting him on the Evo issue, but the challenger's platform had offered no good alternative. And so the President got four more years, and last night he had given a decent, if not great, speech.

"...together with your help and God's grace, we will continue our journey forward and remind the world just why it is that we live in the greatest nation on Earth. Thank you, America. God bless you. God bless these United States."

The video ended before the thunderous applause, for which Dion was grateful, as he already had a headache. He was sitting in the staging area for the raid, which would be starting as soon as Interpol arrived with the international warrant from the World Court. His team had set up in an empty cargo container.

It had been quite an up-and-down year for Dion. After Claire escaped, Dion and most of the rest of the mercenaries were fired. Schwenkman probably would have been, too, but he quit instead, going to work for a company called Renautas.

Luckily, a security firm based out of Italy called Sicurezza Castiglione was hiring. Signor Castiglione himself had been very impressed by Dion's résumé and had brought him on board. SC's primary client was Interpol, which contracted the company to complete various tactical assignments.

This particular task was a dream come true for Dion. The little twerp Esposito had also been fired by Lamarck after Claire's escape, but he'd gone to work for Interpol directly to help round up Evos who had crossed national borders. According to Castiglione—who was leading this raid himself—Esposito had tracked down a woman named Abhaya Bhatnagar in the Czech Republic and had learned the location of the headquarters of the Petrelli Movement.

It turned out that the movement was based on a boat, which was why Interpol had had such trouble finding them.

But the best part for Dion was that the little bitch Claire was supposedly on that boat.

She'd played him, back on the *Charles Darwin*, and had gotten his ass fired, and he was so very much looking forward to repaying her for that.

He should've expected it from a damn Cowboys fan.

Castiglione entered the cargo container, together with an inspector from Interpol. Dion put his tablet away in his pack.

The inspector was a short man with a day's beard growth. He spoke with a British accent in a very raspy voice. "We've got our warrant. The people on that barge are wanted for dozens of violations of international law. They're also extremely dangerous, so proceed with caution, please."

Castiglione said the same thing in Italian for the people in the unit who didn't speak English, and then everyone stood up and checked their weapons one last time. As Dion went over his P90, he thought about how very little caution he intended to use with Claire. It wasn't as if he could actually do permanent harm to her, but that just meant he could shoot her all he wanted. He intended to dump his entire magazine into her. It wouldn't hurt her for long, but it would make him feel a lot better.

At Castiglione's order, they moved quickly across the dock and boarded the barge with the words HIGHLAND DREAM stenciled on its hull. They moved in formation through every deck, through every corridor, through every room.

They found absolutely nothing.

Dion, along with three of his colleagues, checked the engine room, the point farthest from where they had boarded and therefore the final place to look.

The engines seemed to be in good working order, though they were currently shut down.

And then he looked under one large lever and saw a device standing on its own.

It was an explosive.

Sonofabitch!

"Bomb!" he yelled as he turned to run out of the engine room, his three companions on his heels. He kept yelling, "Bomb!" over and over again as he hurriedly disembarked, accompanied by Castiglione and the entire rest of the unit.

The barge exploded in a very loud, very bright conflagration. Dion held his hands to his ears, but it wasn't enough to keep them from ringing.

The inspector came running toward Castiglione. "What the hell happened?"

"*Caccio*, they knew we were coming," Castiglione said in his heavily accented English. "There was no one there."

"How is that possible?" the inspector asked. "Our information had two dozen Evos living on that damn barge!"

Dion couldn't believe the cop was dumb enough to ask that. "They're *Evos*, for Chrissakes. Didn't you read comic books when you were a kid? Strange powers beyond those of mortal men and all that crap? They *do* this."

He winced as the ringing in his ears got worse. *One of these days, Claire...*

CHAPTER TWENTY-FOUR

27 SEPTEMBER 2013
ABBAZIA DI SAN GIOVANNI, SPILIMBERGO, ITALY
2013 had been the best year of Claire Bennet's life.

In 2011, she had been the public face of the Evos, which was a whirlwind of insanity. In 2012, she had been on the run as the secret face of the Petrelli Movement, which was a great big bundle of stress.

Then they got word that Interpol had captured Abhaya and gotten information out of her, including the location of the barge. There was no time to move it, and the barge was pretty much burned anyhow.

So Claude got his hands on some explosives, and they left them behind as a present for Interpol. The bomb was designed to go off a good five minutes after it was first touched, so the police would have plenty of time to abandon ship before it went boom.

Some people went back to their homes, others to other safehouses. In addition, Angela provided sanctuary. Angela's husband's family had roots in Italy, after all, including several family members who were part of the order of Benedictine monks that ran an abbey in northern

Italy at the foot of the Dolomites—the mountain range that further north became the Swiss Alps.

Claire had taken them up on that offer of sanctuary, as had several others. Now she'd been here for ten months, and she'd never ever been so happy and content.

Over those months, most of the others gradually took their leave of the abbey. Sister Domenica—or Menighina, as everyone called her—treated the Evo guests like family, feeding them and taking care of them, but many of them grew bored and wanted to get back to reality.

Claire thought they were all insane. Reality was bombs and swimming through turbines and secret servers and clandestine messages and getting buried alive and having your head sliced open and waking up on a coroner's table in mid-autopsy.

Here, there was the beautiful, quiet countryside, delicious food, fresh fruit and vegetables, and excellent wine. (The monks made their own wine, both for their own use and to sell; it helped keep the place solvent, as there wasn't a lot of money in being a monk or nun anymore. There certainly wasn't as much call for illuminated manuscripts and the like.) The bed she slept in was more comfortable than the one in her dorm at Arlington University, and every day she saw green grass, beautiful trees, and lovely mountains.

Outside the abbey, people wanted to kill her, even though she couldn't actually die. Why would she ever want to leave?

One morning, Claire got up, stretched, and smiled as she saw the sun rise in the east and heard the rooster crowing dawn's arrival. When she'd first come to San Giovanni under the cover of darkness with a dozen tired, scared Evos, she had always considered herself a night person, and viewed getting up early as the greatest sin in the universe.

But after ten months in this place, she couldn't imagine not being up with the sun.

She threw on a robe over her nightgown and opened the door to her room—

—to find a familiar face standing there, smiling, wearing that stupid trench coat.

"Hammer," she said bitterly.

He winced. "I wish you wouldn't call me that."

"What are you *doing* here?"

"I missed you."

She went back into the room, shaking her head. "How'd you even know I was here?"

He smiled. "I have my ways." Then the smile fell. "Besides, things are getting weird out there. More and more of us are going public. People are aware of us now, and it's about equal parts support and hatred. It's a mess. I just needed a break from it, something to make me smile. And honestly, in my life, the only person who's ever been able to make me smile is you, Blondie."

Claire contemplated complaining about that particular nickname, but that would make it harder for her to defend calling him Hammer.

He walked closer and grabbed her shoulders, pulling her toward him. She stared up at his eyes, which were intense. "I miss you. I miss hearing your stupid arguments about what you call your family. I miss the feel of your beautiful hair as I run my hands through it. I miss the taste of your lips. I miss the smell of your skin". He grinned. "I even miss you calling me 'Hammer'. But most of all, Claire, I miss the sight of your smile. That smile was the first thing I saw when I woke up on the barge, and I honestly think that smile is the reason why I'm still alive and giving a damn about being alive."

Tears welled up in Claire's eyes, and she found herself forgetting the arguments, forgetting the bitterness, and remembering those kisses.

And then he leaned in and she found herself kissing him hungrily.

He spent the day with her. She showed him around the abbey. She introduced him to Menighina as a "friend" and she nodded her understanding. Claire wasn't sure if she only thought of him as a fellow Evo or something more, but it didn't matter.

Together, they ate the abbey's excellent food, drank some of their superb wine, and then that night they went out into the mountains.

They made love under the stars, and then fell asleep in each other's arms.

When Claire awakened at dawn, she was alone in the mountains. Hammer was nowhere to be found. She ran back to the abbey, but there was no sign of him.

For the second time, he left her without a word.

A few days later, she woke up in the middle of the night, nauseous.

Even as she ran to the water closet, she knew something was horribly wrong. Since her powers developed, she'd *never* been nauseous.

After she threw up rather loudly and violently, she went to the sink and splashed cold water on her face.

She was going to need to ask Menighina to borrow the abbey's car so she could go into town and buy a pregnancy test.

CHAPTER TWENTY-FIVE

12 JUNE 201
CONCLUDING THE LETTER WRITTEN BY CLAIRE BENNET ON HER LAPTOP

You certainly weren't kidding about the mixed feelings out there in the world. I started actually paying attention to the news after you left, and saw that you were right.

They actually refer to some of the people who want Evos to live in peace with regular humans as "Claireans," which is kinda hilarious.

Anyhow, the plane's landing soon, so I should finish this up.

Who knows, maybe you'll be at the summit? Supposedly, Evos are coming from all over the world, and it'll be a big gathering of peace and harmony. It'll be like Woodstock. Or maybe it'll be like Altamont.

Look at me, making music references from Dad's childhood. Either way, I can't help thinking about what Abhaya said in that e-mail she sent me, asking what kind of a world we were giving to our children. I guess with the twins—Thor and Loki? Harold and Kumar?—on the way, I'm thinking about that a lot now. What will it be like for them?

The part that scares me is seeing Dad again. I don't even know what I'm going to say to him. We've been on opposite sides of this pretty much ever since Central Park. I have no idea how he's going to respond. Rene promised to talk to him before I get there, prepare the ground, if you know what I mean. Rene's known Dad for twenty years, and *he* doesn't know how he'll react, either.

Anyhow, like I said, I'm going to upload this to Micah's secure server. Maybe you'll read it someday.

Claire.

CHAPTER TWENTY-SIX

13 JUNE 2014
EVO SUMMIT, PRIMATECH PAPER, ODESSA, TX

Claire clambered out of the limo that had brought her to the summit.

The driver ran around to the other side of the limo to help her. He had met her at the airport—complete with a sign that said CLAIRE BENNET—and led her to the limo that Angela had provided.

"There are a lot of things I dislike about being pregnant," she muttered as the driver steadied her, "but being unable to gracefully get up or sit down is *by far* the worst."

Smiling, the driver said, "Well, ma'am, at least it should be over soon. If you don't mind my saying so, you're pretty far along."

Claire gave the driver a grateful smile and nod, then looked over at Primatech Headquarters, which had gotten a lot bigger since the last time she was here, confronting Sylar on Level 5.

It was also packed to the gills with Evos and regular people alike, and tons of media. Some of the Evos were even performing—she saw a troupe of dancing shapechangers—

and others were happily displaying their powers.

"I wish it was like this everywhere, all the time."

"Well, ma'am, maybe after today, it will be."

"Hope so." Then she stumbled and caught herself on a parked car. Unfortunately, she did so on a car with a sharp grille in front, and she cut her hand.

"Are you all right?" the driver asked, grabbing her hand.

"It'll be fine," she said with the surety that came of years of watching every cut heal.

She stared down at her hand.

It didn't heal.

"You *sure* you'll be okay, ma'am?"

"Yeah." She shook her head. "Probably something to do with the pregnancy. It'll be fine."

She walked to the main entrance of the summit. A man in a jumpsuit with the Renautas logo who wasn't visibly armed, but who was very obviously security, walked up to her. "Can I help you, ma'am?"

"I'm Claire Bennet." She had stopped using Petrelli once she arrived at the barge. There didn't seem to be any point. "I'm here to…"

"Is something wrong, ma'am?"

But Claire didn't answer. She felt very weak all of a sudden. And the area between her legs was incredibly moist.

Looking down, she saw a puddle of water on the ground—but it was tinged with red.

"Blood?"

And then she collapsed.

She heard indistinct voices around her.

"Get the ambulance over here!"

"Her water broke!"

"She shouldn't have collapsed like that."

"What happened?"

"Her name's Claire Bennet, she's here for the summit, but her water broke and she just collapsed."

"All right, we'll take her to St. Jude's. On three!"

And then, as darkness engulfed her, she heard nothing else...

TO BE CONTINUED
IN *HEROES REBORN*
CHAPTER SEVEN: "June 13th Part 1"

HEROES

REBORN

EVENT SERIES

BOOK THREE

A LONG WAY FROM HOME

KEVIN J. ANDERSON
AND PETER J. WACKS

In times of war, times of change, humanity vilifies anything that is outside the narrowly defined norm. When persecution begins, people turn away and think, "At least it wasn't me."

Remember the man who watched as the Nazis took his neighbors one by one, choosing not to speak out, since it wasn't him they were coming for... Until they finally knocked on his door, and there was no one left to speak out for him.

There comes a moment for each of us when the wool is pulled from our eyes, when we see the world anew... When society realizes that all the Evolved, all Evos, are just loaded weapons, a trigger ready to be pulled.

Things.

And when Evos are put in chains... Who will speak out to say that they should not be oppressed?

—Mohinder Suresh

Sam Conlon pulled the lapel of the trench coat up to cover his neck. The parking garage was empty, dark. He felt like the world had turned to shades of gray, leaving him lost in a Bogart movie.

"You'll test them, and the facility?" The woman's voice came from the shadows behind the next pillar over.

"How do I know you'll wipe my file? Renautas has that much pull with the FBI?"

A sigh softly glided through the air. "We do have that much pull and we will use it, Mr. Conlon. As an associate once said to me just outside the president's office, the toothpaste is out of the tube. There's no returning to what the world was before. We have the power you want, but in order to access it, you must play this out for me."

Faint electric lines, visible only to Sam, appeared in the air as she spoke. A new pattern was emerging. He smiled grimly at her lies. "I'll do it."

He walked away, ignoring her reply as he prepared to turn himself in.

One Month Later

CHAPTER ONE

The Rocky Mountains were splashed with autumnal aspen colors. The tallest peaks, rugged barriers rising from the Eagle River Valley, were crowned with early snowfall—Jacque Peak, Battle Mountain, Searle Pass, Tennessee Pass.

Luther knew them all. He had studied the geography carefully while planning his latest escape.

Ducking and dodging low-hanging branches of ponderosa pines, he ran up the grassy slope, slipping in the wet mulch of fallen needles. Icy air, too thin, burned his lungs.

He could see the large, fenced-in compound of Temporary Assessment Camp Hale spread out in the valley below. Admin buildings, guard houses, rows of barracks (euphemistically called "Common Living Structures") and the maximum-security barracks where the dangerous Evos were held waited for him down there if he failed.

Luther's power wasn't dangerous, but having it was enough to rob him of his freedom.

Most of the other camp inhabitants could say the same. A few *were* dangerous, or so it was rumored. Luther needed to get away. A prison was a prison, no matter how often they told you it was for your own protection.

Arms flailing, he crashed his way through the trees, scratching himself on a tangle of dead branches, but eventually found a rocky outcropping. He climbed it and kept running. His legs were shaky and his lungs felt like they were on fire, but he still had a long way to go.

Behind him he could hear the dogs barking, howling... getting closer.

Luther put on an extra surge of speed, pushing past his exhaustion.

The TAC Hale guards didn't even need the dogs as they pursued him. Out of the corner of his eye Luther could see the brilliant splashes of yellow he left behind, painting the ground with vibrant footprints... As his agitation increased, he lost control over his power and couldn't prevent what the specialist labeled "chromographic leakage."

Stupidest power ever!

To a more sophisticated Evo, the chameleon-like power would have been useful, but Luther couldn't control it, and for some oddball genetic reason, he only had access to the color yellow. So as he ran, his footprints created intense pools of color—the blades of grass turned yellow, the pine needles turned yellow, even the rocks and dirt turned yellow. Add to that the bright orange "work overalls" that all of the "campers" wore...

Yellow and orange. At least I won't get accidentally shot by a hunter.

He hoped he could get away, cover enough distance so that they wouldn't catch him, but he knew it was a long shot. One of these days, maybe the long shot would pay off. Just not today, unless he caught a lucky break.

Luther gasped in the ten-thousand foot elevation. That struggle to breathe was the reason the original Camp Hale had been built during World War II—as high-altitude training for the 10th Mountain Division. He had hoped to make it several miles before sunrise, but he couldn't find a trail and the terrain was rugged.

He had gotten lost.

And now, the following morning, the guards had a fading set of neon yellow spots to track him. They didn't really need the dogs.

He was close to the tree line now, and worked his way out of the pines until he saw clear grassy ground ahead—which meant the guards could see him, too. The dogs were eager.

Between heaving breaths, one of the guards on the slopes below, a man named Thomas Rizzoli (but better known around the camp as "TQ"), called out, "Come on, Luther. Don't be a jerk."

Luther mumbled a retort, all he could manage. Stumbling, he ducked back into the cover of the trees, following a drainage wash. The path of least resistance. He didn't really have any plan other than to get away. He had hoped by trekking deep enough into the mountains, he could escape pursuit and eventually find a ski lodge or a mining town where he could get help. It didn't look like that was going to happen.

Not today.

He found a game trail on the downslope and picked up speed now that he didn't have to dodge the trees so much. Downhill didn't hurt, either. Unfortunately, his pursuers also moved more quickly. He stumbled and slipped on the loose turf. The trail was heading down to a stream. Maybe if there was enough water he could cross it, make the dogs lose the scent—better yet, he could use the stream to cover his footprints. Perhaps fortune *would* smile on him after all.

Unfortunately, when the vegetation cleared and he knocked shrubs out of the way, he found himself by a wispy creek that emerged out of a spray of water falling from a rocky ledge above. The trail ended. He couldn't get up the opposite slope. A tear ran down his cheek and he clenched his fists.

Luther sighed and his shoulders slumped. Time to put the mask of the disarming buffoon back on. The dogs came charging in, braying, with Rizzoli and the guards stumbling behind, red-faced, looking annoyed. Rizzoli stopped and mopped perspiration from his forehead. The other guards held the dogs back.

Rizzoli huffed, catching his breath. "You're such a pain in the ass, Luther. This isn't what I planned on doing today. Ruthers is going to be pissed."

Luther sat down on a boulder next to the cool, splashing water. "At least I got farther than the last time. Give me a little credit, TQ."

The guard scowled. "Only one person gets to call me that." He gestured toward the others. "Zap him and let's get him back to camp."

Alarmed, Luther sat up. "No, wait! I'll go willingly."

"It would be easier, TQ," said one of the other guards.

Rizzoli shook his head. "It doesn't matter. The jerk deserves it."

Luther ate 1,200 volts at 19 pulses per second as his breakfast.

CHAPTER TWO

When the team of sweaty guards and barking dogs brought a bedraggled but grinning Luther stumbling back through the main entry gate of Temporary Assessment Camp Hale, the camp's head director and Chief of Operations Deborah Ruthers didn't feel satisfaction or relief. Just disappointment. Deep disappointment.

Luther walked with a wobbly gait, trailing yellow stains on the ground. *A pointless power... no obvious threat. But who could know for certain?*

There was no way to hide from the other campers the fact that Luther had escaped and tried to run—again. Many of them were gathered in the commons, doing their daily duties, going in and out of the barracks, and returning from their busy work-camp jobs. She certainly had enough manpower, and everyone pitched in to do their best to make TAC Hale pleasant. They planted flower gardens, vegetable gardens. They kept the living areas clean, brightly painted, even homey.

Ruthers strived to promote a sense of camaraderie and teamwork. The temporary assessment camp wasn't supposed to be a hostile environment. Renautas had set it up as a sanctuary, a tolerable place for anyone who tested positive as an Evo to come for documentation and assessment, except for the ones held in Max. She didn't like to think about Max, though. Hale, for the most part, was a place to get away from the harassment of being labeled different. Most of these people exhibited powers that were no more dangerous (or useful) than Luther's.

She shook her head as Luther walked through the gate, shaking his arms to loosen himself up, still clearly recovering from a Taser shot. "We're all just trying to do the best we can here," Ruthers muttered to herself. Troublemakers like Luther certainly didn't help.

Many of the campers were grinning. They applauded as Luther made his entrance. He seemed embarrassed; a 35-year-old, slightly overweight man with the beginnings of a paunch. He would have been utterly invisible in society. Nothing to worry about, although his penchant for accidentally turning things yellow would have inconvenienced him in the workplace.

Some of the campers whistled and cheered. "Maybe next time, Luther."

He looked sheepish but grinned and took a clumsy bow. The guards ushered him forward.

Ruthers wasn't amused, but she didn't want to make TAC Hale feel like a prison. She wanted the campers and the guards and the Admin staff to get along, to be a team. That's what the temporary assessment camp was supposed to be, and Ruthers believed in it.

She began to speak, and the unruly campers fell silent. "Look," she said, "I can understand that some of you feel trapped. But right now leaving isn't a viable option. Renautas and I are doing everything we can to make TAC Hale like a... summer camp. It's minimum security. The fences are here for your own protection, and you really should stay here. Don't we let you watch the news? You've seen what it's like out there after Odessa. That's why we built Hale. To protect you. So that we can assess you, give you free room and board, try to make you comfortable. Why would you want to run away from this? To be persecuted on the outside?"

She could see them nodding and considering. They all knew the story, and none of them were really violent rebels. For herself, she could have had a nice job in private security in Denver, but Renautas had offered her a big bonus and a temporary assignment running the newly built camp in the mountains, where the nearest towns were nothing more than off-season ski resorts and dying mining towns.

TAC Hale wasn't a government facility, but *was* operated under presidential mandate. She saw a few of the campers grumbling at her words, obviously dissatisfied, but they knew what she was saying. They knew of the turmoil out in the real world. They knew the violent prejudice against Evos.

They—the innocuous ones here in Camp Hale—were the ones at greatest risk. They weren't heroes. They didn't have powers strong enough to protect themselves. They were just targets. "I know it's an inconvenience, and I'm trying to give you as much freedom as possible. Neither the guards nor the Admin staff—nor I—really want to be here any more than you do." She raised her voice. "But this is the best chance for you and for us. Just wait for things to settle down in the real world. You're safe here. It's for your own good."

From their expressions, she could see that the campers—most of them, at any rate—believed what she was saying.

So did Ruthers.

CHAPTER THREE

Andrew Meek had a queasy, sinking feeling in his stomach as he and his friend Reggie went back to work. He had heard all the promises and propaganda, and he'd had no choice when they shipped him out here from Denver for "temporary assessment" in the mountains not far from Leadville, Colorado.

He just didn't believe it.

He didn't trust the government, or Renautas, or whatever logos or labels they put on the buildings. Protective enclosures were still fences, and living commons were still barracks… and innocence was still guilt.

Reggie was smiling, showing bad teeth from a childhood without orthodontia. "Makes ya wonder how long we would have survived out in the real world. Right, Andrew?" he asked as he picked up their janitorial equipment and headed for the next set of barracks. "That's nothing ta sneeze at." With a twinkle in his eye, Reggie turned to Andrew, squinted his left eye in a spasmodic wink—and Andrew sneezed.

"Stop that, Reggie," he scolded. Reggie's "great" Evo power was that he could trigger a quick sneeze. Quite a dangerous, destructive power, no doubt.

"No harm, no foul," Reggie laughed.

"We've got two more sets to do before lunchtime. You do the toilets in this one. I'll do the next." Andrew didn't argue about the sneeze because Reggie considered it a victory. The two of them had been assigned janitorial and groundskeeping duties along with a dozen other volunteers. Everyone in TAC Hale was expected to pitch in and carry their own weight, though Ruthers was careful not to give the impression that it was a forced labor camp. If campers helped out, a small stipend was placed into a holding account for them to make up for their time away—if they ever got out of TAC Hale.

Andrew didn't mind the work and found that *not* having a job made his time here much worse, mind-numbingly boring. He had never worked at anything that would even remotely be considered a glamorous job. Five years as a civil-service employee pushing papers around for the City of Denver had primed him for tedium.

When he tested positive for the Evo gene, he was whisked off here to the mountains two hours away. He had had no choice in the matter, even if they made it seem like he did, and his boss had given him no reassurances that he'd have his job back "when" he got released. Equal employment opportunities for Evos were still a very murky legal gray area. Andrew knew not to count on it.

Reggie wheeled the cart up the ramp and into the office trailer, then pulled out the vacuum while Andrew grabbed the trash bag. He couldn't hide his uneasiness. Already knowing the answer, he still asked his companion, "So you really believe the line that this is all for our own good?"

Reggie snorted, "Hell, yes. Look around. We've got beds, a comfy home, free food—and pretty decent nosh, too. I've worked harder jobs for way less." He lifted the vacuum hose. "You've seen the violence out there. What it's like. It's not safe fer us to be out on the streets." His thick eyebrows drew together. "There's lotsa bad blood out there, Andrew. I don't wanna be strung up and gutted by somebody who had a cousin in Odessa or some angry high school football player who blames a big zit on an Evo with acne powers. If they come at me with torches and pitchforks, what'm I gonna do? Make 'em sneeze? I can't defend myself. What'll you do? Give 'em a chill? We ain't all like Claire Bennet. No. We're safe here, and thank God for Renautas. *Doing good is good business.*"

Andrew was still uneasy, but he couldn't argue with Reggie, though he mistrusted his friend's blind enthusiasm. If Evos were indeed being held here strictly for protection, and to help measure and assess whatever abilities they had, then he could have accepted it. But he suspected that Renautas and the government had brought the Evos here to TAC Hale to control them. Even the Evos like him and Reggie and Luther whose powers were simply ridiculous.

How can we be a threat, and how are any of our abilities useful?

Andrew's ability was to drop the ambient temperature ten degrees. He could raise a few goose bumps or give someone a chill… How was he supposed to turn that into a weapon? Make his enemies gradually catch a cold? He sighed as he finished dumping wastebaskets, then went over to the janitorial cart so he could gather up the bathroom cleaning supplies.

They finished the office barracks and moved out. In the main open area next to the community gardens, Luther, looking a little worse for wear, was pitching in, pulling weeds while other campers around him laughed. Andrew was never sure if Luther was raging against the world and hiding it, or just a complete tool. Reggie glanced through the chain-like fence up at the steep mountains that surrounded Hale. Beautiful postcard scenery, the White River National Forest.

TAC Hale had been set up in less than a month. Highway 24, which ran from Interstate 70 down to Leadville, had been a main thoroughfare, but to increase security around the camp, it had been "closed for road construction," although supply trucks came through without any difficulty. Traffic was minimal, and only the most diehard hikers made the extra effort to get here without the road access.

Luther was pointing to the slopes just above the tree line. Reggie frowned. "I woulda never made it half that far," he said. "I woulda started to climb those hills and blown my aneurism clip." He rubbed the center of his chest self-consciously.

Andrew gave him the janitorial cart to push as they moved away from the Admin barracks. "Yeah, you certainly don't put yourself in line for anything too stressful, Reggie." He pulled out the clipboard, checked off the Admin barracks, and flipped the page. In the center of the camp, inside another line of chain-link fences—this one topped with coils of razor-wire, with access granted only through a guarded sally port—was the cluster of four maximum-security barracks. "We're on call to do Max tomorrow, not today," he said.

They were allowed inside the second set of fences, but only up to the foyer of the barracks. They weren't allowed any contact with the Evos being held inside. The truly dangerous ones.

"I'll bet they're doin' secret training exercises," Reggie said. "Training to do covert ops for the government!"

Andrew looked at him in surprise. "Is that what you think goes on in there?"

"Those are the powerful ones, you know," Reggie said. "People who can fly or throw fireballs or teleport themselves. Could be they've even got Mohinder Suresh in there working for them."

Andrew groaned. "Come on! Suresh is who caused all this. That explosion in Odessa."

"*If* he really did it," said Reggie.

"You're a conspiracy nut," Andrew said.

"I read Hero_Truther. Some things don't add up."

The fact was, Andrew didn't know what went on in the Max barracks, or who was actually dangerous. All he knew was that before all this, many of their powers had been hidden or undiscovered. The public had had no clue that Evos existed. No one had worried about persecution... And then a cheerleader had thrown herself off a Ferris wheel, the whole world watching as she fell to her death. But she stood back up, healing and emerging without a scratch. Claire Bennet, the name heard round the world. Her and those attempts. Then more and more and more Evos came out... And fear spread, alongside the wonder.

Reggie continued, "They don't want us anywhere near Max barracks on certain days because that's when the real mysterious testing and experiments take place. It's when they teach 'em to be all secret-agency and stuff!"

"Or it could be," Andrew suggested, "that they just don't need janitorial services on Tuesdays and Thursdays."

Reggie grinned. "Think what you like. This is a temporary assessment camp. They's trying to figure out if we have useful abilities so we can become secret operatives, powerful agents... *heroes*!"

"Right," Andrew said, shoving the cart over for Reggie to

push. He didn't disagree—not in the slightest. He believed that Renautas had set up the temporary assessment camp to keep the truly dangerous Evos locked up in places like the Max barracks, but also to test and determine the threat level posed by people like him and Reggie. What he didn't believe was that the camp had been set up for altruistic purposes, to turn them into useful secret agents.

As each day went by in the camp, he felt more sharp, focused, cold, and above all, scared—justifiably so, he believed. He could see which way the wind was blowing.

It was only a matter of time before he and the other inmates were reassigned to Max Security. He remembered the stories his grandfather had told about surviving the concentration camps in Nazi Germany during World War II. Andrew had even gotten his grandad's numbers tattooed on his own wrist when he lost his Papa. The gas chambers would be installed any day now, and the government would "take care" of all the problematic Evos like himself and his comrades here in TAC Hale.

Andrew Meeks' minor cool-down power would be just as useless as Luther's if he wanted to escape.

CHAPTER FOUR

Inside her office in the main Admin building of TAC Hale, Chief of Operations Deborah Ruthers finished setting up the chessboard, turned the black pieces to face her, and adjusted the line of pawns.

Everything was ready.

It just was a distraction while she waited; she was far more interested in the upcoming Webchat conversation. She looked at the clock. Still three minutes early, but she decided to log in, just in case. She turned the large monitor screen toward her and called up the contact icons. She always enjoyed these conversations with Erica Kravid, though they felt as intense as the chess matches she played with Sam. Kravid was ostensibly her boss, but Deborah was sure that the woman was playing a game, using her as a pawn.

Ruthers tapped the green phone button and saw the dark hair, large eyes, and stony expression of Erica Kravid, head of Renautas, when the call connected. Kravid was Ruthers' direct boss, and even though she was busy managing the large corporation, she took a close interest and a direct hand in the running of the temporary assessment camp.

"Doing good is good business" was the motto of Renautas, and Kravid was genuinely interested in Evos of all sorts and all abilities.

"Hello, Deborah," Kravid said.

"Hello, Ms. Kravid."

"You had an escape incident; I read the report this morning." The head of Renautas looked harried. Something was wrong, but Ruthers wasn't sure what.

"It was just Luther," Ruthers said, trying to play it down. "I think it's like a game to him. He's testing to see how good our security is—and in a way, it's good to know our weaknesses. We're shoring them up now."

Kravid pursed her lips and nodded. "Good to know. We can't let any of the dangerous Evos get out."

"They're in Max Security, ma'am, and there's nothing to worry about with Luther. He's not about to bring down civilization by leaving yellow stains on the landscape."

"If that's the full extent of his powers," Kravid said. "Have there been any further results in the testing?"

"None so far, ma'am, but we're diligent. We continue to keep watch and test."

Kravid frowned. "Let me know if anything appears to be threatening or even potentially useful. We need to be sure that these harmless Evos aren't just playing possum. The whole point of allowing them autonomy is compromised if you can't control them."

"Understood, ma'am."

"And I don't want to hear about another escape. If a low-powered Evo can get out, then you're at risk for worse."

"With all due respect, ma'am, these people are here for their protection. I'd rather not have to act like a prison warden."

Kravid's eyes narrowed. "With all due respect, these

people are dangerous. Renautas has invested heavily in their containment, and if we want to see a return on that investment, we must be able to control the threat they represent. Now, are you up to that job or not, Ms. Ruthers?"

Deborah looked down at her desk. She was gripping one of the white pawns so hard her knuckles were turning white. "I'll make sure that security protocols are upgraded right away."

"Good." Erica Kravid's lips twitched. "See that you do."

The screen went blank as the other woman hung up. Ruthers put the pawn back in its spot on the board, then massaged her palm to restore circulation. A slight sound caught her attention, and she looked toward the door of her office. Sam Conlon stood there, waiting for her. A rail-thin, olive-skinned, balding, middle-aged man of indeterminate ethnicity and amazing intelligence. Sam was the smartest of all the campers at TAC Hale.

He was looking at her intently. "I see your runaway pawn is giving you trouble. Are you ready for our match, Director? I can come back later…"

She smiled and gestured to the board. "Already set up for you."

CHAPTER FIVE

Gossamer connections spun across Sam's vision, personal holograms superimposed on reality. Everything fit. Everything connected. The chessboard to the director to him to the files… and that was only the thread he was currently following. The interconnected movements of the world were laid out as a clear pattern for Sam Conlon. He could choose his path on the web of "fate" in a way nobody else could. And the idiots around him thought he was just good at puzzles.

Sam smiled warmly as he settled into the chair and glanced at the waiting chessboard. He knew she looked forward to these games, liked his conversation, and enjoyed keeping her abilities sharp. She liked to think of herself as a friend to the euphemistically named "campers"—as if they were all in this together, a team. Nothing could be further from the truth.

Ruthers seemed happy and cheerful, but Sam could see the lines in the air that connected her to the computer. The warden—that was how he thought of her—was still reeling from the conversation with her boss, and it would make her distracted and careless. Sam would have to play her carefully. Luther's escape attempts were useful for the distractions they provided.

She shook her head and refocused on him. "So far, you've been able to beat me six out of ten games, Sam, but I intend for us to keep at it until we're evenly matched. At least."

"It's always good to have goals, Director," he said, discreetly failing to note that his win record against her was actually seven point three games out of ten. It was pointless, since he could easily beat her ten out of ten games, but he knew that wouldn't go over well. Losing at the right time was just another pattern that bolstered her confidence.

Because she was playing white, she moved the first piece, her standard opening: pawn to king four. Sam did the same, placing his king's pawn opposite hers. She studied the board intently, mapping out moves in her head. Sam kept his gaze on the pieces as well, though he barely devoted five percent of his attention to playing.

He had already seen countless moves ahead, a feat that any average player could accomplish at this stage of the game. What made Sam different was that he saw only one line—the line she would actually play. It was a reflection of the fading patterns left from her call with Kravid. The stress she had endured in that conversation determined the sloppy mid-game she would set up more surely than any knowledge of strategy she possessed.

Ruthers liked to keep tabs on the prisoners, and she claimed that she enjoyed Sam's insightful conversation, although she did most of the talking. He knew that she would be horrified if she ever found out what he actually thought and saw.

"I keep watching," she said, "and the news really concerns me. I know two things—one is that society will be better off with the non-threatening Evos kept apart. And the other thing I know is that Evos like you, Sam, have to be protected from the prejudices of society." Her words were like a background drone. She often repeated these same thoughts in their encounters.

"Some people might question that, Director," he said, "with all the signs going up in cities these days. 'We don't serve Evos.' 'Evos need not apply.' So many of us getting fired from our jobs. What you see as protection, many of us see as a violation of our civil liberties. History shows that the oppressed always rise up."

"It's just a backlash," she said, moving her king-side knight. "People are scared because you're something new, something different. They'll adjust. People are good at heart."

He responded—too quickly—and scolded himself. He'd make sure to pretend to contemplate his next move. "People may be, but I'm not so sure society is as kind as the average person."

"After the disaster in Odessa, people are afraid. You know, and I know, that Evos are just people like anyone else, even if they are 'different'."

"I wish everyone thought like you," Sam said.

While they played, Sam was analyzing the office, examining the connections he saw in the air. There were so many levels of the game he'd have to track if his plan was going to come off. Beneath it all there was a simmering anger that he couldn't let interfere.

Before so many Evos had started to come out, posting videos of themselves and their abilities, Sam had used his skills to become a chess tournament champion, and he could easily have been a grandmaster. But then he realized that it was better to keep a low profile than to show off his freakish talent… That was before the disaster in Odessa changed everything.

Now, as always, he could simply look at the world and see the tapestry, see the web of interconnections as physical colored lines. It was like living his life inside a tapestry, walking around through the tangled skeins of fate.

And he could follow them, like a giant three-dimensional conspiracy diagram. The yarn, strings, and thumbtacks that formed connections between photographs and scribbled notes on the walls of paranoiacs—for Sam Conlon, they were all real. He could see the secret ties that bound people into alliances or feuds. He saw a nexus that resembled the Renautas logo, a sunburst of countless lines extending out to all of the people in the camp, people unable to see the strings that bound them all. But Sam saw them.

He picked up his bishop and moved it to a completely random position. The director's brow furrowed as she tried to understand his strategy. He simply assumed he could adapt to whatever she did next.

"You're playing a good game," he said.

"I'm trying," she muttered as she moved her queen-side knight, trying to keep one step ahead of him.

He slid his queen forward, threatening the knight.

Smiling, Ruthers moved her bishop. "Check," she said.

"You're keeping me on the run," he said.

Everything was changing so fast… He was aware of the growing backlash against Evos, and foresaw even more darkening strands in the future than the director did. On the radio, especially on the programs the guards listened to, he had heard the rantings of the media blowhard Jimmy Rourke as well as several less talented but louder imitators. He caught himself curling his fingers into a fist as he thought about it and carefully relaxed his hand.

Ruthers was still talking about keeping the Evos safe here in the camp. "The only ones who have to worry are the Evos with uncontrolled powers, the ones who mean to cause us harm. I like to think that everyone here in my camp is innocent and innocuous, but there are dangerous Evos as well. You have to admit that." She raised her eyebrows.

Sam nodded slightly. "Of course. But safety is an illusion. There are dangerous Evos only because there are dangerous people. Being Evolved isn't what makes us a danger."

Ruthers frowned, studying the board in silence.

Sam was worried that he had pushed too far. Giving her a win right now would distract her. After her next move, he studied the chessboard. Consulting the lines, he set the wheels in motion for the least obvious way to expose his king to checkmate.

CHAPTER SIX

Inside the small guard breakroom connected to TAC Hale's mess hall and the adjacent community center, Thomas "TQ" Rizzoli lounged back in his chair, confident that he could squeeze another 20 minutes out of his break. After all, what was going to happen? His feet were sore from running around in the mountains chasing after that idiot Luther.

He was going to suggest to Ruthers that they all deserved time-and-a-half; then she would have to make the case to Renautas. It wasn't likely to happen, but there was no harm in asking. For now, Rizzoli would get a little bit of unauthorized bonus time rather than being out there with the Evos.

They had invited him and the other guards to play games during their downtime, but Rizzoli wouldn't be caught dead doing that. Who knew what kinds of powers they had? He was sure they were all just cheaters. No, he preferred to sit here listening to the chatter of the guards as he played Evernow on his tablet. He was getting addicted to it, fast. On the radio in the breakroom Jimmy Rourke was ranting so loudly that Rizzoli imagined he must be spraying saliva all over the microphone.

"If the Evos aren't a threat, then let's take them at their word. Okay, let's forget about Odessa and all the people that died there. Let's forget about people who can fly or travel through time or see through walls. How many times have the liberals wanted us to register all of our handguns? Isn't an Evo with superpowers more dangerous than a handgun? A million times worse, if you ask me. The right kind of Evo can twist the minds of a crowd, turn them into a mob, make them go hysterical. Even the worst mass shooter could only kill a handful of people."

"Damn right," grumbled one of the other guards.

"Oh, shut up, Clint," retorted another one. "If they could twist our minds, the Evos here would make us forget about them and then just walk right out of the camp."

"It's a plot," said Clint. "What if they're biding their time?"

"What if you're full of crap?" The other guards laughed.

"Always a possibility," Rizzoli piped up as he continued to move his character through the amazing fantasy world of Evernow, starting a fight with a pair of animated demon bandits. With a polite knock, Reggie and Andrew came into the room, hauling the janitorial cart.

"Here to pick up the garbage," said Andrew.

Rizzoli absently waved them into the room. The guards were laughing again. "Take the radio with you. Jimmy Rourke is full of as much garbage as anything you'll find here."

"He's got some good points," Clint said defensively.

On the radio, the commentator continued. "As I was saying, we should take them at their word if they say they're harmless and don't intend to hurt us. Okay, then they have to take us at our word. We don't mean them any harm, either, but we need to protect ourselves. It's perfectly reasonable to ask for universal testing and to exercise due caution until they prove they're as harmless as they say. Get 'em registered."

Rizzoli looked up and saw Andrew staring at the radio. He didn't go for the constant ranting bullshit of Rourke, and he had worked here ever since TAC Hale had opened its gates. Sure, he supposed some of the Evos were dangerous, but he loved the German Shepherds in the kennels here, and they could be dangerous, too. They just needed to be handled properly.

"Don't worry about it, guys," he said to Andrew and Reggie. "That's why you're here in the assessment camp. So we can clear you and let you get on with your lives."

"Oh, we're happy enough here," said Reggie. He looked around at the lounging guards. "Can I bum a cigarette?"

"I'll give you a whole pack if you make Clint sneeze." Rizzoli glanced up briefly from Evernow.

Clint grumbled peevishly. Reggie grinned, squinted his left eye, and the guard explosively sneezed. Reggie said, "For a whole pack, I'll make him sneeze twice." All the other guards guffawed.

A female voice called out from the door to the guard room, sending Rizzoli's spine thrumming. "Hi, TQ. I'm on my way to the mess hall, but the weather channel says it's supposed to get really cold tonight. I hope you can keep yourself warm."

All the guards turned, muttering. One whistled. Alexa stood in the doorway, beaming, practically glowing. She was a gorgeous, curvaceous blonde who made Rizzoli's pulse race like a hit of cocaine.

"I… I will," he said, putting his game down and straightening up in his seat. He felt himself flushing. He was having a hard time breathing.

"Of course you will," grumbled Clint. "How else is he going to keep warm?"

"Maybe she has some suggestions," said another guard.

Alexa was beaming at all of them. "I just wanted to say hi. Bye now." She flounced away, and Rizzoli felt his throat go dry.

"Why does she call you TQ? You never explained that," asked the resident skeptic, Antonio. Rizzoli lifted his chin in pride. All the guards knew that Alexa flirted with him and that they sometimes met in private. "It stands for Total Quality," he said. "She knows it when she gets it… and she's certainly getting some." He laughed low in his throat.

Andrew and Reggie were both fidgeting uncomfortably as Jimmy Rourke got even more outrageous on the radio. Rizzoli barely moved as Andrew yanked the wastebasket out from under his desk. Clint offered a pack of cigarettes to Reggie to make another guard sneeze, and Reggie did his trick again, much to Clint's amusement.

Rizzoli caught Andrew's eye and nodded toward the radio. "That's the way it is outside. You should be glad you're in here."

"I'm happy as can be," Andrew said, his voice oddly flat.

CHAPTER SEVEN

In the mess hall for the evening meal, Andrew was given his tray of delicious gourmet fare—soupy tuna noodles with a side of canned green beans—but by now he knew not to get his hopes up. Back in Denver he'd eaten a lot of prepackaged dinners and fast food, but he knew what a good meal was and sometimes he liked to cook, even if it was just for himself. This was… nutrients, not food.

Reggie was off glad-handing some of the camp personnel, everybody's friend, and Andrew wanted to spend time with some of the other campers. He saw Sam Conlon sitting by himself. The man wasn't antisocial so much as preoccupied. Sam stared off into space as if seeing things no one else was aware of. There was an invisible "do not disturb" sign up around him.

Andrew chose to sit next to Dorian Avey, a bony young man whose once well-trimmed Afro was now growing in all directions because he refused to cut it until he got out of the camp. Dorian's uninviting food sat in front of him, barely touched, as he played with a paper clip—standing it upright, balancing it on the tip of one finger as he spun it around.

"Hey, Dorian," Andrew said, taking a seat next to the man.

"Andrew." Dorian stared at the paper clip and concentrated. The metal wire glowed red hot and *melted*, turning into a little puddle of metal on the mess hall table and leaving a burn mark.

"Look at that," Dorian said sarcastically. "Terrifying!" He blew on the melted metal, which hardened quickly, and then he brushed the little lump away. He slid his tray over to cover the scorch mark on the tabletop.

"I can spontaneously melt *two whole grams* of metal at a time, and only within two feet." He rolled his eyes. "I'm such a menace to civilization."

"I think they just don't know what to do with us," said Laina, sounding nervous and uncertain, "so they're overreacting."

Andrew blinked. The drab young woman with mouse-brown hair was sitting right across from them. Andrew hadn't seen her sit down, hadn't noticed her at all. Laina liked to hang out with them. Enigmatic was the word that sprang to mind; Andrew found he had to concentrate just to remember her, to see her there. It was the oddest thing.

"When things start to get really bad," Andrew said, "I doubt anyone will notice you."

"I hope not," Laina said and picked at her tuna noodles. She was skittish and shy and often seemed embarrassed when Andrew made an effort to pay attention to her. Laina didn't talk much, but she seemed to like the company.

"There you are," said Alexa, carrying her tray over. "I didn't see you."

"You know I usually eat with these guys," Laina said.

Right now, even though Alexa had her hair tied back, wore no makeup, and was dressed in a shapeless sweatshirt and sweatpants—seemingly trying to look as nondescript as possible—she still exuded animal magnetism. Andrew tried to give up his seat to her, but she waved him away.

"I'm just fine here next to Laina. Don't give me any special treatment."

Embarrassed, he sat down.

Alexa frowned at the cafeteria food. "Look at all those carbs. And I bet there's nothing natural here. How am I supposed to keep my figure when this is the kind of food they provide?"

"Keeping your figure never seems to be a problem for you," Dorian said, dropping a metal spoon into his ceramic coffee cup. He touched the spoon and concentrated again, and it heated up just enough to warm his coffee.

Alexa looked at Laina's food tray and frowned. "They didn't give you any apple cobbler? But you like apple cobbler."

Laina shrugged. "They missed me when I went through the line."

Alexa got up, looking annoyed. "Well, that doesn't happen when I'm around. I'll take care of you." She went up to one of the guards standing by the dessert line in the cafeteria. Andrew watched her, marveling at what she could do. He didn't understand it, but he knew it had something to do with her powers. She smiled, stepped up close to the guard, and it seemed like a light bulb went on. The guard, glowing with pleasure, couldn't move fast enough to help her. Even the fiftyish woman in the hairnet and dirty apron dishing out food quickly brightened and served up more apple cobbler. Alexa came back with three portions. "Here's an extra one if somebody wants two."

A couple of tables away, Andrew noticed Sam watching her intently.

"I wish I knew how you pulled that off," Dorian said.

She lowered her voice. "Just a little bit of pheromones. The right manipulation here and there, just to give people the warm fuzzies, make them want to keep me happy. They don't even realize they're doing it. I can make them think I'm absolutely gorgeous, and they'll trip over themselves just to get a smile from me."

"You are gorgeous," Andrew blurted out.

"Am I?" she asked. "Am I really, or is that the pheromones talking?" She sighed. "They don't know half of what I can do—and I don't dare show them, because then they really would be scared." She giggled. "It's enough for me to know that I can make any of them stand at attention anytime they're near me."

Andrew glanced at the door and the fence beyond it, unconsciously rubbing at his tattooed wrist.

CHAPTER EIGHT

Deborah Ruthers spent the morning going over the budget and supply paperwork for TAC Hale. And when she finished with that joyous task, she completed the detailed incident report and security analysis for Luther's escape attempt. Sam's words about danger haunted her, so she focused on the tedium of bureaucracy.

Besides, Erica Kravid had demanded it.

If she'd been a different type of person, Ruthers might not even have filed a report in the first place. Luther had been apprehended, no harm done. And other than the hole cut in the chain-link fence, there had been no damage. The guards, despite their grumbling, could use a bit of exercise and response training. In fact, since Luther posed no threat at all, his escape and apprehension could actually be considered an effective drill.

Sighing, she put the pen down and pinched the bridge of her nose. Were she honest with herself, she would admit that Kravid felt more like an enemy than anyone here at the camp. Whatever that woman was up to, Deborah was positive she was being used by her boss. To what end, though? These Evos were harmless.

But Renautas didn't see it that way, so Ruthers picked her pen back up and returned to the paperwork. She knew there wouldn't be any docking of pay or official reprimand, though Erica Kravid would express her "concern" strongly enough that Ruthers would demand her people to be more vigilant, crack down a little.

"Excuse me, Director Ruthers?" The woman's voice was accompanied by a soft knock at her door. "Thanks for seeing me. It's just a quick request." Alexa Konig stood there smiling, her blonde hair loose, her blue eyes sparkling. The campers were allowed regular amenities and personal possessions, but somehow Alexa seemed to have access to all the makeup any woman could ever want. Ruthers squinted. Maybe Alexa wasn't even wearing makeup…

Pushing her chair back, Ruthers looked back at her report on Luther's escape, closed the file, and stood up. "I have lots of paperwork this morning, Miss Konig. I didn't know you had an appointment."

Alexa flashed a smile that belonged in a toothpaste commercial. "Oh, Francis let me in, but don't be too hard on him."

Alexa rarely had an appointment when she came to visit, but somehow the director's moat dragon always found a way to let her in. Deborah didn't like that.

"What is it today?" Ruthers opened a file drawer and put the report of Luther's most recent escape next to the printed copies of the previous two incident reports. The man was persistent but completely inept. His attempts weren't getting any better.

"It's not for me," Alexa said. "It's for my friend, Laina."

"Laina? I'm sorry, I don't recall a camper named Liana. I was sure that I knew everyone by first…" Her brows furrowed as her voice trailed off.

"Laina Jacobsen," Alexa said. The corner of her mouth twitched.

Ruthers sat back at her desk and called up the personnel roster on her screen.

"She and I share a room," Alexa prompted her.

"Ah, there she is. Sorry, I didn't recall her. How odd. What do you need?"

"It's what she needs," Alexa said. "Her mattress is falling apart. She doesn't complain, but I know that her back hurts every day now. If you could upgrade her, get her a new bed…"

Ruthers frowned. "Try as I might to take care of all of you, this isn't a bed-and-breakfast, Miss Konig."

"But you do keep insisting this isn't a prison camp, and a fairly minor change would be a big help. I'd really appreciate it." Alexa came closer to the desk, and Deborah's throat went dry.

She felt flushed. The young camper was an extremely beautiful woman with perfect skin. And how did she make her hair so lush, as if she'd just come out of a salon? Ruthers was startled at her reaction. She'd never been attracted to a woman before. Shaking her head, she scooted her chair back.

"I don't have the budget for that," she said, resisting the easy way out. But Alexa was persistent.

"The guard bunkhouses have much better mattresses. It wouldn't cost you anything, and if we're all part of a team, shouldn't we all have the same amenities? Laina would be so thankful. She'd come here personally to express her gratitude. Wouldn't you like that?"

Ruthers tried to resist but realized that there was no good reason not to. "I suppose if I keep the campers happy, then we'll all be happy." She called up a requisition form on her screen and submitted the order. Ruthers realized that she felt uncomfortable, wanted Alexa to leave… but also wanted her to stay. She frowned. "Now, if there isn't anything else…?"

Alexa opened her mouth to reply but was interrupted as alarms went off throughout the camp.

A buzzing sound on the intercom vied for Ruthers' attention. "We're done here, Miss Konig. Please get somewhere safe. *Now.*"

Her phone rang and she grabbed it. "What is it?" she shouted over the ear-splitting alarms.

A shaky voice answered, "There's a fire in Max Security. One of the Category-V Evos is awake and loose—the Firestarter. He found something combustible."

"How did he wake up?" Ruthers shouted.

"We'll figure that out later, ma'am. We've got a fire to put out… and an Evo to control."

"Tranq darts immediately," she said. "Everyone needs to be armed. Call the volunteer fire crews in." She was already bolting for the door, ignoring the frozen Alexa. She had to get everyone to the high-security barracks immediately.

What had started out as a dull day of paperwork was rapidly becoming a worst-case scenario.

CHAPTER NINE

When the alarms rang Andrew recognized the sound. "That's a fire, Reggie!"

Campers began to scramble in confusion. "Come on, we need to get to the muster point." He grabbed Reggie's arm.

Reggie seemed confused. "A fire? Maybe it's just a drill?" They had both been trained for the fire-suppression team.

In fact, Reggie had volunteered for just about everything possible, and Andrew had seen no harm in it. They earned brownie points with the guards and the Admin staff, and Andrew figured it might improve his chances if the situation at TAC Hale turned sour and Renautas stopped being a benevolent protector.

As they ran out of the barracks—they had been "on break" from their janitorial duties—Andrew saw a flurry of activity and heard shouting. Alarms were still ringing throughout the compound, along with air-raid sirens. Inside the inner set of fences, an inferno had broken out in the maximum-security barracks.

Reggie stared. "Guess it ain't a drill."

Andrew grabbed his arm just as something exploded

and a column of fire and smoke erupted. Debris bounced off the inside of the Max fence.

"Wow," Andrew said.

The sally port was open. Teams rushed in, and Andrew and Reggie knew what they had to do. Reggie rubbed his chest... "I'm not sure. This is somethin' else, Andrew. We should leave it to the guards, don't ya think?"

Andrew shook his head and moved away; Reggie followed, still protesting. Fire extinguishers were being brought in from the other buildings as staff and campers alike desperately fought the flames.

Of those inside the Max perimeter, Andrew, Reggie, and one other camper wore the TAC Hale jumpsuits. They rarely went inside the second fence, but Andrew didn't hesitate. He grabbed an extinguisher while another group quickly rolled out fire hoses, running to hook them to a standpipe near a hydrant in the middle of the compound. The extinguishers just needed to buy 45 seconds so the hoses could be primed.

"That's a big fire," Andrew said. "How the hell did it start?"

More guards were shouting. He recognized many of them from their day-to-day routine. All of them were carrying rifles—tranquilizer guns, he hoped. Others carried sidearms, the straps on their holsters unfastened. It seemed an odd thing to bring to a firefight. Unless...

"Maybe one of the training sessions for the Max Evos went wrong," Reggie said. "Do you suppose they've got a firestarter in there?"

"I know they've got a fire," Andrew said. He unclipped the nozzle of the fire extinguisher and ran toward the flames on the side of the building, blasting white gouts of vapor at the blaze near the main entrance. One wall of the secure barracks *exploded* outward. Flames, splintered support beams, and siding flew out in an eruption that made the firefighting guards scatter.

Andrew grimaced as the heat hit him and reflexively triggered his ability. The temperature only dropped from "burn-you-alive" to "sweat-lodge" heat, but it was enough. Four of the guards took up positions near him, unshouldering their rifles and crouching down, aiming at the fire as Andrew sprayed it with foam.

"What the hell?"

A figure emerged, sheathed in a halo of red and orange. A man—clad only in tattered, blackened strips of what remained of a TAC Hale jumpsuit. His skin was red and glowing, and the air around him shimmered. He held a crackling ball of fire in his hand. In that moment, as this demon stepped out of the maelstrom, wielding death in his bare palms, Andrew understood what an Evo with true power looked like.

"Open fire. Use your tranqs," screamed one of the guards.

A volley of feathered darts flew out—and vaporized on impact. The curls of feathers turned into puffs of flame. The maddened Evo stepped away from the debris of the collapsed wall. He hurled his fireball and the armed guards scattered, desperately reloading as they moved. The Evo sparked a second crackling ball in his other hand. Camp personnel raced toward him with their fire extinguishers blasting away.

Andrew was still gripping his extinguisher but couldn't force his knees to unlock. Steam geysered and the escapee flinched from the clouds of cold vapor. He threw the fire in his left hand at one of the firefighting volunteers, engulfing the man in flames. He barely had a moment to scream before the fire extinguisher in his hands exploded, shredding him into gobbets of flesh that sprayed in all directions. The escaping prisoner seemed disoriented and enraged, a true monster. Something had triggered him to unleash this extreme violence. Andrew finally unfroze and grabbed Reggie, hauling him back before they were incinerated.

"Still think they're training secret agents in there, Reggie? Covert operatives?" Andrew gasped, ducking for cover.

The flames were spreading in the maximum-security barracks. One of the guards managed to take a shot, striking the Evo with another tranq dart that vaporized just as the others had. Finally the firehoses arrived. Three people carrying heavy nozzles that came alive like water-spitting pythons. They blasted the man, spinning him around, and he screamed as the cold water hit his ember-hot flesh. The water jets pummeled him, but the moisture immediately flashed into steam.

He rose, screaming in a basso roar of challenge as he tried to dodge the jets, but they drove him back, pouring more and more water on him. Clouds of steam thickened. Andrew could barely see, but he knew the fire was still crackling and spreading across the blasted walls of the security barracks.

"I don't think that guy's been trained very well," Reggie said.

Under the bombardment of high-pressure water, the Evo's glow finally faded. His power surge was washed away, leaving him hunched over, drenched and bedraggled, surrounded by a dense fog bank of hot steam. He sobbed. Most of his clothes were gone, and he was shivering.

Loud gunshots rang out. Rizzoli had pulled out his

sidearm and fired four times, each one hitting the shivering prisoner center mass. The man jerked and thrashed. Two other guards, equally keyed up, also opened fire. They mowed down the Evo with a dozen shots that pocked his pale, wet body.

Reggie stared in abject horror.

Andrew fought down vomit.

Another guard, Clint, yelled, "Don't just stare. The barracks are still burning." Somebody shoved Andrew's shoulders and he staggered ahead, aiming his fire extinguisher and blasting at the smoldering walls where the escapee had blown his way out. Rizzoli stood over the bloodied, mangled body of the Evo.

"I don't know how he woke up, but he was dangerous. Someone get medical here *now*! We have a man down." As Andrew fought the fire and worked his way inside the barracks building, he found halls filled with steam and smoke. With the vapors swirling around him, he caught his first glimpse of the interior of the maximum-security barracks. Chambers with metal doorknobs melted away were evenly spaced on either side of the hallway. The closest door was in splinters, no doubt kicked open by the escaping firestarter. Spraying his fire extinguisher stream from side to side, Andrew moved forward. The chambers contained people in flimsy hospital gowns, all of them supine on hospital beds, connected to tubes and monitors. *This* was the fate of the other Evos? High-powered prisoners kept in medically induced comas? Held here, asleep, where they wouldn't cause trouble. *Couldn't* cause trouble. One of them, though, had somehow awakened, then broken out…

He stared, took a step toward the next room when a guard yelled, "Hey you! That's a restricted area. No prisoners inside."

"I'm part of the fire crew," Andrew quickly said. His heart started pounding. He was suddenly worried that now that he had discovered this dark secret, they would sedate him and lock him away—even though his powers were trivial.

"We've got it handled. Work on the outside or get back to your living quarters. TAC Hale is on lockdown right now."

"Yes, sir," Andrew ran back out of the Max barracks.

Outside, the steam was finally dissipating and the smoke had died down. Andrew passed the bloody, mangled body of the dead firestarter sprawled on the ground in front of the barracks.

Rizzoli stared down at it. His pistol shook in his hands.

"He was dangerous. The tranq darts didn't work... There was no choice."

His words seemed hollow to Andrew.

CHAPTER TEN

Even with the emergency crackdown and curfew at TAC Hale, Laina was more comfortable than she had been since her first day at the camp. She was still uneasy, uncertain of her future, and she knew that the guards, the staff, and the campers inside the large fenced-in compound were all frightened and on edge. But Laina wasn't thinking about that at the moment.

Night shrouded the women's barracks, a comfortable darkness for Laina, and she snuggled into the sheets on her new mattress. It was both soft and firm, and stretching out to rest—finally—was no longer painful. The guards had brought it in late that afternoon, just before dinner in the mess hall.

They had to look up the paperwork to find her quarters, checking her name against the roster. She wasn't surprised none of them remembered her. That had always been her form of self-protection, especially in recent times as the world grew darker and people began to seek out individuals like her. She knew Alexa had pulled strings for her, and as she lay back after saying goodnight to her friend (who slept on the other side of the small room), Laina decided just to enjoy the peace for a moment, to let herself relax.

She pulled the blankets up to her chin, warm and cozy against the chill, and stared at the ceiling. She wondered what they would do when full winter set in and plunged TAC Hale in feet of snow. Laina decided not to worry about that now. She just wanted to be invisible, to be quiet and have peace…

There's always a person in school, in meetings, or at parties who somehow never got noticed. Early in life, Laina had discovered she was that person; she didn't try to call attention to herself, but she also didn't actively hide. When others scanned a crowd or looked at the faces of people in a room, they somehow skated right over her, only occasionally turning back for a second look.

She had seen a Woody Allen movie in high school, *Zelig*, about a man who seemed to be everywhere but noticed by no one. That was exactly it! Laina had laughed so loudly that others in the theater actually noticed her. That was her life, up on the screen.

She'd thought it was just her lot in life, but it wasn't until her mid-teens that Laina realized her power was something more than that. When her abusive stepfather, who somehow *did* manage to see her, began to prey on her, stroking her arm, pinching her, hugging her. Her mother didn't notice, but Laina felt the sickening intensity of his attention increasing until one night her stepfather slipped into her darkened bedroom. Laina had wanted to throw up.

Helpless, with nowhere to run, Laina had huddled under her sheets, focused on going into another world, muttering a mantra to herself, "Don't see me, don't see me, don't see me."

Her stepfather stood there, confused. He studied the room for a while, turning one way then the other, and finally he wandered off. Once she realized what she could do, she chose to deflect people's attention—especially her stepfather's—more and more frequently. She moved out on her own as soon as she could, which turned out to be easier than she thought it would be. Rent was no problem when the landlord constantly forgot that there was anyone living in the apartment.

She had lived under the radar for several years—until the Evo summit meeting and the massive terrorist explosion in Odessa, Texas, had rocked the world.

Laina still had to interact with society on occasion, and eventually she was caught unawares at a testing checkpoint. Once marked as an Evo, she found herself on a list, and ultimately she was rounded up by bureaucrats who focused only on names and numbers and didn't notice anyone in particular. That was the day she discovered the limit of her power. She had tried to avoid being caught. Imagined herself as a modern-day Anne Frank, hiding in plain sight...

But the power to go unnoticed among her fellow citizens turned out to be useless on bureaucrats who didn't see Evos as humans.

CHAPTER ELEVEN

No matter how much she tried to reassure the campers and staff, Director Ruthers knew it was going to take more than a day or two for everything to get back to normal. She felt harried and desperate. The investigation continued inside Max Security to determine how the incapacitated Evo had woken up and broken free. She was appalled at the fire in the barracks, but even more so at how the firestarter had been gunned down.

She had ordered tranquilizer darts only—but had seen with her own eyes that the darts were completely ineffective. Rizzoli and the other guards had disobeyed orders, but they had brought down a threat with the only force that would actually work. Even now, with a day's contemplation behind her, she had no idea what she might have suggested differently. It felt like the Evos were forcing her to treat Hale more like a prison with each passing day.

In a way, she was more upset that the destructive Evo had been shot out in the open, in plain sight of so many campers. But they'd also seen the man ruthlessly murder one of the staff firefighters. Yes, the guards' actions had been justified, but now she was forced to increase security for the Max barracks while repairs were being made. The campers were placed under heavy restrictions. Many of their freedoms had to be taken away, at least until things calmed down. *If* things calmed down…

She opened up a Webchat application on her screen, knowing she had to contact Erica Kravid. She would report all the facts. Be contrite, but offer no excuses. But before she could click on the icon for Renautas and Kravid, the insistent Webchat contacts tone announced that another high-priority call was incoming. Erica Kravid—as if the hard-faced businesswoman had the power of precognition herself.

As soon as Ruthers' face appeared in the split-screen video, Kravid narrowed her eyes. Her expression was drawn, and she was clearly upset. "What the hell happened there, Deborah? You assured me the camp was under control. It obviously isn't."

"We've had a very difficult 24 hours, Ms. Kravid," Ruthers said. "I can assure you that I've restored calm."

Kravid looked deeply skeptical. "You'll excuse me if I don't take your word for it. I want a full report. Your preliminary notes are sketchy, and your staff can't seem to agree on what happened. But that firestarter outburst—which I believe your guards handled appropriately, by the way— wasn't the only Class-A screw-up for Renautas today."

Ruthers was shocked to hear that. "My incident only involved one maximum-security Evo escapee. I think something went wrong with the medical monitoring apparatus, and the drugs may have caused brain damage or some kind of delusional hallucinations. We've double-checked the monitors, and I can assure you that all of the remaining high-powered subjects are secure and incapacitated."

"Good," Kravid said. "But we're beginning to think that

Evos of any power level cannot be controlled. Even..."
Kravid glanced away from the screen briefly. "Luther is a
problem for you."

Ruthers heard an ominous tone in the woman's voice
and knew not to ask further. She felt even more uneasy.
"I understand, ma'am. I have Hale as secure as it can be
right now."

"Of course. Now, I've got plenty of work to do. Please
send me your full report—and I mean a *full* report—as
soon as possible. Maybe we'll learn some lessons we
can apply to detect other potential situations before they
get out of hand. In the meantime, I need to consider the
possibility that we may have to put all your prisoners under
for now." Kravid signed off, and Ruthers turned away from
her computer screen to face the door to her office. She was
startled to see a thin, mousey-looking, brown-haired young
woman standing there.

"Who the hell are you?" Ruthers said.

"Laina, ma'am. Laina Jacobsen. You delivered a brand
new mattress for me yesterday, and I just came to say thank
you."

Ruthers yelled, "Who told you to let her through?"

Her assistant scrambled to the door of her office, looking
harried. "I'm sorry, Director, I didn't see her." He took
Laina's shoulder and started to usher her away.

"I just wanted to say thank you," Laina said quietly as
she was whisked out of the Admin building. Ruthers looked
after her and felt a deep chill. She wondered just how much
that young woman had overheard.

CHAPTER TWELVE

Although they noticed more guards on duty in the mess hall, the campers were allowed to eat at their usual time. Andrew didn't feel much like socializing, but he spotted Dorian sitting at their usual table with a double helping of food he had somehow wrangled.

Meh, why not? He walked over and sat down.

When Andrew looked pointedly at the creamed beef piled high over a mound of mashed potatoes, Dorian shrugged and said, "A precautionary measure. Got to keep my strength up. Who knows? They might crack down and put us all in solitary with nothing more than bread and water." He scooped up a forkful of the food. "Though flavor-wise it might be an improvement."

"Look. All that stuff you talk about, how it's only a matter of time for us... I don't think it's your imagination, Dorian," Andrew said. "After the fire and that guy getting shot... I saw things. TAC Hale isn't just a camp to protect us."

"Never thought it was." Dorian shrugged and shoveled another forkful of food into his mouth.

Alexa sat down next to them. She was out of breath and wore an urgent expression on her face. Laina tagged along beside her, quiet and shy as always. Somehow Alexa didn't seem as pretty today. Her baggy sweatshirt, loose hair, and washed-out face made her seem almost normal.

"Laina overheard something in the director's office you all need to know."

Andrew and Dorian turned their attention to Laina.

In a quivering voice, the wallflower described the Webchat session on which she had discretely eavesdropped. "And they're… they're… talking about locking us all up in Max," she concluded.

Andrew swallowed hard and fiddled with his fork. He glanced at the table on the other side of the room where Sam Conlon sat by himself, as usual. He seemed to be examining several blades of grass he had plucked from the yard. Staring at them, shifting them in his fingers. Then he looked down at his food tray, rearranging his knife and fork, staring at them, then glanced over at the wall, at the guards. His gaze flitted over to the table where Andrew, Dorian, Alexa, and Laina were sitting. A slight smile twitched at the corner of his mouth. Then his eyes slid past them and moved onward.

Andrew lowered his voice and leaned closer to his companions. "Reggie and I were helping to put out the fire yesterday. We were in lockdown and I was in shock so I couldn't tell you, but we saw things… saw things we weren't supposed to."

Dorian's eyes went wide. "You saw the fire dude get shot? You were right there, weren't you!"

"A lot of people saw that," Andrew said. "No, it was even crazier. I got inside. The fire was everywhere. When the Evo was trying to escape, he blasted a hole right through the Max wall. I went in with my fire extinguisher. Doing my duty, you know. But inside were a bunch of rooms, and people in comas, linked up to medical stuff. Like hospital machines. Somehow the one guy woke up and broke out, but there are others there, and a ton of them." He shook his head. "Reggie thought the advanced Evos were being trained for secret missions, and while I always argued that it was a prison. But that—that's way worse."

Dorian snorted. "Of course Reggie thought it was all going to be okay. He's an idiot."

Alexa said, "It's only a matter of time before they make this whole camp maximum security. What are we going to do about it? I don't want to end up… just…" Alexa turned her head away.

"Look, they killed one guy already. What if they do the same to us because we're too much trouble?" Dorian said. "We have to escape."

"It's been tried before," Alexa said as she wiped at her eyes.

They all looked over at Luther, reminded of his serial failures. Luther and Reggie were horsing around by the guards, making them laugh as if neither of them had a care in the world. Luther made a big, bright, yellow splash on the painted cinderblock wall. Reggie reached out to touch it gingerly—as if afraid it would smear wet paint on his hand—but nothing happened. Luther then clamped his hand on Reggie's shoulder, turning his sleeve a bright yellow all the way down to his elbow. Reggie squinted with his left eye and made Luther sneeze. A cloud of yellow vapor exploded out of his mouth and nose. The guards guffawed.

"Luther's an idiot, too," Dorian said. "All right, deciding to escape is one thing, but how are we going to get out of here?"

Andrew said, "We need to make a plan."

Dorian said, "Luther never made a plan."

Andrew nodded. "That's why he always fails. We need to know how we're getting out, and what we'll do once we've succeeded. There are rumors… Canada. The free zone for Evos. A safe enclave in Saskatchewan, I think."

"Well, that narrows it down," Dorian said with biting sarcasm. "Saskatchewan's not *that* big of a province, is it? Of course, we'll need to get to Canada first and over the border."

"There's an underground railroad that leaves out of L.A.," Alexa said. "That might be a better bet."

"First we have to get out of this camp," Andrew said.

"Leave that to me." They were all surprised to see Sam Conlon standing right by them with an intense look on his face. He had never spoken to them before, other than the normal pleasantries. "I could just about tolerate our imprisonment when it was safer in here than out there, and Luther was keeping them," he gestured toward the guards at the gate, "occupied with his bumbling antics. The pattern is changing, though. I've been watching it over the past two days. Strands of possibilities coming together, tangling up… being severed. Forever. We have to move before it's too late. Before more people die."

CHAPTER THIRTEEN

Bright sunlight shone through the windows of the Admin building. Even now, two days later, the smell of smoke permeated everything. Fractured, jagged lines of probability spun around Sam. It was difficult to contain himself, to not just rage against the world. So many endings, and so few ways for Evos to survive. But the surest way to die was by losing his head and not playing the game. So he choked down the rage and fear, instead smiling warmly at Deborah Ruthers.

The director, sitting in front of the chessboard with a nervous smile, pretending that everything was fine and getting back to normal, was oblivious to all the tangles. She thought Sam was either oblivious or gullible. He was neither—but he could pretend.

"Thank you for meeting with me again, Director," he said. "I know you've been through a great deal of stress the past few days."

"We'll get through it," she said, "though it may be difficult, even unpleasant for some of the campers. Their safety—and the safety of my staff—is of the utmost importance. And so I've had to announce a series of temporary protective measures."

"Protective measures? You mean like a crackdown? If you start treating people like prisoners, they'll start acting like prisoners..." Sam let the sentence trail off. He was baiting her with the word *prisoners*, using it as a litmus test to see where she stood.

"Yes, there will be some campers who assume the worst," Ruthers said. "But after the recent incident, I think it's wise to exercise caution. We don't know the extent of the powers people here have, Sam. Maybe some of them are hiding abilities. They could be dangerous, like that firestarter. First and foremost, safety for everyone *must* be my byword."

Sam moved a rook out of the way of a potential knight fork, and Ruthers studied the board. "What sort of crackdown are you talking about, then?"

"Please don't use that word, Sam. It's just going to create ill-will between the campers and guards if you do."

Sam nodded. "You're right, of course. So then, what type of *protective measures* are you thinking of?"

She slid a pawn forward. "I think we should just call them "safety measures," temporarily at least. I'm going to limit the number of television channels the campers can watch. They'll still have the weather channel and sports, the entertainment programs from the major networks. Everyone's already on edge. I don't need to rile them up or provoke them by flashing people like Jimmy Rourke in front of them."

"So will you censor the guards' TVs to prevent them from listening to Jimmy Rourke, too? He's about as inflammatory as they come, and they talk about him in front of us all the time."

"That's a good idea, Sam."

Sam fought for control of his voice as he spoke the next words. "You've always been reasonable, Director. Even when plenty of people in the outside world are not."

She moved her queen's bishop into an obvious pin. Sam spotted the error but didn't take advantage of it. He pretended to study the board. Ruthers was leaving a lot out of the conversation. Increased guard rotations, live ammo, active k-9 patrols instead of kenneling. Erica Kravid was no doubt imposing these strict measures through Ruthers.

"With the new crack... safety measures, sorry, I hope we'll still be able to play chess," he said. "I enjoy the games we play." He moved a pawn, leaving his knight hanging, sacrificing it intentionally. Sam found his visits to the director's office very useful, and he needed to protect them for the time being. His eyes drifted to the filing cabinet.

"Of course," Ruthers said. "I'd like to maintain contact with the campers. Try to keep spirits up, you know?"

"I'm not a typical camper." Sam knew exactly what she was asking of him. "I tend to be a loner. I can try to reach out and spend more time with other people, I suppose."

"Yes, I've seen that you stick to yourself. I've watched you in the mess hall and in the volunteer details. I appreciate the offer, Sam. I think you should go ahead and try to be more social. You can listen for me. You may hear rumors."

"Do you want me to become a spy, then?" he managed a tone that flat-out said, *You're asking me to spy for you*.

Ruthers frowned, "No, not at all. Being a spy implies that there's an enemy. I want this camp to function smoothly for *everyone* here. All I'm asking you to do is help me with that."

Sam knew that these new "safety measures" would make any escape attempt more challenging. Keeping Ruthers in his pocket would give them an edge. "Of course.

Our matches have helped keep me sane, and I, for one, am grateful to you for it. I'll help you as best I can."

"Thank you, Sam."

He nodded and returned to the game. They kept playing for a while, but he could tell her head was elsewhere. She hadn't even noticed his hanging knight.

He smiled. "Do I need to let you focus on work? You seem out of it."

"I guess I'm just distracted today, preoccupied with everything that's been going on here. Sorry. I feel like I'm getting attacked from all sides these days. Call this one a draw?"

Sam stood to go, not arguing with her. "We are no threat to you, Director," he lied. "But I'll keep an ear out for you."

She didn't respond.

CHAPTER FOURTEEN

Alexa had her marching orders, and she intended to do her part to realize the escape plan. Sam Conlon stepping forward with a plan had been a surprise. Everyone knew he played chess with Ruthers, and he was easily the smartest person here, so his intercession had been a blessing. Especially once he revealed that his skill at chess was tied into his power, though he still refused to reveal exactly what it was he could do. It was just—he had always been a quiet person, someone who hadn't talked much with them. He was older, and his libido must be waning because he demonstrated no attraction for her whatsoever, which was hard to wrap her head around.

But Alexa hadn't tried to turn on the pheromones. It was nice to have someone who treated her as an ordinary person for a change. He acknowledged her ability, although she had explained it only briefly. She understood that he was a master problem-solver, someone who could put all the pieces of an intricately complex wheels-within-wheels puzzle together. She and her companions were confident that he could find a way for them to escape. Before he could create the plan, though, Sam needed to know everything about all the pieces. He required specifics. He gave her the whereabouts of a list of data.

"Get this for me. I'm sure you know a way."

"What is it?" she asked.

He just gave her a cool smile. "I need to *know* the pieces we have to work with, the resources available." His gaze hardened. "And that means I have to find out exactly what's inside the Max barracks. I've seen the connections in the director's office. This is the name of the file I want, "code numbers." I can figure it out from there. I think most guards will have access to it, but they won't be able to understand it."

Alexa smiled. "Leave it to me."

Unlike her friend Laina, Alexa's problem had always been that she was noticed *too* much. That certainly had its advantages, and she could turn on the charm at will. She could be the prom queen. Everybody liked her, wanted to please her. But that was only her self-defense mechanism. After she had learned how to use her power, she worked very hard to diminish its effect.

Sex appeal, the release of pheromones in the outside world—and even here within the restricted areas of the camp—made her a magnet for wolf whistles and wide-eyed stares. She did her best to wear unattractive clothes, to leave her hair down, sometimes tangled. Nothing that was the least bit attractive… But others saw what they wanted to see. And if people were going to dehumanize her, she was damn well going to use it as a weapon to get an edge.

Alexa tried not to pull strings too often, but she knew how to get exactly what she wanted. Like now. She had flirted with all of the guards, and if she really turned on the charm, she could make them fall all over themselves. They whistled, they smiled at her, they tried to think of things to give her (although there wasn't much by way of luxuries in TAC Hale).

But Thomas Rizzoli, "TQ", was entirely wrapped around her finger. Outside in the camp commons, she walked up to him while he did his rounds. The other guards saw and began to whistle and laugh. She could see a flush spread across Rizzoli's cheeks. No doubt his pulse was racing.

"I need to talk to you, TQ." She stroked his cheek. "You can help me, and no one else can."

He could barely get a word out, so she continued. "I need something."

He stammered. "D—don't you always?"

She smiled seductively, released just a few more intense pheromones. "And don't you always want something from me, TQ? We make a good team." She stroked his arm, making him shiver. "If you play your cards right, we can both be *very* satisfied."

He squirmed.

She amped it up a little more.

A sheen of sweat covered his face, and she knew he was in no position to suspect her request. "I need a file, TQ. It's just a list. Nobody will notice it's gone. And it doesn't really mean anything to me. It's just a favor I owe someone else." He started to ask a question, but she cut him off. "Don't you want to keep me happy?"

"Of course," he said "but you... you're asking for... data from the director's maximum-security files."

"It's just a list," she repeated, cranking the pheromones up again. "And I'm dying of curiosity. Besides, what would I ever be able to do with it? If you want something from me, then I need something from you. Indulge me."

The thing Thomas Rizzoli wanted most in the entire universe was to indulge her. "How about a kiss?" He reached forward but she backed away, holding up a finger. "The anticipation will just make it better. You can have everything you want—once you deliver."

"I'll deliver," he said. "Tonight. I'll set up a time. We can meet in the storage shed."

Once it was dark and she knew Rizzoli was off duty, Alexa headed to the storage shed. She had no idea how difficult it would be for him to obtain the file, but Sam said it would be accessible to the guards, and the escape couldn't succeed without it.

Since Rizzoli was cleared to work inside the Max barracks, she figured he could just copy the file she had requested. She pulled open the door to the storage shed, glad that she had put on a jacket; winter was coming, and the nights were getting frigid. Rizzoli was five minutes early, but she was ready, waiting for him. He was nervous, breathing hard. When he saw her, he yanked a folded sheet of paper out of his uniform pocket before she could even say hello.

"This is the list," he said. "I got you what you wanted." He reached forward, grabbing her shoulder, but she gently pushed his hand away.

"Not until I see it," she said. She took the paper from him, looking down the columns. Twenty numbers— room numbers, she supposed—and a series of letters and numbers, code names. One had been x'ed out. The man who had been gunned down, probably.

It was a list of incomprehensible codes to her, but to Sam it would be a list of the most powerful Evos held incapacitated in Max Security. She folded the paper and slipped it into her pocket, then slid forward into Rizzoli's arms. He kissed her sloppily and she touched his cheek, pushing out as many pheromones as she could. His carotid artery was thrumming against the side of his neck, and his face turned red.

"This will be good," she whispered in his ear. "Very good."

Rizzoli kissed on her cheek and her neck. He was breathing heavily and his voice was hoarse. "It'll be good this time. I'll show you what a real lover is."

"I can't wait," she said. She licked his earlobe, buying time for her pheromones to do their work.

Rizzoli cried out and clutched her, groaning with disappointment. He looked away, staring at the ground.

She smiled. "Oh, no, not again."

The guard's shoulders slumped. "I'm sorry. I thought I could hold it back this time, but you're so damn sexy."

She stroked his face. "Don't worry. One of these days we'll actually make it happen." He was still panting as she disentangled herself and said, "I *might* even give you another chance." She walked over to the door of the storage shed. "See you later, Too Quick."

CHAPTER FIFTEEN

When Sam studied the information that Alexa had delivered, he saw an entirely new set of probabilities, bright colors snaking out and creating dominant patterns that had been nonexistent moments before. She was there, the one he needed.

He smiled and tapped the paper. "Well done."

Alexa seemed quite pleased with herself. Laina was full of questions, but Alexa just tossed her hair. "It was no trouble at all, and I can guarantee that TQ isn't going to be revealing any details."

As Sam pored over the printout, Andrew came up to him. "Why did she work so hard to get that? What do the codes mean?"

Sam paused for a moment, considering whether or not to reveal all the details. He decided to only feed them what they needed to know. Sam pointed to the numbers. "These are the rooms in Max. It looks like they've got 19 extremely powerful Evos in there. It was 20 last week. These code numbers," he traced the column with his finger, "contain different types of information. This is a designator for male or female, this denotes the age. But this…" He indicated the string of randomized letters at the end. "This is a code for the type of demonstrated or suspected abilities the individual possesses. That's the interesting part."

"How do we interpret that code?" Dorian asked.

"That's my job. Deciphering this will be easy enough; it'll just take a little time." He turned to look at Andrew. "You've seen the inside of Max. Give me details about the setup of the rooms, the beds, the monitors. Once I identify the Evos with the right kinds of powers, then we'll move on to step two."

Andrew frowned. "Let's be sure to spend enough time planning what happens after we get outside the fence. Luther's screwed up over and over again because he has no place to go. Highway 24 is closed, blocked off for miles in either direction. The mountains are awfully rugged—I'm worried about whether or not we can actually get anywhere once we get out."

"Obviously," Sam said, "we'll need to make detailed plans. Everyone will have to choose where they'll go. We're much better off if we split up. Staying together will only get us caught."

Alexa said, "If we can just get far enough away, there are plenty of ski resorts, mountain towns, vacation homes, abandoned mines—even the Interstate, if we head far enough north."

"That would require transportation," Laina said.

"Then that should be part of the plan," Sam said. "If we can get transportation, we can go anywhere. You all need to spread out, carry word to other Evos about what's happening here."

Alexa smiled and took Laina's arm. "If we can get to a freeway, *I* can get a car to stop, so long as the windows are rolled down. Guaranteed."

Andrew still looked concerned. "But even once we get over the fences and, make our way from the camp, they'll be hunting us down. After the recent events, Director Ruthers is going to pull out all the stops. She'll never let us get away."

"They'll even set the dogs on us," Laina said.

Dorian flinched, then flipped his paper clip against the wall. "I joke about our abilities sometimes, but if you're going to force us to ally with super-powerful Evos, how do we know they'll listen to us? Why should they follow our plan? Once we free them, they'll just do whatever they want."

"I'm counting on it," Sam said as the pattern sparkled like kaleidoscope crystals in his mind. "We're not going to ally with them, sadly. But we will turn a couple of carefully selected ones loose and let them do their thing. We're just innocuous misfits with no useful powers. We'll have our chance, and we'll carry this fight to the outside world. When we get away, we just have to make sure that catching us is the lowest item on the director's priority list."

Andrew sucked in a breath as he suddenly got it. "The Max Evos are going to create an emergency? You're going to use them as a distraction, aren't you?"

"Exactly," Sam said. "Jimmy Rourke says we're just like weapons. Well, then, it's about time we armed ourselves."

CHAPTER SIXTEEN

The plan, the possibilities, the people. Sam used them all. The misfits, as they called themselves now, worked as usual, followed their daily routines—but they had much more on their minds. Their powers had all been tested and documented by Sam.

Andrew Meek's ability was indeed nothing more than dropping the temperature by ten degrees, though the extent of his influence was hard to measure. Dorian Avey could melt small metal objects, but not at a great distance and not any large quantity. Laina Jacobsen was able to deflect attention. But Sam didn't know how to quantify that. Alexa Konig had reasonably extensive pheromone skills and could manipulate people.

She was the one, besides Sam himself, who was hiding her Evo talents the most. Sam was fully aware that many people would be terrified of an individual with such intense and manipulative sex appeal, and Sam knew that the Renautas Corporation would find her power extremely valuable. Bottling it could create a whole new industry.

Once he had all of their skills cataloged, Sam was able to examine the patterns and direct how they might pool their abilities. He watched the weather station obsessively, studying what was expected in the upcoming days and nights. He had the misfits subtly practice their abilities in pairs. Their powers were all weak, innocuous, and unremarkable—though in his opinion, that was only because their captors hadn't yet figured out how to make them remarkable—but Sam Conlon could work with synergy, combining the small bits so they would wind up greater than the sum of their parts.

And it was going extremely well.

Seventy years ago here at Camp Hale, the 10th Mountain Division had trained in rock-climbing, winter survival, mountain ascents, and cross-country hiking and skiing, as well as trailblazing in the wilderness. The Evo detainees at Temporary Assessment Camp Hale faced nothing so rigorous. But Sam knew he could provoke the misfits into demonstrating how powerful they really could be. He smiled. He intended to demonstrate exactly what supposedly harmless Evos could do.

One order stood above all else: don't disrupt the routine. The guards couldn't be allowed to notice that something was amiss. Sam suggested that Andrew and Dorian work together. Dorian would melt small pieces of metal, while Andrew would drop the temperature to cool them quickly. They practiced making new shapes. Laina and Alexa also combined their abilities. Alexa would make other Evos and camp personnel uncomfortable by spiking their hormones, dousing them with carefully tailored pheromone mixtures she exuded. Then Laina would "wallflower" to deflect attention. Normally a loner, Sam joined the others for nightly meals in the mess hall. The misfits seemed delighted at what they had accomplished.

Andrew said, "I was always worried about hiding my

abilities and ensuring that no one would believe I could do anything with them. Now I can see possibilities. Thanks to you, Sam, I think we might have a chance."

Dorian nodded in agreement but added, "We need to know more about the plan. So far, we've been training up some decent parlor. How are we actually going to get out of the camp? Do we just break through the fences and run away? And how do the Max prisoners fit into the picture?"

"And when is it going to happen?" Laina asked. "We can't just jump the fence after dinner and run for it."

"Luther has proven that for us time and again," Sam agreed. "We'll slip away, but first we have to create the mother of all diversions. Thanks to the list Alexa got me, I've been able to identify the right Evos in Max Security. It'll be up to Andrew, with Dorian's help, to get inside Max, bypass the medical monitors, and awaken them."

"Reggie and I are still working occasional janitorial shifts just outside the Max barracks," Andrew said. "Even with all the reconstruction from the fire, there's no way they'd let us get inside—I guarantee it." He swallowed hard. "And Reggie's not going to help. He believes everything is for the best, that this camp is a resort and we're one big happy family."

"We have to keep this confidential," Dorian said. "We don't want that idiot blabbering."

Andrew seemed sullen. Sam explored all the possibility lines around him and spotted a potential danger.

Andrew said, "I was careful, and I only mentioned it once. He wants to join us here in the mess hall, but he has no idea what we're doing."

Alexa was alarmed. "This is where we have our planning discussions. Don't you dare let him eavesdrop."

"He won't." Andrew shook his head. "I was careful.

Once, only once, when we were cleaning in the outer entry to the Max barracks, I broached the subject. Reggie looked horrified. He thinks that we have everything we need here and that it's dangerous outside. The good news is, I spotted the power leads you were asking about, Sam, and he didn't catch me at it."

"It *is* dangerous out there," Laina said.

"Reggie's convinced that Ruthers is keeping us safe," Andrew continued.

"Then he doesn't suspect anything, right?" Sam asked, although he could easily determine the answer just by looking at the strands of colored lines that intersected all of the campers. He needed the team to reach the right conclusions so that he wouldn't have to reveal the extent of his abilities.

Andrew shook his head. "I don't think so. When we're working, we talk a lot of B.S., and this was just more of the same."

"Good," Sam said. "Keep going, then. Assemble the pieces. You all know what to do."

Laina, managing to remain unnoticed, had slipped into the Admin offices and gotten detailed maps of the vicinity around TAC Hale. The mountains and trails, the Jeep roads, the passes and mining towns. Much of the surrounding countryside was designated a wilderness area. And with Highway 24 closed off, there was very little traffic. Alexa proved herself just as cunning by "requisitioning" all the tools they needed from various guards. Bolt cutters for breaking through the fence. Circuit testers, super-glue. As the two updated the team, Sam smiled and nodded, satisfied.

Dorian was astonished. "How the hell did you do that?"

Alexa smiled. "Just a little sweet-talking. It wasn't too

difficult." She raised her eyebrows and said ironically, "Let's just say I may need to use that 'TQ' nickname for more than one guard."

Sam looked intently at all the misfits. "That's almost all the pieces. I'll brief each of you on your specific part of the plan." He watched the probability lines spreading out. "Soon, we'll be free."

CHAPTER SEVENTEEN

Just as tensions in the camp began to fade, Luther made another escape attempt. This time the response was swift—and harsh. Alarms went off and the guards rushed in. Luther managed to cut the electricity to the outer chain-link fence, but he didn't even make it through the barrier before the dogs were set loose and he was surrounded, then apprehended. He held up his hands in surrender, looking abashed. The guards didn't seem at all amused. They all carried live ammo now. Rifles and handguns. But at least they didn't bother to unholster them for Luther.

The misfits watched the escape attempt from the commons, up past curfew thanks to Sam's manipulation of Ruthers. It had been easy enough to convince her—once she had asked him to spy on the campers' morale—that each of them was an opinion-shaper amongst the other campers. He used that to get a bit of private late-evening commons time.

"He's an idiot," Dorian said. "Now he's got everyone on high alert, and that screws up our plans."

Sam sat staring off into space, preoccupied but intensely focused on the plan. "No," he said. "It just means we have to be more careful. Nothing has changed. If anything, he's done us a favor. Things running too smoothly would be a red flag."

"What the hell does that mean?" Dorian asked.

Sam studied a blade of grass. "It means that Luther has shown them that the new security system functions the way they want it to. It sucks for Luther, but this is for the best. We needed him failing, getting caught. When we make our move, everyone will be just a little complacent. Right where we want them to be."

"You're a cold bastard, Sam Conlon. Is everything just a game for you?" Dorian was upset and was taking it out on everyone.

"Far from it." Sam shook his head. "Nothing's a game. It's everyone else that tries to make it into one, desperately seeking to exert some modicum of control over their environment, over their lives. We're the lucky few. We can change the world. That's why they hate us, don't you see? We're different *because* we don't have to play games."

Dorian clenched his fists and turned his back on Sam to stare out the window. "Just do your job, get us out of here."

Sam looked through the window at the wilted plants in the garden. They had all died in the recent late-autumn hard freeze. "I will. That much I promise you. They can no more stop us than they can stop the winter from coming."

"Yeah, yeah. Whatever, dude."

Andrew stepped between them, although neither man was actually looking at the other. "Sam... I know you have this whole bigger-picture smart-guy thing going, but we're just ordinary people with a sucky genetic fluke. It feels a lot like you're talking down to us right now."

Sam looked at Andrew. The pattern that resulted in their escape was not as bright as it had been. He focused on the moment. "I'm sorry. I see the world differently. Look, I'm angry that we're being used, too. That we're being kept like cattle in this slaughterhouse. I know I come off as cold, but you guys... You're all something special. I get frustrated that you don't see it for yourselves, and I'm not that good with people—which is why I usually just keep to myself. I didn't mean to upset you."

Dorian turned back around. "It's cool. Sorry I got pissy, too."

"I feel like we're all walking on eggshells around here," Alexa said.

"Renautas is watching very closely," Sam said. "So it's only natural that we're all tense." He sniffed the air once more, sensed the moisture and humidity. According to the meteorologists on TV, the weather was due to change, and he saw the patterns in the bent blades of grass. The timing wasn't optimal, but with the way the group was fracturing, the escape would have to be sooner rather than later. He made his decision.

"Andrew and Dorian, you need to be ready. The escape will have to be tomorrow night."

"Why tomorrow?" Alexa asked. "Is something going to happen?"

Andrew paled. "I don't know that we'll be able to get into Max Security then."

"You will," Sam said.

Alexa pressed, "What's happening tomorrow night?"

"We escape, Alexa." Sam looked at Andrew. "That's when we'll need you the most."

"Me?" he asked, stunned.

"Yes. Ten degrees... That's the key. Everything will hinge on you," he said.

Sam looked at the misfits hunched around the table in

the commons. They would have to push the limits of their abilities to make this work. And once they succeeded in escaping, once they were long gone, everyone would see that they weren't so innocuous after all. Working together, they could change the world. At least, they could change it for Sam Conlon.

CHAPTER EIGHTEEN

By the next evening, all the misfits knew their parts. Sam had precisely communicated the components of the breakout and their tightly time-constrained responsibilities.

He had seen in their faces and actions that they had always considered themselves worthless. Their powers were of no consequence. Their lives had led nowhere, or rather, to a prison euphemistically called a protective camp.

But they had learned otherwise now. They had an air of confidence and determination. Security was tighter around the camp, and they had less freedom of movement. Sam knew that if they had made their escape attempt several weeks ago, it would have been a breeze, except that the team wouldn't have been ready. And Sam wouldn't have had everything he needed.

Now they would just have to try harder. It wouldn't be easy. Probability gave them about a 60% chance. *If* they followed his plan exactly, it would be 100%. But... there were so many ways a single misstep could ruin everything.

After dark, as the drop in temperature made the damp air feel even more cold and miserable, he sent them each of them out to their assigned locations. Then he headed to the large janitorial storage shed where the camp's stockpiles of cleaning chemicals and equipment were kept.

Andrew Meek had left it open for him as requested. That was the easy part. Andrew and Dorian would have a much greater challenge ahead of them. Sam began counting under his breath. "Time to start."

Inside the poorly lit janitorial shed, he quickly pulled jugs down from the shelves, studying the labels, separating them into groups while he recalled some basic chemistry. He looked up, and even in the bright lights of the camp's security poles, he could see all the colored lines spreading outward. He started unscrewing the tops of chemical bottles and thought of his other team members while counting under his breath. Chess pieces in his own unique game. Cue Alexa.

It was no coincidence that his favorite opening was the Danish Gambit.

Alexa stood at the entrance to the fenced-in kennels where the dozen German Shepherds were housed. The dogs were content, but even happy dogs bark and yip. They had seen her approaching and stood up, shaking themselves. She'd always liked dogs, especially big dogs, but these German Shepherds weren't pets. Their handler, a Hispanic man named Antonio, came out of his small office next to the open-air kennel. The office was a converted industrial container, and several space heaters blasted out warmth as he emerged. He pulled a padlock from his pocket and locked the office behind him. Glancing over at Alexa, he shook his head, then pulled a pack of cigarettes from his pocket.

After Luther's attempted escape the previous night, Antonio was ordered to stay with his dogs even in the dead of night so they could be ready on a moment's notice. Upon seeing their handler, the dogs started barking and whining, expecting to be fed. The rest of the camp was used to the barking, and nobody would notice.

"Shouldn't you be back in the living quarters?" Antonio asked. He pulled out one of the smokes and lit it.

"Why would I stay there when I could come and see you, Antonio?" She had worked her charm on him before, flirting with him, building up his desire for when she would need it—tonight.

"I'm sorry about the other night," she said. "But I'm glad you were so excited."

"That doesn't usually happen to me," Antonio said. "If you'd like to try again…" He took a drag of his cigarette and exhaled a thick cloud of smoke, glancing meaningfully back at his little shack.

"I'd definitely like to try again," Alexa said, trying not to scrunch her nose at the smell, and stroked his cheek. He was sweating.

She pointed at his shack. "We'll have plenty of privacy in there."

Antonio couldn't agree fast enough. He ground out his cigarette, shakily opened the padlock that held the metal door shut, and swung it open. Warmth and light spilled out.

"After you, lover boy."

Antonio entered the transportainer that was his home. He was so eager to find them a makeshift bed that he didn't notice Alexa pulling a rock from her pocket. With a quick swing, she clocked him across the back of the head and he crumpled. She swung the metal door shut. Even if he woke up sooner rather than later, the padlock would hold him for some time. Eventually some other guard would hear him yelling and pounding on the door, but by then the misfits would have escaped.

Alexa hurried over to the kennel cages, and the dogs started barking and growling. They could sense that something was amiss. These were vicious trackers, and they would happily growl and snarl and scare the crap out of any normal prisoner. But Alexa wasn't worried as she opened their cages. She tweaked the composition of her pheromones and let loose a blast. Even those who suspected how powerful her sex appeal was never guessed that Alexa could alter the chemical composition of her pheromones to make them just as effective on animals.

Except Sam Conlon. Somehow he had known.

Now all dozen of the German Shepherds began panting, sniffing, and wagging their tails, and they followed her as she led them away. When they had all trotted out into the main camp, she altered the chemistry again, turning them loose to run wild.

Inside the janitorial equipment shed, Sam had pulled down and emptied several Styrofoam coolers, and now he began to pour jugs of chemicals into them. He measured perfectly without hesitation as he created his concoctions. He was still counting under his breath. He said quietly to himself, "Laina… bishop to king four. Force their move by threatening a line on the queen for me."

Tense and sweating, they made their way to the Max barracks, keeping low, Andrew in front, Dorian glancing anxiously from side to side. But Laina slipped them right past the guards. She held on to their hands and muttered her quiet mantra, "Don't see me, don't see me, don't see me."

The sally port was too problematic, used only for large deliveries, but the regular guard gate was open.

"How did you manage that?" Dorian whispered.

Andrew shushed him.

Laina kept concentrating.

They carefully made their way to the outside of the barracks. New plywood barriers had been placed on the damaged walls. Much of the siding had been torn away and new insulation had been added. But the repairs were far from complete.

Laina said, "I have to stay out here. I'll keep everyone's attention off this doorway, but you get inside."

"We know the Evos we're supposed to find," Andrew said. "Sam was very specific."

"He better know what he's doing," Dorian muttered, "or we're all toast."

"Burnt toast," Andrew added.

They opened the door to the Max barracks. Laina stood against the wall, placing her hands against the building on either side of the door. She closed her eyes as a guard walked around the corner on patrol. Andrew and Dorian had just slipped inside, and Laina concentrated harder. "Don't see me, don't see me, don't see me."

The guard walked right past, not noticing that the door was partly open. She heaved a sigh of relief, hoping she had given Andrew and Dorian the time they needed.

Then dogs started barking and snapping in the camp, creating a commotion. The guard who had just passed by turned, stared out into the main camp, and then ran to see what the trouble was. He didn't even look back at the Max barracks. The guards at the sally port also looked up. The camp was on high alert, but at least their attention was focused elsewhere.

"Hurry…" Laina muttered.

Inside the janitorial storage shed, Sam coughed and choked. His eyes were burning, tears flooding his vision, but he kept mixing the chemicals, counting under his breath. Styrofoam began to bubble in the first cooler as he emptied the last bottle into the final cooler and replaced the lid. Moving quickly, he stacked the filled, churning, reacting coolers like Styrofoam Lego blocks up against the wall of other cleaning chemicals.

Still counting under his breath, he walked out of the storage shed and closed the door behind him. Everything was precisely on schedule.

"All right, rooks. Do your jobs. Free the king and queen." He walked calmly to the rear of the storage shed. There he found a junction box behind a maintenance bunker, next to a larger transformer box. This was a subsidiary fuse box, a forgotten standby junction—and an unexpected point of weakness.

As the dogs began barking and running loose, Sam used the wire cutters on the main wires leading out of the junction box. It really was foolish for them to have neglected such an obvious vulnerability.

Around the camp, backup manual locks engaged as the electronic security system went down.

CHAPTER NINETEEN

With the dogs turned loose and the security power out, the guards were in turmoil, rushing to close ranks. Andrew felt his heart pounding as he and Dorian worked their way deeper into the Max barracks. They kept a low profile but moved as swiftly as they could. Andrew had the list—three specific Evos they had to liberate, after which they would free everyone else they could in the 5-minute window they were given.

The three most important were designated Y35F, who Sam had nicknamed "Allergy Guy," X23R, who he called "Resonance Girl," and X46R, "The Seer." Andrew wasn't sure he even wanted to know the scope of what they could do, why they had been considered so dangerous that Renautas kept them locked up here in comas. He was sure he'd get a chance to witness their abilities before the night was over.

"This one," Dorian said in a hushed voice as he stopped by a locked door. He rattled the knob. "It'll be tricky."

Andrew said, "I know. I'm ready when you are."

Dorian nodded, then slipped a few paper clips out of his pocket and held them in the palm of his hand. "You sure you're ready?"

"I'm ready."

Dorian concentrated. His hand glowed, and then the paper clips glowed even brighter as they melted into a puddle of metal. He tilted his palm, letting the liquid drip across his fingers into the doorknob's key slot.

Andrew clasped the knob, focusing. Soft sizzling, popping sounds came from the knob as he dropped the temperature by ten degrees. It was enough to swiftly harden the molten metal inside the handle, and as the metal solidified around the lock's tumblers, it became a makeshift key. He turned it in the lock, opened the door, and stepped into the room.

X23R was a young African-American woman, eyes closed and face slack. The medical equipment next to her bed was softly beeping, connected by leads to the comatose woman. Plastic tubing ran from one of the machines to her nostril. Andrew rushed forward, shut off the monitoring device, and pulled the leads off of her. Dorian removed the tubes and then slid a net of electrodes from her head. Almost immediately she began to stir.

"While she wakes up," Andrew said, "let's find the other one, Allergy Guy. I wonder if he can make people sneeze like Reggie."

Dorian gave him a sour look. "Let's hope he can do a lot more than Reggie. Otherwise, we're screwed."

Alarms were ringing now, and guards were running around the camp, shouting. Andrew hoped that Laina was doing her part to divert attention. They needed just a few more minutes. They came to the second door, the one with the code designator Y35F. Dorian melted his paper clips again, and together they fashioned a second key. Inside they found a middle-aged Caucasian man whose collarbone-length beard showed just how long he had been kept unconscious. His cheeks were jowly and his skin hung loose. He had obviously lost significant weight while in the induced coma. They quickly disengaged the medical apparatus, beginning the steps that would revive him.

As he began to stir, the two moved on to the third room, repeating the process. As they pulled the electrodes off of the third patient, a Native American woman in her fifties, they were surprised to see her eyes immediately snap open. Cloudy white irises cleared, revealing deep brown eyes.

She sat up and rubbed her shoulder. "Thank you. I'll be fine from here."

The two looked at each other, and Andrew shrugged.

"I'll get the dude," Dorian said. "You go check on Resonance Girl. We need both of them with us, at least for the time being—and then we'll turn them loose." His eyes twinkled.

Andrew raced back to the first room to find the young woman already sitting up in her bed. Her movements were stiff, unlike those of the older woman. Her eyes were confused, her expression angry. "Where the hell am I?" Her voice was a croak. She grabbed the side of the bed and it began to vibrate. Andrew could hear it hum.

"We're here to rescue you. Renautas built this maximum-security holding area to keep dangerous Evos sedated. I don't know how long you've been here, but you're free now."

"And who the hell are you?"

"I'm another Evolved. But… my powers are pathetic compared to yours. Still, they're holding us all here in this camp."

She released the edge of the bed. "Why are you rescuing me?"

Andrew peeked out into the hallway. This was taking too long—they wouldn't be able to release any other prisoners. He didn't think Sam would be too happy about that, but he had said that these three were musts, any others were bonuses.

He frowned, then looked back to the woman in the room. "There's been a crackdown. Sooner or later they'll get rid of us all. Some of us are planning a break, and we're freeing everyone we can first."

Resonance Girl rubbed her arms. She swung her legs over the side of the bed. "Well, that's just great. Why should I go along with your plan? I don't know anything about it."

"We don't need you to," Andrew said quickly. "We're just turning you loose. It's every Evo for herself tonight."

"Fine," said Resonance Girl. "I'll shake things up. Thank you."

"You're welcome." Andrew hovered in the door.

Out in the hall, Allergy Guy was storming along in his hospital gown, furious. Dorian ran alongside him. "We're on your side. We're letting her out. We're letting you out. We aren't here to tell you what to do." Allergy Guy shot Dorian a withering glare, then looked up to see Andrew and Resonance Girl emerging.

"You're one of them, too?" he asked her.

"I'm my own person," she said.

"So am I."

"Go on. Run away," said Resonance Girl, looking at Andrew and Dorian. "I've got some payback to deliver."

She quickly worked her way down the hallway, touching doors and humming. Each door she touched dissolved under her fingers. The man followed, unplugging machines in each room.

Andrew and Dorian were shocked. This was what it meant to be a powerful Evolved. These two had released half the hall's prisoners in the time it had taken the two misfits to work on a single key. There was no sign of the third prisoner they had released. Still in their hospital gowns, the pair reversed direction and walked past the misfits to the exit. Neither of them noticed Laina as she dropped her arms and uncovered the door.

Dorian grinned. "I kinda want to see this."

"I just want to get out of here and away," Andrew said.

As soon as they emerged from the Max barracks, the air-raid sirens went off. Allergy Guy lurched forward, brash, furious, and uncaring, ready to meet the onrushing guards.

Andrew recognized Rizzoli in the lead, yelling, "The Max Evos are loose. You! Stop! Don't make me shoot!" He drew the pistol holstered at his side and took a bead on the escaping prisoner.

The man didn't pause, but merely lifted his hand, fingers splayed. Rizzoli shuddered and seized up. Gasping and clutching at his face and throat, the guard dropped his gun. His eyes puffed up and went red, streaming tears. His nose started gushing a waterfall of snot. He staggered back, but Allergy Guy kept coming.

Andrew stared. Reggie could make people sneeze as a joke or parlor trick, but this guy could throw everyone into full anaphylactic shock. The man gestured with his hands, and all the guards around Rizzoli collapsed in allergic seizures. He walked right through their ranks, with Resonance Girl following on his heels.

Dorian gaped in amazement. "We should take them with us. There's no way the camp personnel could stop us if they were on our side."

Andrew narrowed his eyes, frightened. "No. We have to follow Sam's plan. Think about it. With Evos that powerful, Ruthers can't let them get away. We're better off on our own. Staying with them would be signing our own death warrants."

* * *

Tucked behind the corner of the mess hall, Sam watched the events unfold—and he wasn't disappointed. Barking guard dogs ran amok, endangering the entire camp. Ruthers had emerged from the Admin building where her quarters were located, in full uniform and shouting orders. More guards came rushing from their barracks.

It was total chaos.

Perfect.

Alexa had done her part, and now he saw that Andrew and Dorian had also followed through. The two powerful Evos had emerged from Max and were working their way toward the main gate. He watched the guards fall into choking spasms thanks to Allergy Guy. Sam suspected that most of them would live, though he didn't doubt that the powerful Evo had the ability to kill—if he chose to. It all depended on how angry he was right now.

Resonance Girl was the real gem, though. She walked over to the side of the guards' barracks, touched the wall. It looked like she was trying to catch her breath, but Sam knew otherwise. She hummed, raising and lowering the pitch until she hit just the right frequency. The walls vibrated, shook, quaked until the whole building was trembling.

Sam watched, curious. It was as if the building was being hit by a high-magnitude earthquake. Windows shattered and walls crumbled, structural beams fell in, the roof collapsed. Siding exploded outward. The few guards still inside ran out, yelling.

He knew the destruction was just beginning. Sam narrowed his eyes as he saw the bright red lines in the air streaking out, ricocheting, connecting, terminating. Then, just as he had predicted, loud gunfire began to ring out. The game had gone to the next level. He shook his head sadly. If only there had been a way to get some of the Max Evos out alive…

If either of these two survived, it would only be because more of the released prisoners would soon be joining the fray.

Alexa tried to stay out of view, creeping between the buildings, making her way over to the Max barracks. She didn't think she was behind schedule, but she saw no sign of Laina. The dogs were running loose, creating pandemonium throughout the camp, and the guards weren't much better. All their efforts to get things under control were only making matters worse—and then they encountered the escaped Max prisoners.

The security power was out, but alarms were still ringing and the lights were on, casting long shadows... Good places to hide. Alexa was getting nervous, though. She hadn't connected up like she was supposed to—and she knew how intricate Sam's plan was. She edged toward the back of the double fences surrounding the Max barracks but saw no one. Where were they?

"Laina," she whispered. She kept walking along, whispering as loud as she dared. "Laina."

Suddenly a hand reached out and grabbed her arm. She hadn't seen anything, but her friend was right there.

Laina looked frightened and harried. "Keep quiet," she said. "I'm concentrating." But she held on to Alexa's arm, and Alexa sensed that no one was going to notice them—not right now.

When the two powerful Evos went on the rampage, Andrew and Dorian ran away from the maximum-security barracks. "Don't you think we should wake up the ones they didn't get to?" Dorian said. "Think of the damage. It would show everyone why they shouldn't keep people in camps like this."

Andrew disagreed. He thought that more than anything else, it would result in more camps. "Now's not the time for a philosophical discussion. Sam said at least those three and others if we could. The ones they released are on them, and I don't think it'll throw off Sam's plans. We're on a schedule, Dorian." Andrew just wanted to get away, wanted to get to someplace he could call home, somewhere safe.

They headed back toward their own barracks to retrieve the heavy bolt cutters that they had buried in the garden bed. Alexa had "requisitioned" them, but they needed to hide them for a time. Andrew ducked down, digging around in the dirt until his fingers found the hefty handle. He gasped with relief, his breath curling out in steam in the cold night air.

It was going to be a miserable night of running through the mountains—but he welcomed that kind of misery. He pulled the bolt cutters loose. Dorian had retrieved a second set of wire cutters so they could shut off the electricity in the fences in case killing the main breaker hadn't done the job.

"Come on, let's go," Andrew said. "Get to the rendezvous point at the fence so we can cut our way through and be out of here." He turned and saw Reggie standing right there, staring at them. His mouth was open and his eyes were wide.

"What are you guys doing? There's a lockdown. You should be in your bunks." Then he looked down and saw the wire cutters as Andrew's words registered in his mind. "You're trying ta escape. Hey," he began to shout. Poor, dumb, likeable Reggie began flailing his hands. "You can't run away! You'll ruin it for everyone."

Dorian was right there, though, and he slammed his hand against the center of Reggie's chest. He concentrated, closed his eyes. He *pushed* and his hand glowed. Reggie began to spasm and shake. Then he reeled back against the outer wall of the barracks.

"What did you do?" Andrew cried, running to catch Reggie as he fell. Reggie's mouth was opening and closing. He gasped like a fish, but then his skin went gray and his eyes shut as a blood vessel burst near his heart.

"Same thing I do to the paper clips." Dorian said. "He always talks about that aneurysm clip… Not much difference, really. He was going to turn us in."

"You killed him."

"I think the aneurysm killed him, or it could be the melted clip in his heart. But I had to, dude. He would have gotten us caught." Dorian shook his head and grabbed Andrew's arm. "Come on, we've got a job to do. You know Reggie would never have survived in the new world… At least, not in any world where I want to live."

Staggering, Andrew almost lost his grip on the heavy bolt cutters. Reggie lay dead beside the barracks. Although he was a bit of an idiot, he had also been a good friend. Andrew suppressed a low moan deep in his throat and felt tears streaming down his cheek. But there was no time for emotion, not if he wanted to avoid getting caught.

CHAPTER TWENTY

As the camp erupted in chaos—precise, perfectly planned, and well-orchestrated chaos—Sam walked calmly to his destination. Running people attracted attention. Without their handler to manage them, the dozen guard dogs ran wild, barking and snarling at everyone—prisoners, guards, staff. Most of the power systems were out, thanks to the wires he had cut at the junction box, sheathing parts of the camp in darkness. The alarm klaxons, independently powered, echoed through the mountains.

But of course the real excitement had started once Andrew and Dorian set loose Allergy Guy and Resonance Girl. Those two Evos were far better than a flyer or a speedster.

He made his way through all the turmoil, casually strolling. It was like Moses parting the Red Sea, the way that commotion just missed him, leaving a calm path. He stepped easily into the shadows between barracks just as a guard came running around the corner, racing to respond to another emergency. Without even changing his pace, Sam emerged at the exact moment the guard was out of sight. It was all a matter of recognizing the patterns… patterns that no one else could see.

As some guards rallied to round up the dogs and confront the two Max prisoners that were on the rampage, others were pleading with campers to get back inside. Sam smiled. The third prisoner... She was long gone. He could already see her pattern fading into the tree line, well past the fences.

Then several shots rang out. The timing was perfect. Those shots drew the eyes and ears of everyone at TAC Hale to the center of the compound and the main gate. As he made his way to the rendezvous point where he would meet up with the rest of the misfits, he saw Luther running past, utter panic on his face. His gangly legs and arms were flopping as he tried to get away, but he had no idea what he was doing. He wailed, and as he ran, his power left yellow streaks everywhere.

Sam saw the lines changing, the red strands, the connections broken, and he knew that even his perfect clockwork plan could not account for the persistent penchant of other people to make the wrong move. Something had happened that had changed the pattern.

Andrew Meek, normally cool and reliable, was a wreck, looking distraught and shaken. Dorian seemed grim but sickened. "He killed Reggie," Andrew blurted out.

"I had to," Dorian snapped. "He was in the way. He was going to turn us in, and then we'd all be sunk."

"Andrew, he's right," Sam said. "Look around you. We'll never have another chance to get away from here."

"Well, Reggie didn't deserve... None of us deserves this. How many times have you said it yourself? We're all innocent, supposedly. How the hell can we say we're innocent when we just killed one of our own?"

"Just because he's an Evo doesn't make him one of us. He was a lapdog for the guards here. I'm sorry, Andrew, but what's done is done. We have to move on. Right now our priorities are survival and escape." Sam looked at the lines, reconfigured his plan.

Andrew and Dorian had the necessary tools. Sam glanced around at the darkness, the shadowy areas around the fence, the places where the lights had gone out. He chose a better spot. "You going to be okay, Andrew?"

The other man nodded and gulped. "I have to be."

"Good," Sam said. "This way."

They reconnected with Alexa and Laina exactly as planned, and Sam guided them over to the poorly repaired section of the chain-link fence where Luther had made his previous escape attempt.

"That's our best bet. The electrified portion of the fence is still down," Sam said. "Even if cutting the power didn't work, we're safe here."

Alexa let go of Laina's hand. "Everything's happening just the way you said, Sam, but I still think the plan is falling apart. We're screwed. Every guard in camp is mobilized now."

Laina blurted, "They're everywhere! We'll never be able to sneak out."

Sam smiled at them, a magician about to perform the big reveal. "I needed them mobilized. We were never going to try to sneak out. Right now they're running to respond to other emergencies. Believe me, they're not worried about us. We weren't just creating a distraction for time to escape, but also for time to run. Right there, Andrew," he pointed to the fence.

Andrew took the bolt cutters and began to snip the temporary wire closures that held the fence together. Sam had told the director, had warned her that it wasn't just Evos who were dangerous. That everyone could be a threat... if provoked.

Playing against Sam had taught Deborah Ruthers a thing or two, though. Just as Andrew finished clipping the fence and tossed the bolt cutters aside, she stepped around the corner of the Admin building, looking flushed, disheveled, and angry. "I thought all this mayhem seemed a bit too planned, a bit too convenient. I thought you'd go here. Why?"

The misfits froze, stared at her, and collectively groaned. Sam shifted his weight and stepped between Ruthers and the rest of his group. "Because you're just a pawn, even if you thought you were the queen. You wanted to make a beautiful place where we were all happy little prisoners, but there you stand holding us at gunpoint. Don't you see the truth yet... *Director*?"

Ruthers' hand crept toward her holstered gun. "How much were you playing me this whole time? Using me?"

"I was... doing what had to be done," Sam said. "It was obvious to me that things were getting worse. Whatever title you give yourself, you're here to keep us imprisoned. Ask yourself, what is TAC Hale going to look like in a month? A concentration camp—a death camp? You weren't playing against me, Director, I was playing against Kravid."

"I know damn well what my boss wants. You should have known I would never allow Hale to turn into that," Ruthers said. Her hand gripped the pistol in its holster.

"You're wrong, Deborah." Sam saw a fluctuation in the patterns and held up his hand behind him, warning the rest of the misfits not to move. "It's only a matter of time before something happens and your job goes away. A few deaths here or there, and then we're all in Max. This camp will never survive. That's the Renautas endgame. Control us like any other asset."

Andrew interrupted, pleading, "We don't mean any

harm. We never did. We're just trying to make a life for ourselves."

"You've tested our abilities," Dorian added. "We can't hurt anybody."

Sam watched the director carefully. He needed her alive; otherwise, no one would get the guards organized at the gate, and they would be caught by Rizzoli. Ruthers' fingers were alternately squeezing and releasing her pistol.

"We'll take our chances out there," Alexa said. "Please?"

"We were held here against our will, and you know we're not dangerous," Sam interjected, thrusting a thin, sharp knife of words at her. "No more than a non-Evo," he said. "You have bigger problems than us right now."

The director's face fell, and a single word cut quietly through the pandemonium of the rest of the camp as she drew her gun. "No."

The line of sight through the buildings was perfect, allowing Sam to watch the main gate over the director's shoulder. The next few seconds played out in slow-motion for him. In the center of the camp, Allergy Guy was charging into the rallying guards, and they dropped, coughing, sneezing, spasming. Sam thought he intended to walk right out the front gate, leaving the debris of collapsed personnel behind him.

He was arrogant.

The guards had fallen behind him. Allergy Guy was right out in the open, and one of the camp sharpshooters, finally taking the necessary action, opened fire with a long-range rifle—the kind that didn't use tranquilizer darts. Two loud shots echoed over the camp's klaxons.

Allergy Guy's shoulder and abdomen erupted in a spray of blood, and his lifeless body was thrown to the ground by the impact of the high-powered rifle rounds. Resonance

Girl screamed and slammed her hands onto the ground. Her scream warbled, shifting octaves, and the ground around her exploded in a series of ever-widening concentric circles. Half-frozen divots of dirt flew everywhere as she used the raw earth like a pineapple grenade. All of the guards Sam could see went down, as did half the structures in the camp.

Standing up, she walked to the closed main gates and touched the thick brick posts that held them in place. The gate shuttered and shook. Finally the bricks crumbled, the gates shattered. More gunfire rang out, but everything was vibrating and shimmering around Resonance Girl. She turned around, glared at the people facing her, and slammed her hand down onto the ground, pressing her palm flat against the pavement—unleashing a second round of seismic tremors.

Sam sprang forward and tackled Ruthers. The gun went off between them, then flew from her hand as they hit the ground. A spike of rebar three feet long had impaled itself right in the spot where Ruthers had been standing.

She stared wide-eyed at the vibrating spear.

Sam rolled to the side, clutching at a sleeve that was wet with blood. "Are we really the ones you need to be worrying about?"

Torn, but knowing her duty, Deborah stood and retrieved her gun, refusing to meet Sam's eyes. "I can't waste time trying to stop you."

"We'll take our chances in the outside world." Andrew crouched next to Sam, helping his injured friend.

Ruthers shook her head, then turned and sprinted toward the center of camp.

Sam gestured at the fence. "That's our cue to move."

Alexa's eyebrows furrowed. "But you just got shot."

Sam grimaced. "It was a calculated risk. I get hurt saving

her, she lets us go and focuses the guards on what's going on over there. Worth it. Now, we need to get moving."

One by one the misfits clambered through the hole in the chain-link fence and crept out into the cold, damp night. Just as they left, exactly on Sam's timetable, a massive explosion engulfed the janitorial shed back inside the compound. The chemicals he had set up inside the Styrofoam coolers had eaten through their containers and mixed. The massive explosion coated the compound in a napalm-like substance.

As the escapees fled toward the mountains, breathless, Sam said, "Conserve your energy. We have a long trek ahead of us. This is about stamina, not speed."

CHAPTER TWENTY-ONE

Warden Ruthers had run out of good options more than an hour ago. Over half of her guard staff had been incapacitated by Eddie Jax, the allergy-wielding Evo freak who now lay dead, gunned down.

Necessarily eliminated.

It was a perfectly defensible action. Ruthers would have no difficulty at all explaining that to Erica Kravid. In fact, the hard part would be justifying why it had taken so long. And how she had allowed such a disaster to happen in the first place.

The guards had managed to catch most of the freed Evos before they regained their wits and get them back into their holding comas. Kravid was going to be pissed. Stacey Terrell, the angry young woman with the resonating powers, was clearly more concerned with causing massive destruction than simply slipping away unobtrusively like Sam Conlon and his co-conspirators.

As Ruthers ran into the middle of the fray, calling for assistance, she saw the young woman standing next to the Admin building that housed her offices and quarters, as well as all of the camp records—the main facility at the heart of TAC Hale. She slapped both hands against the wall and set the entire structure vibrating, shuddering.

Ruthers had been waiting for this moment. According to the files, Stacey focused sound waves through her palms, using her own voice to find a structure's resonance. With her distracted, bullets would be able to break through the sound shell around her. Ruthers waited until the building's windows began shattering and then yelled, "Take her out! Now!"

Many of the guards were still struggling to recover from their massive allergy overload. Rizzoli had staggered to his feet. He pulled out his handgun and opened fire at the resonating Evo. Other guards struggled up and did likewise, emptying their clips.

Through the chaos of the walls of the Admin building coming apart, the resonating Evo went down in a hail of bullets, her flesh turned to hamburger. Warden Ruthers stepped forward. The explosion in the janitorial shack was still burning. Chemical fumes and smoke roiled up into the air. The firefighters would need special equipment to put that out.

But she suspected that might have been just a diversion. She walked up to Stacey's corpse, which was slumped at the base of the Admin building. There was a red smear among the numerous bullet pockmarks in the wall.

Ruthers felt sick.

As the guards recovered, fighting off the Evo-triggered allergic reactions, a breathless, stunned calm began to return to the camp. Fires still raged. Destruction was everywhere, but they had somehow come out of it with minimal deaths. There were only a few bodies that weren't moving. "Get medical equipment," she shouted. "I need field kits. We have people down. MOVE!"

Rizzoli and the others capable of moving scrambled to follow her orders. She was still reeling, though. Ruthers dreaded another disaster yet to come. Now that it was safe, her support personnel ran up to her.

She turned to two of her computer technicians. "We need to know exactly how those Evos got out of Max. They were dangerous, and they should have been incapacitated. What the hell happened to our security measures? Find out—now!"

Before long Rizzoli returned, still wiping snot from his face. His eyes were bulging and swollen red, but he cleared his throat and told her that they had found the body of Reggie lying dead outside one of the barracks. As the braver guards finally finished rounding up the dogs and chasing them back into their kennels, they discovered Antonio the handler locked in his transportainer.

The dog trainer approached the warden, looking aghast at the destruction that had swept through the camp— devastation that he had missed. He seemed contrite and was blubbering, deeply embarrassed. He was holding a compress against the back of his head. "It was Alexa. She tricked me, knocked me over the head with a rock. I'm sorry, ma'am…"

"Alexa?" Ruthers had seen her with Sam Conlon in the small group of campers trying to escape. Then she remembered that Reggie was a close companion of Andrew Meek, who had also just gone through the back fence. Looking pale, one of her computer technicians stepped up. "Warden Ruthers. You'll want to see this. I've got footage from the few cameras connected to the backup generators."

"Finally some answers," she said. "Show me."

The tech handed her a tablet. Her gut sank as she watched. Sam Conlon and his conspirators hadn't cared in the least that they might be caught on film. Everything had happened so fast. She clearly saw Alexa turning the dogs loose—they seemed like slobbering puppies instead of vicious guard dogs.

Another set of images showed Sam entering the janitorial storage shed and then leaving a short time later... not long before the whole place exploded. More importantly, she saw Andrew Meek and Dorian Avey walking right into the maximum-security barracks, and the two dangerous Evos leaving just a few minutes later.

"No," she corrected herself out loud.

She had to stop thinking that way. Those two weren't the only dangerous Evos. Not at all. Sam had shown her the truth.

The final, most sickening, image showed Dorian Avey placing his palm against Reggie's chest and killing the man. Killing him in cold blood. A man who was obviously their friend. She felt a cold, disgusted burn inside. Kravid had been right. They weren't just playing possum. These supposedly innocuous misfits had been behind all of the turmoil in the camp tonight. The destruction, the deaths... They weren't harmless at all... not by a long shot.

She realized her mistake. She had let them go. She had thought they were unimportant, not worth the effort, a very low priority. Now she saw that they were the masterminds, the instigators—the worst ones of all. She should have shot them all on the spot.

"Barnes! Rizzoli! Applebaum! Veksman!" Ruthers called together a group of guards, her best trackers. It was time for a hunting party. They had to catch the escaped prisoners—she could no longer think of them as mere "campers."

"Recapture them," Ruthers said. "We can't let them run loose. If they resist, kill them."

"Yes, ma'am," said Rizzoli. "They're too dangerous to be out in the world." He and five of the best guards took their weapons and headed out into the thin fog of the damp autumn night. As she watched them go, Ruthers was appalled at herself, wondering how much she had been manipulated all along.

She was going to put an end to it.

Now.

CHAPTER TWENTY-TWO

In the dark, making their way through the underbrush, across drainage ditches, fighting through dense stands of willows and then up the slope without a trail—the misfits made far slower progress than they had hoped.

"It looked so easy on the maps Laina brought us," Dorian said. His tone suggested that the wallflower girl should have known better.

"It'll get better once we're clear of these willows," Andrew said, having no idea whether or not that was true. "We've made it this far. We got out of the camp. Now we just have to keep moving far enough away to be safe."

Sam had been quiet since they left the camp, clutching at his shoulder and glancing back occasionally at something only he could see.

"Luther made it this far," Alexa said, "Several times, in fact. We're better off than Luther. He left a bright yellow trail of breadcrumbs wherever he ran."

Even so, the guards had begun tracking them. Andrew could hear the shouts behind them, saw the lights. The trackers weren't hindered by trying to stay quiet and hidden.

Sticking together, they worked their way up the slope to

where the trees were patchier and the boulders gave them some shelter. But Andrew knew they couldn't hide. They would be found soon enough. They had to keep moving.

As they panted hard, cold steam curled out of their mouths. Andrew's clothes were clammy, and he was sweating even in the evening chill. Finally Sam paused the group and gave him an intent look. "Now it's time, Mr. Meek. This is your big show."

"What can I do?" he blinked, surprised.

"I've been monitoring the weather. This is the final piece of the puzzle. Heavy moisture in the air, a cold night—a ten-degree drop will make all the difference. The question is, how far can you extend it? Just how far can you push?"

"Let's find out." Andrew concentrated, calling on his power. He drew the heat out of the air, and just at the condensation point, fog appeared, rolling out from him in all directions. The moisture that had been hanging heavy in the night air now became a smokescreen for them. Mists that swirled and thickened and appeared out of nowhere, quickly spreading out across the side of the mountain. Andrew grinned, panting. "I did it."

Dorian laughed. "Good job, buddy."

Andrew was amazed.

"If the conditions are right, even a small power can become a big one." Sam grimaced, then added, "Hold on one moment." He pulled off his outer shirt and tied a sling around his injured arm. "I knew you all had the potential to become much more effective at using your powers—you just needed to be pushed. To be shown that there was a way."

Andrew gawked. This was a side of their leader he hadn't expected. When the chips were down… he was tough.

Sam gritted his teeth as he tied the final knot. "Let's move out."

They ran on into the fog, leaving the guards farther behind. Andrew paid no attention to the time, just continued to run, focusing on keeping the temperature lowered... although running soon became plodding.

They fought their way through the trees peppering the slope. The guards were still behind them, closing in despite the thick obscuring mists. They struggled through deadfalls.

Laina twisted her ankle on a hidden stump, but it was just sore, not sprained. Unfortunately, the route they had taken followed the contours of the landscape, and the guards could guess where they were going. They kept hurrying along, unwilling to look back. Andrew could spot the glow from pursuing flashlights.

Shouts echoed behind them, interspersed with the crack of branches.

He concentrated, pushing against the limits of his power, and made the fog even thicker. He climbed higher on a ridge, choosing to go up and over a rocky ledge. Sam, Alexa, and Laina were following close behind. In the thick mist, Dorian got separated and wandered down a different game trail that took him lower. The mist swirled and the fog cleared in a patch. Andrew spotted Dorian below them and farther to the right.

"Dorian, we're up here," he whisper-shouted, but his reply came in the form of loud yells from the guards who were closing in.

He heard Rizzoli. "They're close. Keep moving."

Dorian looked up, searching for them. But as the fog thinned and swirled, another clear line of sight opened up. The loud crack of rifle fire echoed, thunder in the close mountain pass, and Dorian staggered. He cried out in pain, then fell forward, still. Blood welled from his back. Even through the mist Andrew could see the red spreading on his TAC Hale jumpsuit.

"My god," Alexa cried.

Andrew grabbed her arm. "Quiet."

They could have run. But as the guards closed in, Laina huddled next to the other misfits. "We can't outrun them," she said and then squeezed her eyes shut. Alexa slipped her arm around her while Sam stared at them.

He didn't seem worried. "Everyone hold hands," he whispered.

They did as instructed and formed a human circle. Andrew sat there, contemplating. He felt just as miserable as he had when Reggie died, and he was having serious second thoughts about their plan to escape. But there was no way around it, not now that the guards were shooting on sight.

Laina began to mutter, concentrating hard as one of the guards shouted, "There's footprints. They went up this way over the rocks."

Below, by Dorian's body, Rizzoli stopped to examine his handiwork. Then he turned and followed the rest of them up to where the escapees were hiding. But as the guards approached, Laina's voice was a consistent thrum that faded into a faint whisper, "Don't see us, don't see us, don't see us."

The group of searching guards, also panting and exhausted, climbed up through the bushes, pushed their way around trees, stumbled on the loose dirt of the slope. "I can't find them anywhere," somebody said. "Where the hell did this fog come from?" The guards were going to walk right past them.

Andrew saw Alexa tense up. Her eyes flashed, and then she concentrated as well. "Pheromones can do a lot of things," she said quietly, and her expression hardened as she *pushed*. A wave of calm, quieting sensations exuded from her. Even Andrew felt a deep contentment, a sense of peace... a sleepiness.

Laina's head drooped as she nodded off, but Alexa dug her fingernails into the young woman's arm and she woke up. She also jabbed Andrew. Sam, somehow, was perfectly awake.

The guards moved slower. They yawned, and as they walked by they seemed overwhelmed, tranquilized by her relaxing pheromones. As Laina continued to whisper her mantra, the guards became more and more disoriented. They drooped almost in unison.

One by one they sat down to rest, shaking their heads drowsily and then slumping onto the ground. Finally all six were asleep, unable to overcome the intense induced stupor. Alexa, shuddering and looking drained, was barely able to sit up straight.

But Andrew's anger kept him awake. He stood up and looked back down the slope to where Dorian's body lay, his jumpsuit covered with blood. They had gunned the man down in the mist. He was just trying to get away from a prison that was undoubtedly about to get much worse. They'd have locked them up and sedated them just like the Max Evos. Fire raged in his veins.

They had provoked this. Neither Andrew nor Dorian nor any of the misfits had wanted to be in that camp. They didn't need any "temporary assessment." They just wanted to be left alone. Yes, there had been mayhem and disaster in the camp tonight, and some people had died—including Reggie—but they had brought this upon themselves. Warden Ruthers and the guards, and especially Renautas. It was their own damn fault!

And they had killed Dorian in cold blood.

He found a greater depth in his power, stretched harder than he had ever done before, and reached out into the air, finding that he could squeeze out another few degrees. Deepening the cold another ten degrees was enough to bring on a hard freeze and to distill snow, thick blanketing snow, instead of fog.

"It's below zero," Alexa said, shivering.

"For them," Andrew said, looking at the sleeping guards as snow began to fall all around them. "If we move, we should be out of it soon enough."

"Interesting," Sam said. "Frankly, I hadn't seen this coming from you, Andrew. It's rare that I am surprised."

Frost formed over the sleeping men. Alexa stood up, frowned down at her pet guard, and her expression turned into a different kind of ice. She spit on his sleeping form. "Not so quick anymore, are you?"

"Let's go. Time's wasting," Sam said. "Once we get far enough away, we need to split up. We've all got copies of the maps."

The misfits headed out, no longer pursued, making their way far, far from the camp.

CHAPTER TWENTY-THREE

Brilliant golden rays of dawn shone on Ruthers as she stood in the ruins of her camp. Her calm and perfect camp—the place where she had just tried to do her best for everybody. She'd wanted it to be a safe place for those Evos who were no threat, who were being unfairly put upon, suffering prejudices and suspicions. She should have known better.

How much have I been played all along? She stared at the body bags. Handlers were zipping them up and hauling them away to the compound's morgue. Three of her guards dead. Four campers—*prisoners*, she corrected herself—as well as the two monstrous Evos who had escaped from Max Security.

Rizzoli and the team of guards hunting down Sam Conlon's group of escapees had fallen silent three hours earlier, failing to respond to repeated radio inquiries. After about half an hour, Ruthers had been unable to write it off as poor reception in the foggy mountainous terrain.

She had sent out a secondary team. This time she had included Antonio and his dogs. She expected—hoped and dreaded—to hear word soon. She continued to feel disgusted with herself, and she was convinced that Sam and his group were going to get away. They weren't inept, spontaneous buffoons like Luther. This was much more sinister, much more dangerous. They had a well-thought-out, detailed escape plan, and they hadn't cared how many bodies they left behind or how much destruction they wreaked on TAC Hale.

She had meant it to be a safe place for all... The prisoners were confined to their barracks as a temporary precautionary measure, but she suspected it might become permanent. There would be more fences erected. She knew that. Increased security and far fewer freedoms. The Evos had proved where their loyalties truly lay.

Her radio crackled; it was Antonio with the second tracking party. "Warden, ma'am. We found something. We managed to track them."

"Have you found the escaped Evos?" she asked.

"One of them. The one named Dorian. He's been shot. He's dead."

She swallowed, not sure whether to rejoice or feel dismay. "That's one of them, at least."

"But Warden... Hold on. I think I see something." Ruthers only had to wait a moment. "I found the team. They're all together, lying on the ground. They're frozen to death, ma'am. Every single one of them. It's like they just lay down to sleep and the snow covered them. I don't see any signs of a struggle."

"The Evos did it," Ruthers said. She didn't know how, but she was absolutely certain. "Bring their bodies back," she said, then drew a deep breath. "Including the dead Evo." Part of her just wanted to leave the man's body lying there in the open where the scavengers could dispose of it. But she supposed Renautas might want to study it, dissect it. Learn from it.

She walked back to the makeshift office her I.T. crew had set up, her mind made up. She keyed into the P.A. system and made an announcement across the entire camp. "After the events of last night, from today forward all of TAC Hale will be considered a maximum-security installation. Privileges will be revoked and harsh punishments will be instituted for anyone who breaks our rules. Fence security will be increased and appropriate defensive measures will be taken. All remaining guards will be armed."

The rest of the day was spent dealing with that decision. She drafted and signed an order that all volunteer campers in the labor force were to be withdrawn. She knew Renautas would send in enhanced contract support personnel—if Erica Kravid didn't simply shut down Hale. Ruthers hoped she could make that extreme response unnecessary through her preemptive measures.

"We won't let our guard down again," she said. She found she had hardened enough that she didn't even dread contacting Erica Kravid to deliver her report. She didn't want to delay. Early in the afternoon she pulled out a tablet and opened Webchat.

Staring at the head of Renautas on her tablet screen, she delivered a crisp, ruthless summary of everything that had happened. And she watched Kravid's face grow darker and grimmer.

She finished with, "No, Ms. Kravid. I do not believe there can be a safe minimum-security compound. It is my recommendation that from now on all Evos must be detained with maximum protections against their abilities. It doesn't matter how innocuous their power may seem. What has been proven here at Hale is that each and every one of them carries a risk. They must be dealt with accordingly—if only to protect ourselves."

Kravid blinked, then sighed. "I'm afraid I have to agree with you, Deborah. Once a subject has been identified as an Evolved human, we cannot predict how they might use their powers, or when they'll turn against the rest of us. We can't afford to take any further risks." She shook her head, looking sad. "And their powers could be so valuable if only they were made useful and employed for the benefit of humanity in general."

Ruthers shuddered. "I can't help but think of how many more seemingly harmless ones are running loose in society." Her throat thickened, and she felt tears burning her eyes—tears of shame. "And because of my failings, Ms. Kravid, there are now four more on the loose and out of control."

CHAPTER TWENTY-FOUR

The misfits had travelled far from TAC Hale, rising up through a drainage wash, over a ridge, then picking up a hiking trail that had been abandoned in the past year. At the head of the trail, where it emerged into civilization, Sam stole supplies from a resort shop. They all changed clothes, ditching their prison oranges. After consulting the maps, they split up to follow their own plans. They had each developed ideas of where to go that they did not revealed to the others, just in case one of them was apprehended and Renautas decided to use "rigorous" interrogation methods.

But Alexa and Laina weren't going to split up. They were a team; they were synergy, blonde bombshell and mousy wallflower.

Once they all got far enough away, even in the wilderness of the Rocky Mountains, there were possibilities. Plenty of them. Mountain towns, ski shelter huts, unoccupied vacation homes.

But Alexa had no intention of hiding. She couldn't use her abilities if she pretended to be a pioneer mountain woman. Once the misfits had gone in their separate directions, Alexa and Laina made their way down to the closed Highway 24, conveniently blocked off by perennial "road construction" to deny access to the temporary assessment camp.

Once they found the abandoned road, they holed up in the thick trees and just rested during the next day. After nightfall they hit the road again, walking and walking. It was only seven miles past the road closure barricade to the old mining and tourist town of Minturn.

Laina had been scared and quiet for a long time, but she looked confident now as they headed into the town. Seeing the early morning traffic picking up, Alexa said, "Since the camp itself is low-profile, I doubt they'll broadcast stories about our escape all over the news. They'll have their own operatives searching for us, but if we can just get far enough away..."

Laina looked at her. "I can help us stay hidden, if that's what we need."

Alexa flashed a smile. "We don't need to stay hidden, we just need a ride."

Upending her usual routine, Alexa did her best to make herself attractive—then worked on Laina, who was full of questions. "How are you going to use your pheromones on passing traffic? You won't be able to get close enough."

Alexa laughed, "Pheromones? Girl, if two pretty and lonely-looking young women standing by the side of the road can't get a mountain redneck to stop and offer a ride within five minutes, then we're doing something wrong."

She was right. Alexa let her hair flow free, tucked in her shirt, showed as much cleavage as possible. The first car stopped seven minutes later. Alexa jokingly blamed the delay on the sparse early-morning traffic. The driver was a grinning middle-aged man—married, so picking up hitchhikers was probably his only form of excitement.

He rolled down the window and smiled at Alexa. She leaned closer and flashed her radiant smile back. At that point the pheromones wafted over him, and he couldn't even think straight.

"Where are you girls needing to go?"

"We'd like to get to Vale, ten miles east," she said, "and if you could loan us some money for new clothes, we'd be very grateful." She touched his shoulder.

He was already digging for his wallet but Alexa said, "You can wait until we get there."

Laina climbed into the back while Alexa slid into the front seat. The man was eager to drive off. "It wasn't on my way but… anywhere you want to go."

"Thanks," Laina said, but he didn't hear her.

"If you could hurry, that would be great," Alexa said, and the man peeled away excitedly.

Sam Conlon walked alone, his left arm bound to his midsection with a more traditional sling. Clouds blocked the moon, but even in the darkest night, bright, interconnected lines wavered in the air, guiding him along the best possible path. He moved without hesitation. He could look through the darkness at the pattern he had woven and see where all the other misfits had gone. He felt good, knowing they had survived to carry on the fight.

Because he could move at a good pace, knowing exactly when to duck for cover to avoid being seen, he made excellent time. The Interstate wasn't all that far away, and he crossed it that next night. The traffic was busy, even this far into the mountains, headlights coming from both directions along the double-laned highway. But he timed his steps and simply walked across the road. It didn't matter that it was an Interstate freeway; by looking at all the lines and probabilities and patterns, he could walk easily through the gaps in traffic, not even pausing to look both ways. The cars swept by, and he doubted they even saw him. It was like the old videogame Frogger. The gaps appeared when he needed them to, and he made it across Interstate 70 as if it wasn't even there.

Farther north he found the expected set of railroad tracks, and he arrived just as a long freight train was passing, going west toward Grand Junction. From there he could go anywhere. The train was rolling lazily along, going up a gentle grade. Sam walked directly toward it, and just as he reached the tracks, an open boxcar rolled up. He reached out and grabbed a handle, easily swinging himself up, perfectly timed… just as expected. He was all alone in the open rattling car. He leaned back against the wall, relaxing, knowing it would be a long ride.

Andrew had made it as far as Crescent Junction, Utah, out in the desert. It was a sharp contrast to the cold snap on the night of the escape. The air was hot, the sunshine bright. Crescent Junction was basically only a gas station and a couple of forlorn fast-food joints. But there was also a truck stop with a lot of through traffic.

He didn't have to work hard to play the part of the bedraggled-looking hitchhiker heading across country. His problem was that he seemed so poorly prepared. On the other hand, his appearance attracted the helpful nature of certain truckers.

He held his thumb out, watching as the big eighteen-wheelers lumbered along, slowly rolling toward the stop sign before the Interstate onramp.

One trucker stopped and leaned out his window. "Where you heading?"

"Far away," Andrew said. "I've always wanted to see the West Coast."

"I'm only going as far as Las Vegas," said the trucker.

"Good enough," Andrew said. "I've got a lot of things on my bucket list."

"Well then, let's take care of one of them," said the trucker. "Hop in." He looked up, shaking his head at the baking sun, "Aren't you hot out there?"

Andrew laughed as he climbed into the cab. "No, the temperature's always just fine to me."

CHAPTER TWENTY-FIVE

There was no sign of the escaped misfits, but the newly titled "Warden" Ruthers knew that Renautas had sent out teams. Specialists were combing the area, and she didn't have the personnel to bother with it. It was out of her hands. She had already made the big mistake of letting them get away in the first place, and now her primary focus was rebuilding TAC Hale to make sure such a debacle never happened again... assuming the camp didn't get shut down.

She sat at her desk, looking down at her cold coffee. Her stomach was upset, churning with acid and tension. She didn't need any more caffeine.

What had happened here at what was supposedly a showpiece camp for Renautas to prove that Evos could be peaceful and profitable—not just the escape of the supposedly innocuous misfits, but the deaths of the prisoners and guards and the rampage of the three super powerful Evos... The firestarter, the allergy twister, and the resonator. And the seer... She was just gone. That one had slipped under her radar the night of the escape.

Ruthers had failed miserably. She had expected Erica Kravid would want her head on a platter, but instead Kravid insisted that she would be given a second chance. *If* she got her act together.

The camp would be a much harder, bleaker place, but she couldn't bring herself to feel sympathy. The Evos had done it to themselves, were reaping what they had sowed. She had thought them harmless, innocent creatures to be protected.

Nobody was harmless. It was humans that needed to be protected from them.

CHAPTER TWENTY-SIX

Except for Dorian, who'd been gunned down by the guards in the mountains, all the misfits got away. It was indeed a perfect plan. Sam had known that from the very beginning. He had hopped off the train in the main track yards in Grand Junction, a large enough city that he could blend in with plenty of homeless people for a time if needed. He'd always been able to manage one way or another. It was all part of the puzzle.

By himself as usual, he walked toward a small auto-repair shop on the outskirts of town, arriving two minutes after another customer. This customer had gone straight up to the counter to talk to a grizzled old man in an oil-stained work shirt. They were discussing a car in the shop, bickering over what needed to be done.

The proprietor said, "Let's go in the back and have a look." He came around the desk, and the two of them walked out the back door into the repair bay, out of sight. One second after they disappeared, Sam opened the door and walked directly over to the desk. Without a pause, without looking around, he approached the phone, picked it up, and punched in a number he had memorized. He listened to it ring.

When the voice on the other end answered, he started talking.

"Ms. Kravid, this is Sam Conlon calling in."

"Good," she said. "I was expecting to hear from you yesterday. What did you find out about the others?"

"It was exactly as you had expected, ma'am. Even the supposedly harmless Evos learned how to put their powers to good use—destructive use. All that was required was to place them in a high-pressure situation. Given what I discovered in the temporary assessment camp, any one of those Evos could become dangerous under the appropriate circumstances. I'm positive about that."

Kravid paused on the other end of the line. "That's one way to look at it. Another possibility is that many of those Evos could have useful or profitable abilities if they were properly directed."

"Like me, you mean," Sam said.

Kravid murmured in agreement. "I'd like you to come in so I can have a full debriefing. I need to know the full extent of how you pushed them into using their powers. Regardless, you've proven to my satisfaction that even harmless Evos cannot be allowed to run loose. When can I expect you back at Renautas Headquarters, Mr. Conlon?"

He looked at the phone, considering. "I think I'll skip the debriefing. I got what I needed. Just remember, no matter how powerless we are, we're still stronger than you. Checkmate, Ms. Kravid. Checkmate."

"Don't do this, Sam. We had an agreement. We will find you, and whe—" He hung up the phone. He walked calmly out of the auto-repair shop, the door closing behind him at the exact second the proprietor and customer returned from the repair bay, still discussing the job.

A Native American woman in her fifties stood outside

the door. It was the third prisoner they had released. "You're the one I saw. You can change everything with my visions. Thank you for freeing me."

Sam smiled. The moment she had opened her mouth, everything had changed. Now he wasn't just seeing the patterns of what existed, but also the patterns of everything that could be. It all blossomed from the single thread that connected him to the woman standing before him. His eyes glowed with the power unfolding in him.

He nodded in reply. "Shall we go save the world?"

CHAPTER TWENTY-SEVEN

Static briefly sounded as the call was disconnected. Erica Kravid looked across her office at the empty sword stand and clenched her fingers. Conlon had actually had the temerity to hang up on her.

She clenched her fingers into a fist, her knuckles going white. To an outside observer, she would have looked calm. She was breathing evenly, despite the intense anger heating her veins. She narrowed her eyes and spoke aloud. "Think it through, Erica. What does he know? What does he know?"

Sam knew something, obviously. But what? It seemed like the last six months had been a long series of failures and surprises. Noah Bennet, Hiro, Molly Walker's disappearance, and the cherry on top of it all: Camp Hale. Her prototype for a non-invasive Evo containment system was worthless.

And now Sam Conlon had slipped through her fingers. Some days it felt like her foundation was more cracks than stability.

She stood and walked to the front of her desk, grabbing a tablet. Sunbeams sliced through the electric lights, creating patches of natural warmth in the room, warmth she gladly basked in. She slid aside a coffee cup and perched on the edge of the desk, tilting her head back and closing her eyes as the sun struck her face.

Warmth. A smile slowly spread. Her eyes snapped open, looked down at the tablet in her hand. "You can't win, Sam. Ultimately, you're just an annoyance."

Images slid under her fingers on the tablet until she settled on a file named Sunstone Manor. It was a brute-force solution, but it could fix so many problems. She flipped open the file and stared at the picture of Matt Parkman.

Kravid pivoted, jabbing a finger down on her phone and scooping up the handset. "I want Sunstone Manor ready to be fully operational in two weeks. Get me Parkman."

She hung up and went back to the files. Ruthers was now disposable, as was almost everyone at Hale. She studied pictures. Hale wasn't going to work. She had made the right call. It couldn't have worked any other way, and there was too much at stake to play nice. But that left another problem. A lot of people that she didn't need to be wasting resources on.

She picked the phone back up. "I want all Max prisoners, and I do mean all of the maximum-security Evos, moved from Camp Hale to Sunstone Manor. Sunstone will be operational in two weeks; have them ready. Everyone at Hale that is not a necessary asset is to be terminated."

She listened intently for a moment, then shook her head. "The useless Evos and staff alike will have to be dealt with. Everyone that isn't being moved to Sunstone is to be terminated once the transfer is complete. We cannot risk *anything* about Hale or Sunstone Manor leaking to the public. Understood?"

She listened to the reply.

"Good." She hung up the receiver and went back to thoughtfully studying Sam Conlon's file.

CHAPTER TWENTY-EIGHT

The alarms were ringing in Camp Hale. The air-raid sirens had gone off in the middle of the night, and everyone was on edge. Warden Ruthers was pleased to see how swiftly the guards responded.

Antonio had all of his German shepherds ready to go, barking and snarling but completely under his control. Ruthers emerged from the Admin offices and stood on the porch under the harsh, bright lights that shone down on the camp compound. They were stadium-powered lights that allowed no masking shadows, no comfortable darkness. Everything the Evos did had to be done under harsh illumination. No secrets.

"What's happening?" Ruthers called out as one of her guards rushed by. Since the disastrous events of two weeks ago, all guards had been thoroughly briefed and retrained. Every one of them knew what to do, and every one of them understood that their jobs—and possibly their lives—were on the line if they screwed up again.

"Another prisoner has escaped, Warden. Gone through the fence."

"How did that happen? We're supposed to have increased security."

"It's Evos, ma'am. Who knows what they can do."

"*We* have to know," she shouted. "We have to defend ourselves against them."

Another guard ran up, but he didn't seem quite as alarmed. "There were yellow stains on the ground and on the fence, Warden. It's just Luther. He's trying to run—again."

The first guard groaned, but Ruthers was not amused. "I don't care that it's only Luther. He's an escaped prisoner. That's all you need to know."

"Sure, Warden," said the second guard, "but we'll track him down. He's leaving yellow stains all over the ground. We'll round him up in no time."

Ruthers felt bitter bile boil up inside her throat. "Can't control its powers... Isn't that the problem with all of them?"

As the hunting teams were assembled in the main yard of the compound, other guards kept watch on the remaining Evo prisoners in their barracks, not letting them come out into the night. They were awake, though—she could see their silhouetted faces in the windows of the barracks.

"We'll need to get out our tranq guns and Tasers," the first guard said. "He usually surrenders and will probably come back willingly, but we'd better make sure."

Ruthers shook her head. "No, we won't take any further risks, not with dangerous subjects like that. We've learned our lesson. Luther has proven to be a persistent troublemaker and a repeat offender. Even if you bring him back, he'll just try to escape again, and again, and he might take others with him. He's a danger to society." She drew a deep breath. "Carry high-powered rifles when you go find him. Take him down. The Max transport to Sunstone

Manor is tomorrow; we can't afford this distraction. Kravid will have my head if there are any problems."

The guards were shocked, but she put her hands on her hips and reaffirmed her command. "You have your orders. Take him down. There's no such thing as a harmless Evo."

ABOUT THE AUTHORS

Duane Swierczynski ("Catch and Kill") is the author of several crime thrillers, including the Shamus Award-winning *Fun and Games*, the first in the Charlie Hardie trilogy, as well as the Edgar-nominated and Anthony Award-winning *Expiration Date*. As a comic book writer, his credits include *Judge Dredd*, T*he Punisher*, *Godzilla Birds of Prey*, *Godzilla* and *Black Widow*. He also collaborated with CSI creator Anthony E. Zuiker on a series of bestselling "digi-novels" which include *Level 26: Dark Origins*, *Dark Prophecy* and *Dark Revelations*.

Keith R.A. DeCandido ("Save The Cheerleader, Destroy The World") has written bunches of other prose starring super-powered beings, including several novels and short stories based on Marvel Comics: the *Spider-Man* novels *Venom's Wrath* and *Down These Mean Streets*, stories in the anthologies *The Ultimate Spider-Man*, *The Ultimate Silver Surfer*, *Untold Tales of Spider-Man*, *The Ultimate Hulk*, and *X-Men Legends*, and the new *Tales of Asgard* trilogy featuring Thor, Sif, and the Warriors Three. In addition, Keith has his own superhero universe in the *Super*

City Police Department stories that include the novel *The Case of the Claw* and short stories in the anthologies *With Great Power* and *The Side of Good/The Side of Evil*, with more to come.

Keith has also written novels, short fiction, and comic books based on TV shows (*Star Trek*, *Sleepy Hollow*, *Supernatural*), movies (*Cars*, *Resident Evil*, *Serenity*), and games (*World of Warcraft*, *Dungeons & Dragons*, *StarCraft*), as well as his own original fiction, such as the fantasy police procedural series that started in 2004 with *Dragon Precinct* and includes numerous novels and short stories, and a cycle of urban fantasy stories set in Key West, Florida, that have appeared in the magazine *Buzzy Mag* and several anthologies and collections. Recent and upcoming work includes the *Star Trek* coffee-table book *The Klingon Art of War*, the *Stargate SG-1* novel *Kali's Wrath*, the graphic novel *Icarus*, the short-story collection *Without a License: The Fantastic Worlds of Keith R.A. DeCandido*, the novel *Mermaid Precinct*, and stories in the anthologies *The X-Files: Trust No One*, *V-Wars: Night Terrors*, and *Out of Tune*.

In 2009, Keith was honored with a Lifetime Achievement Award by the International Association of Media Tie-in Writers, which means he never needs to achieve anything ever again. Keith is also a second-degree black belt in karate (which he teaches as well as trains in), a veteran podcaster, a freelance editor for clients both corporate and private, a professional percussionist (currently playing for the parody band Boogie Knights), and a bunch of other things he's forgotten due to lack of sleep. He lives in New York City with assorted humans and felines. Find out less at his appallingly retro website, DeCandido.net.

Kevin J. Anderson ("A Long Way from Home") has published 125 books, more than fifty of which have been national or international bestsellers. He has written numerous novels in the *Star Wars*, *X-Files*, and *Dune* universes, as well as a unique steampunk fantasy novel, *Clockwork Angels*, based on the concept album by the legendary rock group Rush. His original works include *The Saga of Seven Suns* series, the *Terra Incognita* fantasy trilogy, *The Saga of Shadows* trilogy, and his humorous horror series featuring Dan Shamble, Zombie PI. He has edited numerous anthologies, including the *Five by Five* and *Blood Lite* series. Anderson and his wife Rebecca Moesta are the publishers of "WordFire Press".

Peter J. Wacks ("A Long Way from Home") is a bestselling cross-genre writer. He has worked across the creative fields in gaming, television, film and comics. There are over 3.5 million copies of his stories in circulation. Peter started his writing career in the gaming industry when he created the international bestselling game "Cyberpunk CCG". He moved on from there to work on ABC's *Alias*, and has since also written tie-ins for *Veronica Mars* and *G.I. Joe*. His next novel, *VilleAnne* is co-written with Steven L. Sears (co-executive producer of *Xena, Warrior Princess* and thirty-year veteran of the television business), and debuts in late 2015.

HER**O**ES

REBORN

EVENT SERIES

COLLECTION ONE

Three brand-new short stories based on the fascinating characters and rich mythology of NBC's world-wide hit TV series *Heroes*, and the epic event series *Heroes Reborn*.

"BRAVE NEW WORLD"
BY DAVID BISHOP

A year after the fateful events of the Odessa Summit, the world is a very different place. It's certainly no longer friendly for Evolved Humans—or "Evos"—who are held responsible for what happened. If the government doesn't find you, there are some tenacious and merciless Evo-hunters out there who will.

Based on Tim Kring's original drafts of the script for the season premiere of *Heroes Reborn* and includes content not seen in the TV show.

"A MATTER OF TRUST"
BY TIMOTHY ZAHN

As the number of Evolved Humans increases, so does the
pressure from the governments and people of the world.
Father Mauricio begins searching for a way to help all
Evos after befriending a troubled teenager who possesses
a devastating secret. As a priest, it is Father Mauricio's
calling to protect the innocent and this includes the Evos
who, by no fault of their own, find their lives and
freedom being threatened.

"DIRTY DEEDS"
BY STEPHEN BLACKMOORE

A veteran Federal agent begins investigating the
involvement of ruthless Los Angeles Police Department
detective James Dearing in the death of an Evolved
Human. But when she gets close to uncovering a
dangerous truth, it could cost him everything: his job,
his freedom, maybe even his life.

For more fantastic fiction, author events, exclusive
excerpts, competitions, limited editions and more

VISIT OUR WEBSITE
titanbooks.com

LIKE US ON FACEBOOK
facebook.com/titanbooks

FOLLOW US ON TWITTER
@TitanBooks

EMAIL US
readerfeedback@titanemail.com